DARK WIDOW'S BLESSING

THE CHILDREN OF THE GODS BOOK 25

I. T. LUCAS

1

ELLA

"How do you like Russia?" Misha asked.

"So far, I love it."

"Good." His ugly face beamed as if Ella had just paid him the best of compliments.

Apparently, Misha was a patriot.

What she'd said was true, though. Ella was living a fairytale. Yesterday, while Dimitri had been out at meetings, she'd spent the morning touring the grounds surrounding the mansion, and in the afternoon, she'd had her first horseback riding lesson on her own horse.

After inspecting several, she'd chosen the one the stables manager had recommended. Mariana was a plain looking mare, small and brown, but she had smart eyes and the sweetest temperament. They had hit it off right away.

And the best part was that Dimitri hadn't come back until late at night, and by then Ella had been asleep for hours.

Horseback riding was fun, but it was also very tiring.

This morning at breakfast, she'd told him about all the fun

she'd had the day before, and had even kissed him goodbye when he'd left for another busy day.

Regrettably, in Ella's version of the famous fairytale, her kiss wouldn't transform the prince frog into someone she could love. But then, for the magic to work, the kiss needed to be given from the heart.

Hers had been as fake as it could be.

If her luck held, Dimitri wouldn't be back until late at night again. He'd called earlier, instructing Ella to eat dinner without him. Which meant that she was sharing yet another meal with her bodyguard. Not that she minded. Misha wasn't the sharpest tool in the shed, but he was proving to be surprisingly pleasant company.

"Thank you for another wonderful day, Misha. I had fun."

He shrugged his broad shoulders. "Don't thank me, thank boss. I do what he tell me. He say, Misha, take Ella to stables, I take you to stables. He say, show Ella the mansion, I show you the mansion. He say, take Ella to village…"

She lifted her hand to stop him. "I get it. You do what you're told. But you do it with a smile and a good attitude, and that's what I'm thanking you for. You could've been grouchy and mean, but you're nice. I enjoy your company."

He grinned. "Thank you. You tell boss I do a good job, eh?"

"I sure will."

Ella cut off another small piece of chicken and put it in her mouth. She was already full to bursting, but the chicken, like everything else the cook had served, was too delicious not to finish. At this rate, she was going to get fat fast.

Was horseback riding good exercise?

She wondered how many calories per hour it burned. Probably a lot, but for the horse rather than the rider. Her tiredness was more the result of spending the day in the Russian countryside's incredibly fresh air, and not the actual riding and walking she'd done.

The sounds of Dimitri's purposeful footfalls alerted her to his arrival even before he walked into the master bedroom, and Ella plastered a smile on her face. "Good evening, Dimitri. Would you like to join us?"

He glared at her and then at Misha. "Why are you eating in here?"

Ella had left the door to the master bedroom open on purpose, so no one would suspect Misha of doing something he wasn't supposed to.

Nevertheless, the bodyguard jumped up as if someone had detonated fireworks under his ass. "I'm sorry, boss, but Ella wanted to eat in kitchen because dining room too big. I told her it's not proper for the lady of the house to eat in the kitchen with the cooks and the maids, so she say to eat here."

Dimitri shrugged his suit jacket off and draped it over the back of the chair. "It's okay, Misha. Ella can eat wherever she wants." He bent and kissed her cheek. "How was your day, *lyubimaya?*"

"Wonderful. And yours?"

Look at them, they were acting like an old married couple.

He took the seat Misha had vacated and loosened his tie. "As good as can be expected while spending a day with politicians." He chuckled. "Compared to those vultures, I'm a choirboy."

"Can I go, boss?" Misha asked.

Dimitri waved a dismissive hand. "Yes, and tell the cook to send up another place setting."

"Yes, boss."

"You didn't eat?" Ella asked.

"I did, but it was a while ago, and I'm a little peckish.

Besides, I want to share a meal with you." He reached across the table and took her hand. "After a long day like this, coming home to you is like coming to a desert oasis after a day in the scorching, dry heat of the barren sand dunes."

As poetry went, Dimitri's was so-so. But his words sounded genuine, and it had been a very nice thing to say. Ella wished she could reply with something similar. Unfortunately, she was not happy to see him. Already, she was doing her best to appear as if she was, and trying harder would just make it look fake.

"I'm glad I can be here for you." A big fat lie.

Hopefully, Dimitri was too tired to notice.

As a maid knocked on the open door, Dimitri waved her in. Bowing and smiling, she entered with a rolling cart. After arranging a place setting for him, the girl lifted the lid off a steaming plate loaded with the same assortment Ella and Misha had enjoyed for dinner.

"*Spaseeba,*" Dimitri said.

The girl curtsied. "*Pahalusta.*"

"I should learn Russian." Ella lifted her glass and took a sip. "Most of your staff don't speak any English. In the village Misha and I visited today, there was only one guy who knew a few words. Don't they teach it in schools here?"

"It's an elective. They can learn German or French instead. But the truth is that they have no use for them. Most of these people will never venture outside of their village, let alone outside of Russia."

"That's true of Americans as well."

Dimitri put his fork down. "What second language did you study?"

"Spanish."

"And how good is your command of it?"

Ella grimaced. "Lousy. I never took it seriously."

"There you go." Dimitri picked the fork and knife up, cut off a piece of chicken, and put it in his mouth.

For the next ten minutes or so, Ella talked about her day while he ate. "The people seem to like you," she said after telling him her impressions from the village she'd toured earlier.

According to Misha, there were many more scattered throughout the vast estate. The feeling she'd gotten was of respect and gratitude. It seemed that to the villagers in his territory, Gorchenco was second only to God.

He wiped his mouth with a napkin. "Why wouldn't they? I take care of them."

"Are you like the mayor of these parts? How does it work?"

He waved a hand. "It's more like a feudal lord, but since I don't need to collect taxes, I'm much nicer." He rose to his feet and offered her a hand up. "How about I take a shower while you wait for me in bed?"

It wasn't really a question. It was a command.

"I would like to freshen up too." The bathroom had his and hers separate areas, connected by a big Jacuzzi tub. She had her own shower, vanity, and a toilet compartment including a bidet.

One of his brows lifted, Dimitri eyed her for a moment. "Don't take long."

That had been her plan, but it seemed he was on to her. "I won't." Ella lowered her eyes. There was a question she needed to ask him but was afraid she wouldn't like the answer. "Did you give contraceptives some further thought?" she blurted quickly before her courage deserted her.

Dimitri smiled and took her hand, lifting it to his lips for a kiss. "I did, and I decided against it."

Crap. Her heart sank.

He patted her hand. "I want you to have my children, Ella. I'm getting older, and it's time for me to produce an heir. Before I took over, my father looked after the people living on our lands. I need a son to take over from me when the time comes."

Ella swallowed. "What about my education? You agreed with me that I needed it."

"Being a mother will not interfere with you getting the education you want. You'll have plenty of help. I'll hire nannies and nurses to take care of the baby when you're otherwise occupied."

"And what about my girlish figure?" She was reaching for straws, but that was all she had.

He pulled her into his arms. "When your belly swells with my child, I'm going to love your beautiful body just as much, if not more, than I love it now."

2

VIVIAN

"Mom, I'm hungry." Parker padded into the bedroom and continued into the bathroom.

Mornings didn't feel right in the underground. There was no day or night.

With no natural light to regulate the body's sleep cycle, it was all askew. Or maybe Vivian was just tired after spending most of the night talking with Magnus.

At some point, he'd carried her to her bedroom. She'd been so wiped out after the dancing naked in the woods and the all-nighter with Magnus, that she'd skipped the shower even though it had been kind of gross getting in bed without it. Vivian had had just enough energy to drop the costume wizard robe on the floor, pull a sleep shirt on, and crawl under the covers.

The curse-exorcizing ritual had taken a lot out of her, and then Magnus's revelations had eaten up what little energy she'd had left over.

Her body craved two or three more hours of sleep, and

Vivian didn't want to get up even though her phone's display proclaimed in big white numbers that it was after ten.

She wanted to keep on sleeping and dreaming the strangest, most wonderful dream ever.

Except, it was no dream.

Last night had really happened.

Magnus had told her that he loved her, and she'd finally admitted the same to him, as well as herself.

That alone would have been enough to put a big smile on her face upon waking up. But there was more.

Oh, boy, there was so much more.

As fantastic as Magnus's story was, he'd given her enough proof to convince her that it was true.

Immortals were real. They were the descendants of a race of gods, the same ones that various mythologies had deified. Just like in the myths, those gods had taken human lovers, and a race of immortals had been born. Or near-immortals. Magnus had admitted that they were hard to kill, but not indestructible.

Vivian and her children might be carriers of those godly genes. If they were, their genes could be activated, and in addition to immortality, they would gain a host of other enhancements, some of them great, others a bit peculiar.

The sharper senses, the greater physical strength, and the self-repairing bodies, all of that kind of made sense—there were evolutionary benefits to those traits—but the fangs, the venom, and the males' impulse to bite during sex, not so much.

Bridget could probably explain it better than Magnus, who seemed to have only a superficial knowledge of how and why things worked the way they did in his immortal body.

There must be some biological or survival advantage to the venom system, other than delivering mind-blowing orgasms.

Not that Vivian was complaining. Maybe nature, or whoever had altered the original gods' genes, decided to make sex even more exciting for them. Which given their low conception rate also made sense.

Vivian wondered if all immortal males were as spectacular in bed as Magnus.

Doubtful.

Magnus's sexual prowess was about more than just great technique or staying power, although he had those too. He cared, he paid attention, and her pleasure was always more important to him than his own. That came from the inside, from the soul, and had nothing to do with his genetic makeup.

Just like humans, immortals were probably distributed along the same spectrum of character traits. Only a few were very good, or conversely very bad, while most clustered around the middle.

According to Magnus, not all of his relatives were good. Apparently, every family had a few rotten apples.

In a way, she was glad that not all clan members were perfect. It would have made their village a very dull place.

Vivian opened her eyes and stared at the ceiling.

He hadn't been supposed to tell her about it without getting approval from his boss first. In his excitement, Magnus had blurted out that the clan's secret hideout was somewhere in the Malibu mountains.

The thing was, she and Parker couldn't move into the village if one of them was not susceptible to thralling, and Magnus hadn't tested Parker yet.

Vivian, evidently, was easy to thrall. Magnus had done it to her after each venom bite, making her forget that it ever happened, and even though she understood the reason, she was still peeved at him for getting inside her head without permission.

He claimed that he couldn't read her thoughts, and only got impressions that looked like scenes in a movie, but since thoughts created mental images, what was the difference?

Then again, thoughts usually jumped around from one to the next. So maybe it was hard to read them. The mental images they painted were probably like random scenes from different movies in fast forward. It would be a mess, a kaleidoscope of distorted pictures. At least in her head.

Apparently, communicating telepathically using actual speech, the way she and Ella did, was an extremely rare gift even for these super beings.

Which reminded Vivian that Ella hadn't contacted her last night.

Should she worry?

Gorchenco's Russian estate was in a different time zone though, and Ella might still be adjusting to it. There were eleven zones in Russia, but Ella had mentioned the time in their previous conversation, making it possible for Vivian to figure out which zone the estate was in.

It was late evening over there, so Ella probably wasn't alone. She'd wait until later when their communication had less of a chance of getting interrupted.

Parker opened the door. "Mom, what are you still doing in bed?"

Vivian spread her arms out. "Come give me a kiss, and I'll get up."

Undecided, Parker eyed the bed for a long moment.

He hadn't cuddled with her in bed for years, and she missed that. At twelve and a half, he was still her little boy, with smooth cheeks that were very kissable, and soft hair that she liked running her fingers through.

When he let her.

"Don't tell anyone," he said before diving into the bed and getting inside the circle of her arms.

She hugged him close to her and kissed his warm cheek. "I won't. It's going to be our secret."

One more among many.

If Parker proved to be susceptible to thralling, which he most likely was, they were going to tell him everything.

Vivian smiled. He was going to flip. Parker's superhero aspirations would gain a whole new meaning. He would probably decide that he wanted to become a Guardian.

Like Magnus.

That was another thing he was going to flip over. Except, Vivian wasn't sure which way the flipping would go. Parker seemed to like Magnus a lot, but teenage boys were possessive of their mothers. He might not like the idea of sharing her with a man who was not his biological father.

On the other hand, Parker didn't remember Josh.

Vivian had done all she could to preserve Josh's memory and give Parker a good sense of the kind of man his father had been, but that was not the same as actually growing up with a male role model in his life.

He might like the idea of Magnus filling that void. Vivian certainly did. Magnus was the kind of guy her son could look up to and emulate. And it had nothing to do with the immortality.

Parker's belly rumbled, reminding Vivian that she had a hungry kid to feed.

"What would you like for breakfast?"

"Pancakes."

Hard to do without a stove to cook on. "Other than that."

"I'm sick of cereal."

"I can make you a sandwich."

"I'm sick of that too. Can we go out for breakfast? You said we could if we put on the disguises the lady brought for us."

"True." She kissed the top of his head. "I'll check with Magnus."

He pulled out of her arms and got up. "I'm going to get dressed."

Vivian picked up her phone and typed a text to Magnus. *Can we go out for breakfast? Parker is in the mood for pancakes.*

Sure. Are you ready to go?

Give me ten minutes.

3

MAGNUS

"Aren't you going to blindfold us?" Parker asked as they neared the keep.

He must've recognized the streets leading back to the high rise.

"I forgot to do that on the way out, so it doesn't make sense to do it now. You already know where it is."

Carried away by the kid's excitement at finally getting out of the underground, Magnus hadn't thought of Kian and his paranoia-driven instructions. Besides, in his mind, Vivian was his mate and there were no more secrets between them.

Or maybe it had something to do with how sexy she looked in the dark-haired wig and sunglasses. Stealing sidelong glances at his beautiful mate, he had trouble focusing on the driving, let alone remembering the blindfolds.

As he turned into the parking structure of the building across from the keep, Parker grumbled, "Your boss will be angry at you."

He glanced at the kid in the rearview mirror. "If you don't tell him, I won't."

Parker shook his head. "I don't want you to get fired for something as stupid as this. What if he finds out? He can kick you out and send someone else to watch over Mom and me."

Kian wouldn't do that. The worst Magnus would get was a warning and one of Kian's withering looks. But the kid seemed concerned to the point of being anxious, and that was reason enough to make an effort to comply with the boss's dictate.

Except, there was nothing they could use as blindfolds. "How about you guys close your eyes? I trust you not to peek."

"I can do that." Parker removed his sunglasses. "You can even check to make sure."

Vivian removed hers as well. "I don't really need to close my eyes because I have no sense of direction. Once we are in the tunnels labyrinth, I wouldn't know where we are going anyway."

"Do it, Mom. Do you want to get Magnus fired? If there are hidden cameras on the way, I want the boss to see that both of us have our eyes closed."

"Fine." Vivian did as he asked and crossed her arms over her chest.

Magnus was touched. Out of all the things Parker could've been worried about, the thing that bothered him the most was the possibility of Magnus getting replaced by another Guardian.

When the time came, and he and Vivian tied the knot, Magnus was going to ask Parker if he was willing to become his son and Ella his daughter. The clan had no procedures in place for adopting children, but he was sure Edna could draft something.

The paperwork itself didn't matter. It was the spirit of it.

Magnus wanted Parker and Ella to be considered his children. If they would have him, of course. It wasn't something they should be forced or coerced into accepting.

As Amanda had proven, rituals and ceremonies had the power to alter people's perception. Thanks to that silly ritual she'd enacted, Vivian now believed that the curse had been lifted and that her love for him wouldn't cause his death.

Naturally, the revelation about his immortality had helped too.

What a night that had been.

Magnus couldn't decide what had been more monumental about it, their mutual love declarations, or the secrets he'd shared with Vivian.

For him, hearing her say that she loved him had been the most important part. For Vivian, it had probably been the prospect of immortality for her and her children.

Vivian had loved before. Magnus hadn't.

This was the first time he'd fallen in love, and the feeling was indescribable. Once he'd stopped doubting and let it loose, his love for Vivian had unfurled its wings and soared.

There was no better feeling in the world.

"Magnus? Are you going to help us out?" Vivian asked. "Or can we open our eyes now?"

While daydreaming, he'd parked the car and was just sitting there and smiling like an idiot. It was good that both Vivian and Parker still had their eyes closed.

"Yes to the first one. No to the second. Give me a moment to get the cart."

After loading Parker and Scarlet first, Magnus came back for Vivian and swung her into his arms. "Can I steal a kiss?" he asked in a whisper.

"Yes, please."

Holding her close to his chest, he pressed his lips to hers, and then went in for a quick taste. "So sweet."

She laughed. "It's the pancakes."

Reluctantly, he deposited her in the cart and sat behind the wheel.

She turned her face toward him, peeking at him from under her lashes. "Amanda didn't blindfold me when she took me out last night. So technically, you're off the hook."

"Amanda is Kian's sister. Different rules apply."

"Can she do whatever she wants?"

"Pretty much."

Vivian chuckled. "Yeah, even take a Doomer for a mate."

"What's a Doomer?" Parker asked.

"Oops." Vivian put a hand over her mouth.

"It's my nickname for bad guys," Magnus said. "The bringers of doom."

"Sounds like a video game," Parker said.

Magnus laughed. "There you go. You have a working title for the first computer game you're going to design."

It reminded him that he still needed to check if Parker was susceptible to thralling, and then call Kian. Vivian's slip about Doomers had given him the perfect opportunity to erase just that. A tiny thrall would do.

Parking the cart in the clan's private garage in the keep, Magnus patted Vivian's knee. "You can open your eyes."

"Okay." She winked.

She'd been peeking from under her eyelashes the entire way.

After helping Vivian down, he took Scarlet's leash from Parker and then waited for the kid to look up at him. It took only a moment to erase that one recent image from Parker's memory.

When they were back at the apartment, Magnus asked, "What's my nickname for bad guys, Parker?"

The kid scrunched his nose. "Scumbags? Lowlifes?"

"You've got it."

"Which one, though?"

"Both. It depends on the circumstances."

Parker shrugged and dropped his sunglasses on the table. "Can I play, Mom? Or do you want me to study on a Saturday too?"

Vivian picked up the glasses. "You had a long break already, but fine. No studying on the weekend."

That earned her a hug. "You're the best, Mom."

She laughed and kissed his cheek. "Go play in the bedroom. I want to talk to Magnus and plan the rest of our day."

"Can we go swimming again?"

"That's one possibility."

"Cool." Parker took his portable gaming system into the bedroom and closed the door.

"I guess the experiment was successful," Vivian said.

"It seems so, but I'll ask him again in an hour. The memory is not erased, just suppressed. He might be able to force it up."

She looked disappointed. "Are you going to wait until then to call Kian?"

"No, I'll call him right now, but I'd better not do it from here."

"I'll make us a cup of coffee and bring it to your room."

"Thanks." Magnus smoothed his hand over his goatee.

Kian would not be happy about him issuing an invitation to the village without checking with him first. In case some of his remarks got offensive, it would be better if Vivian wasn't there to hear their conversation.

"Can I have fifteen minutes alone with him? Kian has quite

a mouth on him, and when he's not happy about something, he lets it loose."

She smiled. "I understand. I'll wait here until you're done. You can tell me what he said later."

He leaned and kissed her lips. "Thank you for being so understanding."

Vivian waved a dismissive hand. "Go."

In his room, Magnus pulled out his phone and fired a quick text to Kian first, asking if it was okay to call. The boss worked on Saturdays, but Magnus didn't want to catch him at a bad time.

His phone rang a moment later. "You didn't need to ask. I'll always make time for anything that has to do with Dormants. What's on your mind, Magnus?"

Rather than waste Kian's time with a long preamble, it was better to rip the Band-Aid off and deal with the consequences later. "I told Vivian everything, and I offered to move her and Parker into the village."

"I've heard things were heating up between the two of you. Congratulations."

Magnus hadn't expected such a calm and reasonable response. "Thank you."

"How did she react?"

"I guess it was easier for Vivian to accept my story because of her own otherness. The only part that got her upset was the erasing of the bite memory. She took it as a violation of trust. But after I explained why it was necessary, she accepted it too." Magnus chuckled. "Considering how bad of a job I've done explaining it, Vivian has been taking it remarkably well."

"I'm happy for you. But you can't move her and the kid to the village before she transitions. Until that happens, it is not certain that they are Dormants."

Expecting Kian's response, Magnus had prepared a rebuttal. "Vivian can't go through the transition until we get Ella back. Their connection is our only way of communicating with the girl. And even then she wants for Ella to do it first. An eighteen-year-old should transition easily. A thirty-six-year-old, not so much. Given her age, Vivian wants to ensure there will be someone to take care of Parker in case she doesn't make it. I'm sure you can understand that."

"I do. What it all means, though, is that Vivian and Parker will have to stay in the keep until Ella is rescued and goes through the transition."

Magnus started pacing. "It could take months. After her rescue, Ella won't be in the right state of mind to get intimate with anyone, even a sweetheart like Julian. So no transition for her in the foreseeable future. We can't keep her mother and kid brother locked up in the underground for that long. They are not prisoners, and the kid needs to be out in the fresh air."

Kian sighed. "Look, Magnus. If you bring them to the village, and Ella takes months to attempt transition, and then we discover that she's not a Dormant, Vivian, Parker, and Ella will have too many memories of us to thrall away. They will have to stay in the village for the rest of their mortal lives. It might be okay for Vivian, since she wants a life with you, but it's not okay for the kids."

"What if she's willing to take the risk? Because I'm sure the three of them are Dormants. You have to admit that the Fates wouldn't have done all of this to bring Vivian and her children to us for nothing."

"I'm not a spiritual guy, Magnus. I'm pragmatic. In my opinion, it's best for them to stay in the keep or some other safe place and not take risks. I can find them a secure location above ground."

Kian had a point, but Magnus was convinced that Vivian and her kids were Dormants. "Look, even if we take them to the village, they will not know where it is. Who is going to believe them that there are a bunch of immortals hiding in a secret community in the Malibu mountains?"

"That's irrelevant, Magnus, and you know it. We follow a strict secrecy protocol for a reason. Give Vivian the option. If she is willing to risk her kids' future because of temporary inconvenience, it's up to her. But I strongly advise against it."

4

VIVIAN

"You don't look happy," Vivian said as Magnus returned. "Did he say no?"

He sat next to her on the couch and wrapped his arm around her shoulders. "Kian raised several valid points and asked me to run them by you so you can make an educated decision. You might reconsider after hearing what he had to say."

Vivian put her mug down on the coffee table and turned to face him.

"Let's hear his reservations."

"Despite your strong telepathic ability, there is a chance that you're not a Dormant."

"I'm aware of that."

Magnus rubbed the back of his neck, which meant that he was uncomfortable with what he had to say next. "It might take a long time for us to get Ella back, and after that, I doubt she'll be in the mood to start a new relationship. It could take many months until she's ready. In the meantime, you and Parker are going to accumulate too many memories for us to thrall away safely. Your options would be to either risk brain damage from a massive thrall, or stay in the village for good even though you're not immortal."

What had he meant by that? Would he stop loving her if she didn't turn? How could he talk about erasing her memory of him?

Vivian crossed her arms over her chest. "Unless what you're trying to tell me is that if I don't turn we are over, I want to be with you as a human or as an immortal. I fell in love with Magnus the man, not Magnus the immortal. I hope the same is true for you. Did you love me before discovering I might be a Dormant, or was it only after?"

He pulled her closer to him. "I think I fell for you at first sight, but it took me some time to realize what I was feeling. I've never been in love before. So I wasn't sure if what I was feeling was love or attraction. But there is no more doubt in my mind. I love you and always will."

"I know that there is a but coming up."

"We need to think about Parker and Ella. You might be okay with staying in the village as a human and not being able to leave, but it won't be fair to them. Parker needs kids his age, and we have none in the village. He also needs to grow up, fall in love, start a family, and live a normal life. And other than the issue of friends close to her age, the same is true of Ella."

Vivian slumped against his arm. "You are right. I feel so stupid for not realizing this. I didn't know that there was a limit to the memories you guys could erase. That's why it didn't cross my mind that we could get stuck in the village as humans. We can't go."

"I told Kian that he can't expect you to stay in the underground for months. He said that he'd find us a new safe house."

"That's good. As long as you're coming with us, I don't care where we live. But what about our memories of you? You're already so entrenched in my heart and in my mind that there is no way I'm going to forget you."

"I'm not leaving you no matter what. If you don't turn, I'm going to stay with you wherever you are. And if you need to keep on hiding for the rest of your life, I'll hide with you."

Imagining them living together in a remote cabin somewhere, kind of like the one they'd stayed in before, Vivian smiled. She would homeschool Parker while Magnus would teach him how to hunt and how to fish, and later, when Gorchenco was no longer a threat, they could move back into the city.

There were two big problems with that fantasy, though. One was that she would age while Magnus wouldn't, and the second one was that he would be breaking one of his clan's most important laws to be with her.

A frightening thought entered her mind. "What if Kian replaces you with someone else? He might not have thought about it when you talked to him, but at some point, he'll realize that what he said about the village was also true in regards to you. I'll have too many memories of you to erase, and so will Parker."

"Damn. I didn't think of that. I hope he doesn't either."

Vivian cuddled closer to Magnus. The thought of losing him was unbearable. Maybe after they got Ella back, the four of them could run away and hide somewhere, not only from Gorchenco, but also from Kian.

Except, that wouldn't solve the aging problem.

"I think it's all nonsense," Magnus said. "First of all, even though it feels as if we've been together for months, it's only been a couple of weeks. That's not too many memories. Secondly, I'm sure that you are a Dormant. The Fates wouldn't have gone to all this trouble to bring us together if we weren't meant to be."

It was hard to believe that she'd fallen in love with Magnus in such a short time, but when it was meant to be, it was meant to be. Except, was she willing to risk Parker and Ella's futures based on a belief in fate?

"I think it is best we stay here a little longer. I feel safe in the underground."

"What about when we get Ella? Do we bring her here as well? From one restrictive environment to another? At least in the village she'll have room to breathe."

"What do you think we should do?"

"I say let's move into the village, and as soon as we have Ella, we'll attempt your transition. Waiting for her to do it first will just put an unfair pressure on her to enter a relationship before she's ready."

"But what if something happens to me? Who will take care of Parker?"

"Ella and everyone else in the village. If you're not a Dormant, the induction will not harm you. The only way something might happen to you is if you enter transition and your body can't take it. But even on the super-remote chance that this happens, it will mean that Ella and Parker are Dormants for sure, and they will become part of the clan."

"How? They are not related to you."

"I'll adopt them. I wanted to do that in any case. Only if they were willing, of course."

Vivian's eyes misted with tears. "Oh, Magnus. That's so sweet of you. I don't know what to say."

He pulled her onto his lap and wrapped both arms around her. "I love you, and I want to spend the rest of my immortal life with you. Parker already feels like a son to me, and I'm sure once I get to know Ella, she will feel like a daughter to me too. I just hope she likes me back."

"Why wouldn't she? You're awesome."

"She might not share your opinion."

"She will."

He arched a brow. "How can you be so sure? What if she thinks I'm too European, and not rugged enough? And what if she has an aversion to my Scottish accent and cringes every time she hears it?"

Vivian laughed. "Of all the silly things you could've come up with you found the two things I'm absolutely positive she's going to love." She nuzzled his neck. "Your accent is so sexy. I get all tingly just from listening to you talk. Ella is going to think that I scored myself a major hottie."

"Then it's settled. The moment they agree, I'm adopting both of your kids."

"Don't you want to get married first?"

"In my mind, I'm already mated. But, sure."

5

MAGNUS

When Vivian sniffled, Magnus wasn't certain whether those were happy tears or sad.

"Does it upset you? If you're not sure about it, I'll understand. And Parker and Ella don't need to change their last names either. I know you want them to remember their real father. I'm perfectly fine with them keeping it. You too. My last name is fake anyway. I just chose one that I liked. I don't mind changing it to Takala."

Shaking her head, Vivian wrapped her arms around his neck. "I'm emotional, not sad." She kissed his cheek. "And thank you for offering to take on Josh's last name. I can't think of any man who would've been willing to do that. But all this talk is a bit premature, don't you think?"

"Right. Move to the village, get Ella back, induce your transition, and then a wedding. Not the other way around. But we can move to the village only on the condition that you attempt transition as soon as possible after Ella's rescue. I know you'll need to be there for her and help her settle in, but the sooner you do it, the better. Age is a factor." He kissed her forehead. "I want you to have the best chance of success possible."

She nodded. "I agree. I'm scared, but that's not an excuse. I'm sure it will be just as scary for Ella even with all the reassurances that at her age it's safe."

He kissed the top of her head. "You're a gutsy lady who doesn't back away from a challenge. One of the many reasons I fell in love with you."

Vivian put her head on his chest. "There is one more thing that we need to do before all of that."

"What is it?"

"Tell Parker."

"Right. Do you want to do it now?"

"Sure." Vivian laughed. "He's going to freak out, in a good way." She untangled herself from Magnus's arms and rose to her feet. "I can't wait to see his reaction to your story."

Magnus grimaced. "Maybe you should tell him? I didn't do such a good job with you. I was all over the place."

Waving a dismissive hand, she knocked on the bedroom door. "You did fine. Besides, it's your story to tell."

Parker opened it and looked up at her with a puzzled expression on his face. "You knocked?"

She ruffled his hair. "When a bedroom door is closed, you're supposed to knock. I wish you'd remember that when you barge into my room in the morning. But never mind that. Magnus needs to talk to you."

The puzzled expression turned into worried. "What is it? What did I do? Whatever it was, I didn't mean it."

Magnus chuckled. "You did nothing wrong. Come sit with me." He patted the spot next to him on the couch.

As Vivian pulled out a dining chair and sat across from

them, Magnus thought about the best way to start his story. "Remember how fast I swam in the pool?"

Parker lifted a brow. "What about it?"

"You said that I could win any competition, and you were right. I could win, but there is a very good reason why I don't enter any. It would be unfair to the human swimmers."

Parker chuckled. "And what are you, an alien?"

"Kind of. I didn't come from another planet, but maybe my ancestors did. I'm an immortal."

"What do you mean, immortal? You cannot die?"

"I can, but it's hard to do. I don't age, and my body has remarkable repairing ability. So unless I sustain injuries it cannot fix, like having my head cut off, or my heart cut out, or getting blown to pieces, I won't die."

Crossing his arms over his chest, Parker narrowed his eyes at Magnus. "Prove it."

"Why? You don't believe me?"

The kid sighed and uncrossed his arms. "I kind of do, but then I love stuff like that, and you know it." He glanced at his mother. "Do you believe him?"

She nodded. "I do. He proved it to me last night. Magnus can manipulate human minds. He turned himself into a cute little dragon for me. Not for real, but he made me see him as a dragon."

Magnus frowned. "It wasn't cute. Just small. I didn't want to scare you."

"Can you show it to me?" Parker asked.

"Sure." Concentrating, Magnus brought up the same image of a small, unthreatening dragon.

The kid started laughing. "It looks like Barney."

Magnus dropped the shroud. "Who's Barney?"

"A cartoon for kids," Parker said. "A cute one."

Great. He was telling the kid a secret that should have him enthralled with its scope and magnificence, but instead of being awed, Parker was making fun of his illusion.

"I'm sorry," Parker laughed. "Don't look so offended. But you were asking for it with the face you made when Mom called your dragon cute. I just couldn't miss an opportunity like that to poke fun at you. Please go on."

"No more interruptions."

After making the zipping motion with his fingers, Parker listened to the rest of the story with eyes that kept getting wider and a jaw that kept dropping lower, but without saying a word.

The kid managed to keep his mouth shut until Magnus reached the part about him being a possible Dormant.

"No way! I can become immortal?"

"You might. It's not a sure thing, but I believe the probability is high because of the strong telepathic ability your mom and sister have. If they are Dormants, so are you."

"When will I know?"

When Magnus glanced at Vivian to get her approval, she nodded. Naturally, he wasn't going to explain the process of inducing a female Dormant. If the kid asked, they would have to come up with something evasive.

"One of you needs to attempt the transition, and your mom volunteered to go first. But only after we get Ella back. If your mother is a Dormant, and we will know that only when she starts transitioning into immortality, then we will know for sure that you and your sister are too. The genes pass from the mother."

"Why can't she do it now?"

"Because the transition is difficult for older Dormants, and some of them go into a coma for days. We need your mom to communicate with Ella."

Parker lifted his hands. "Then I should go first."

"You're not thirteen yet."

"I will be in six months. Does it have to be exactly on my birthday?"

"That's the tradition, but it's not an exact thing. I know several guys who weren't ready by thirteen and had to wait until they were older. It has to do more with being at the right stage of puberty."

"The nurse at my school said that puberty can start at nine for boys. I'm pretty sure mine started a long time ago."

Magnus and Vivian exchanged glances again.

This could be the simplest solution. If Parker transitioned, then there would be no more doubt about Vivian being a Dormant, and they could move into the village with Kian's blessing. Vivian wouldn't need to rush into it, and Ella wouldn't be pressured into a relationship.

"We can ask Bridget. If she says you're ready, then you can go first. Provided your mother agrees." He looked at Vivian.

"Are there any risks for boys Parker's age?"

"In all of our history, there wasn't even one case of a boy having trouble transitioning. A few needed more than one bite, but once the transition started, it continued smoothly with no complications. Other than the pain of growing fangs, that is. That was pretty bad. But today there are pain medications to take care of that. When I transitioned, all we had were numbing ointments that tasted so bad I preferred the pain."

Parker lifted a hand. "Hold on one sec. Did you say bite? What kind of a bite?"

Right. Magnus hadn't explained the other function of the

fangs. All he had said was that immortal males had them and used them to fight.

"As I explained before, our fangs deliver venom. In large doses, it can be deadly, but a small dose induces a Dormant's transition."

"Oh."

As Parker started scratching his head, Magnus tensed. The kid's next question would probably be about inducing females.

"So if the doctor says I'm ready, are you going to bite me?"

Magnus shook his head. "In order for a male to produce venom, he needs to get aggressive, which is why a ritual fight is staged between the Dormant and his initiator. Usually, the initiator is close to the Dormant in age."

"I don't want some strange dude biting me. I want you to do it."

"There is no way I can summon aggression toward you."

Parker frowned. "Why not? Because you're big, and I'm no match for you?

Now it was Magnus's turn to scratch his head. "That too, but mostly because I kind of think of you as my son."

Parker opened his mouth, closed it, then opened it again. "Is it because of what's going on between Mom and you? Are you guys going to get married or something?"

So the kid wasn't as clueless as Vivian had thought.

"I love your mother, that's true. And if everything goes well, and if she'll have me, I would like to marry her and for us to be a family. If you'll have me, that is. It's your decision as much as it is hers."

6

VIVIAN

Magnus spilling the beans about the two of them being in love had not been part of the plan. It was too much for Parker to absorb all at once, and given the confused expression on his face, he was going into overload.

This should have been handled more delicately, but after insisting on Magnus telling the story to Parker, she couldn't blame him for messing it up. He'd warned her that he might not do a good job of it.

"I'd like that too," Parker said quietly, and then stunned her by leaning over and giving Magnus a hug.

The big guy wrapped his arms around her son and then kissed the top of his head. "Thank you. You have no idea how much this means to me."

Now, if that wasn't a Hallmark moment, Vivian didn't know what was. As the scene before her started to waver, it took her a moment to realize that her stupid eyes were filling with tears.

"I wish I could film this," she sniffled loudly.

She could reach for her phone and do it, but then it would turn her into an observer instead of a participant. Joining in the hug was a much better idea. The moment she knelt next to them on the floor and tried to wrap her arms around her two guys, Magnus pulled her up and into his embrace, holding her and Parker together.

After a moment, Parker pushed away. "Okay, that's enough mushiness." He glanced at Vivian. "Why are you crying?"

She wiped the tears with the back of her hands. "I'm just so happy."

"And that makes you cry?" He rolled his eyes. "Girls are weird."

Magnus grinned. "But we love them anyway."

"Already you're ganging up on me? Sheesh. At least wait until Ella is back, so we're evenly matched."

"I should call Bridget." Magnus pulled out his phone.

Talking to the doctor in front of Parker wasn't a good idea. Bridget might start asking questions about the two of them and Vivian's transition. "Perhaps it'd be better if you do it from your place," she suggested.

"I get it." Parker pushed to his feet. "You don't want to talk to her with me here. I'll go to the bedroom. You can tell me later what she said."

When the door closed behind Parker, Magnus smirked. "That kid of yours knows much more than he lets on."

"I keep thinking of him as my little boy, and the scoundrel plays along with it when it's convenient for him." Vivian sighed and leaned back against the couch cushions. "The truth is that he's far from innocent, and he is much more mature than I've given him credit for."

"We weren't exactly discreet with our affection for each other, and he's not a little kid. Maybe he was just embarrassed about saying anything, or didn't know how to respond. If my mother started dating someone seriously, I don't think I would've been comfortable acknowledging it until she said something about it. And I'm a grownup."

It was sweet the way Magnus was trying to protect Parker, but there was no need. Vivian thought the world of her son. "The failing was mine, not his. I couldn't be prouder of Parker."

Nodding, he took her hand. "He's a great kid. I'm looking forward to watching him grow into a man."

"He looks up to you. You'd better be a good role model, or we will have words." She pretended to scowl.

"I'll do my best."

"I know you will. I was just teasing. You don't even have to try hard. Just be yourself. You're awesome."

Her praise seemed to embarrass him, and he tried to hide it by turning his attention to his phone.

"Let's call Bridget." Magnus scrolled through his contact list until he found the doctor's number, clicked on it, and put the call on speaker so Vivian could participate.

Bridget answered right away. "Magnus? Is anything wrong?"

"Everything is fine."

"Oh, thank the Fates. I was afraid Vivian had gone into transition."

"Vivian is fine, and she's right here with me. This is about Parker and whether he's ready to transition or not."

"Hi, Bridget," Vivian said.

"Hello, Vivian. I'll need to give him a checkup to see how far along he is. What's the rush, though?"

"I want to move him and Vivian into the village, but Kian prefers to verify that they are Dormants first. Vivian can't attempt the transition because we need her to communicate with Ella. So Parker, being the smart kid that he is, offered to go first."

"I see. This is a good solution. I can't come today because the teams are leaving for New York this evening, and I'm busy with preparing everything for their departure, but I can stop by tomorrow."

"That would be great. Thank you."

"Sure thing. I'll see you tomorrow."

As Magnus clicked the phone off and was about to put it back in his pocket, Vivian put a hand on his arm. "Maybe you should call Kian as well, and tell him of the new plan."

"Right. But what should I tell him? Do you want to move right away, or do you want to wait for Parker to transition first?"

"I think we should take it one step at a time. First, we need Bridget to tell us if Parker is ready."

"And if he is?"

"Then we should wait for him to transition before we move. That way everyone is happy. I prefer not to start my new life in the village with your boss being unhappy with me and thinking that I'm an irresponsible mother."

"He's not going to think that."

"Yes, he is. But regardless of Kian's opinion, I think that's the smarter way to go about it. If Parker is ready, we will know whether he is a Dormant or not in a few days. If he is, then we are good to go. If he's not, there is no reason for us to move into the village. Kian will find us a new safe house that is above ground, and once Ella is freed, she will join us there."

Vivian didn't want to think of the other implication of that possibility. It was just too painful.

Sensing her sudden mood drop, Magnus pulled her into his arms. "Don't worry, love. I'm convinced Parker is going to transition and we are going to have our happy ending, or rather beginning."

7

ELLA

When Dimitri started snoring, Ella slipped out of bed, put on a warm night robe, and padded out onto the terrace.

It had taken tremendous effort to hold the tears at bay until she had been sure he was sleeping, but now that she could finally have a private moment, there was no stopping them. The flow seemed endless, accompanied by sobs that she muffled with the sleeve of her robe.

Ella hadn't cried like that since her ordeal had started. In the beginning, she'd been in denial. After Romeo had delivered her to his uncle, she'd been more angry than sad. Things had gotten worse when Stefano had brought her to the auction house, and she had to strip naked in the viewing room. But then Dimitri had bought her, and she'd been dazzled by his estate, and the elegant wardrobe he'd provided her with, and his private airplane. It wasn't that she craved riches, but it was impossible not to be affected by all of that.

The glitz and the comfort were like rose-colored lenses, altering the perception of her reality, making it tolerable, manageable, and keeping the dark despair from consuming her.

Up until yesterday, Dimitri had done his best to keep up the illusion for her. He'd been decent to her, and sex with him hadn't been the traumatic experience she'd expected. He'd given her time to get used to him and had done his best to make it pleasurable for her.

It had seemed that in his own way, he cared for her and wanted to make her happy.

So despite all that had happened to her, up until yesterday Ella had thought she was in control, at least in some small way. Dimitri had let her believe that she had some room to wiggle. She'd even been naive enough to think that she could manipulate him until the rescue her mother was organizing actually happened.

She hadn't felt completely trapped and hopeless.

But when Dimitri had taken away the most important of her choices, refusing to allow her contraceptives, Ella's illusions had been shattered.

Her rescuers wouldn't make it in time to prevent the pregnancy he was forcing upon her.

She debated whether to open the channel to her mother, but then decided against it. There was nothing her mom could do to help her, and it would only make her miserable as well.

It was cold outside, and several minutes into her self-pity session Ella started to shiver despite the thick robe she had on. Wiping the tears away with her sleeves, she got up and padded back to bed.

Sleep eluded her for a long time, but eventually she drifted off into dreamland. Not surprisingly, her lousy luck followed her there, and instead of dreaming about something nice, she was plunged into a worse nightmare than the real-life one she'd just escaped from.

"Beautiful Ella." Logan cupped her cheek. "Such a treasure. I think I'm going to make Gorchenco an offer he cannot refuse and buy you from him."

As he leaned forward and pressed his lips to hers, Ella tried to lean away, but his other hand held her neck in an iron grip.

"What's the matter, Ella? Don't tell me that you prefer the old Russian to me." He forced his tongue into her mouth.

She tried to push him away, but he was so strong that she couldn't move him even a fraction of an inch. When his hand moved from her cheek and cupped her breast, Ella fought harder, but it was no use. She was trapped, and he was going to rape her.

Ignoring the desperate tears spilling out of the corners of her eyes, Logan left her mouth to suck on her neck.

"Please, don't," she murmured as he scraped her skin, drawing blood.

When he leaned away and smiled at her with glowing demon eyes and a pair of blood-covered fangs, Ella screamed.

And screamed. And screamed.

"Wake up, Ella!" He was shaking her.

"Go away!" She shrieked and pushed with all her strength, not really expecting him to budge.

Except, this time it worked, and the hands shaking her left her shoulders. A moment later, his arms wrapped around her and he smashed her against his body. "Stop it, Ella. Wake up. It's just a nightmare." The voice didn't belong to Logan, and it had a Russian accent.

It wasn't Logan.

She was in Dimitri's bed, and he was holding her and rocking her like a child.

Ella let out a breath and sagged against him. Evidently, the saying about better the devil you know than the devil you don't was true.

"Better?" Dimitri asked.

"Yes, thank you."

"What did you dream about?"

She shuddered. "I don't know where it came from, but I dreamt that Logan wanted to buy me from you."

He chuckled. "And that scared you so much? Should I be flattered? Logan is much more handsome than me."

"In the dream, he was forcing a kiss on me, and when I struggled and begged him to stop, his eyes started glowing like a demon's, and he grew huge fangs. He scraped my neck with them. They were dripping with my blood."

Dimitri leaned back and looked into her eyes. "Have you watched one of those idiotic vampire movies lately?"

She shook her head. "I read a romance novel or two that had vampires in them, but that was a long time ago."

He patted her hand. "The mind is a strange machine. It could've taken a distant memory of a vampire from a book that you read and combined it with a man that you found scary."

"I guess."

"What makes me wonder, however, is why did Logan scare you so much? Did he say something to you when I was gone?"

"I don't think so."

"He either did or didn't."

"That's the thing. I don't remember. Could he have hypnotized me?"

"Why would he do that?"

She shrugged. "I don't know. What I do know is that I never want to see him again. So the next time you meet with him, don't bring me along."

He hugged her closer. “Of course, *lyubimaya*. I would never force you into a situation that upsets you.”

Ella stifled the need to roll her eyes. He was such a hypocrite. As if forcing a pregnancy on her wasn’t upsetting to her.

8

SYSSI

"Shouldn't Merlin be here already?" Syssi asked. "He landed two hours ago."

Kian put his cigarillo down and pulled out his phone. "I don't see any new messages." He put the phone back. "I don't know what's taking them so long. Traffic shouldn't be too bad on the weekend. Do you want me to call him?"

She waved a hand. "No, don't. It's just that everyone is getting antsy. People are hungry, and Amanda is not letting them touch the food until he arrives."

Since Merlin had informed them that he didn't want to share a residence with others, and the only unoccupied houses were at the newly completed section of the village, he was about to become its first resident.

That required a celebration.

It had been Amanda's idea to use the occasion of Merlin's arrival for a ribbon-cutting ceremony to initiate the opening of the new phase.

Except, the guest of honor was running late, the food was

getting cold, and a bunch of hungry immortals were getting more and more annoyed by the minute.

"Why don't you have Onidu start distributing the appetizers?"

"He only has two hands, and there are a lot of people here. Let's wait a little longer."

"As you wish." Kian went back to reading the proposal he'd taken with him to the village square after she'd nagged him to come out of his office.

Her guy was working too hard, but Syssi had learned to live with it. No matter how much help he was getting, or what shortcuts and innovations he applied to better organize his workload, Kian didn't use the freed time to chill. He just took on more work.

"I see him," Anandur said. From his height, the guy could see over the crowd's heads. "He hasn't changed a bit since the last time I saw him."

Kian grimaced. "Is he wearing that long purple coat of his?"

"No coat. Just a jacket. But it's also purple. And his hair is even longer. Does he ever cut it?"

"He must. Otherwise, he would be dragging it on the ground behind him." Kian stood up and offered a hand up to Syssi. "Let's go and greet him."

Walking hand in hand with her husband, Syssi craned her neck to get her first glimpse of Merlin over the small crowd gathered on the village square.

Given the last-minute announcement, many of the village residents had already made other plans for the weekend. Less than half of them had come out to welcome Merlin and watch Kian cut the ribbon to the new phase.

Finally, as people moved aside to let her and Kian pass through, she got to see the famous Merlin in person.

Tall and spindly, he had long blond hair that was so pale it looked white. Woven into a braid, it swung from side to side as he walked, making it look like he had a tail swishing behind him. His beard was not as long, but it still extended over his belt.

None of it made him look old, though, so the resemblance to the legendary wizard he'd been named after was superficial at best.

"Hello, Merlin, and welcome to the village." Kian offered the doctor his hand.

"My pleasure." Merlin shook it without looking at him and smiled at Syssi. "I've heard a lot about you."

"Same here." She gave him her hand, which he lifted to his lips for a kiss. "Good things I hope?"

"That depends on what you consider good."

He laughed. "How true."

Kian patted Merlin's shoulder. "Let's get on with the ribbon-cutting ceremony before we have a riot on our hands. People are hungry."

"My apologies for the delay." The doctor threaded his arm through Syssi's as they followed behind Kian. "I had the annoyance of being subjected to a very thorough inspection at immigration. Evidently, I look like a suspicious character." He winked at her.

"I wonder why?"

"Indeed."

"How come I didn't see you at Andrew and Nathalie's wedding?"

He smiled. "I'm a bit of a recluse, and I don't live in the castle. I have my own cottage an hour's drive away. I intended to come, but there was a medical emergency I had to attend to. Where I live, I'm the only doctor around. Or was. A new human doctor just moved into the area. That's why I came earlier than originally planned."

"I didn't know you served the human population."

"The clan doesn't have much need for my services. Besides, I like working with humans."

"How do you manage that? With your looks, it's not like you can move from place to place and start anew. People must recognize you and wonder how come you don't age."

He waved a dismissive hand. "It's easy. Every ten years or so, I close my clinic and move out. Still, the Scottish highlands are not densely populated, and people know one another. So when I open it somewhere else, I tell everyone that I'm a nephew of that other doctor, and that my uncle moved to America or Argentina or wherever pops into my head."

"And no one wonders?"

"If they do, they think I'm a real wizard." He winked. "And then they are scared to piss me off by asking me questions."

When they reached the place where the fence separating the two sections used to be, they were greeted by Amanda who was waiting for them with a pair of huge scissors in her hands.

"Merlin, darling, I was starting to think you'd decided to ditch the party and hide in a bar somewhere until everyone went home."

"You know me well." He leaned to kiss Amanda's cheek. "Unfortunately for me, Kian told Okidu to deliver me straight here and ignore my requests to go elsewhere."

"That's because I know you too." Kian slapped the guy's back, then turned to the people who'd followed them. "Let's do this."

As everyone clapped, Kian took the scissors from Amanda and cut the ribbon.

"Can I say a few words?" Merlin asked.

"By all means." Kian waved him on. "Just make it short. Everyone wants to get back and eat."

Merlin turned around and raised his arms to quiet the murmurs. "I was told to make this short. So here goes. Thank you for inviting me here. I'm honored to be the first resident of the second building phase, and I pray to the Fates for all these beautiful homes to get snatched up so fast that Kian will have to start on phase three."

As everyone clapped, Syssi wondered what he meant by that.

Merlin could've been referring to their quest for Dormants. As more clan members found their mates, they would need housing. Or, he could've been alluding to the fertility research he was about to start. If more of the clan's females had children, they too would need accommodations.

Hopefully, the Fates would grant them both.

9

BRIDGET

As the twenty-four Guardians Turner was taking with him to New York trickled into the classroom, Bridget handed him the clipboard with his notes. "You should really start using a tablet."

"I'm old-fashioned."

"I'm much older than you, and I switched to modern technology."

He leaned and nuzzled her neck. "Whatever is transmitted electronically, can be hacked. Paper cannot."

"You know that you're paranoid, right?"

"I call it careful. Potato, *potahto*." Turner smiled at her. "My beautiful mate, looking as radiant as ever despite her lack of sleep. But for all the wrong reasons. I missed you in bed last night."

"I had to work out the last details for the six new missions scheduled for next week." She leaned into him. "I'm going to miss you."

"Then come with us. You can work from Ragnar's hotel. Did the new doctor arrive yet?"

"Merlin is here. I should go say hi to him, but I'll do that after you guys leave."

"So there is really no reason for you to stay." He put his hands on her waist and pulled her closer to him. "Come with me. We can work together from the hotel."

She sighed. "I wish I could. Merlin is not going to start working right away. He needs some time to acclimatize, and I need to show him around."

"He's a bit of a prima donna, isn't he?"

Bridget shook her head. "Not really. But he has his way of doing things, and he likes to ease into them. Merlin is more of a country general practitioner than an emergency room doctor."

"That's a shame. I hoped he could take over the clinic starting tomorrow, so you could come with me."

Bridget sighed. "Hopefully, this rescue operation is going to be over in one week. If not, I'll have to come up with more missions for the next one."

"And fly to New York. I don't like the bachelor life."

"I know. I don't like it either. But we have jobs to do." She glanced at the classroom. "I think everyone is here, except for Sylvia and Roni."

"Civilians," Turner muttered under his breath. "No discipline."

Bridget planted a quick peck on his cheek. "Patience, my dear. You need Sylvia, and she's graciously volunteering her talent to aid you."

"I'm not sure I'm going to use her."

"Why not? You know what she can do. Without her talent for manipulating electronic devices, we would not have had the element of surprise in the attack on the monastery. The

Doomers would've seen us coming, and the result could have been catastrophic. Thanks to her, we didn't lose anyone."

"That was different. I don't know if she can manipulate sophisticated equipment like what Gorchenco has on his estate. She hasn't had any military training, which I blame Kian for. He should have seen to it. Having an asset like Sylvia and not drafting her into the Guardian force is a failing on his part."

"You forget that we don't operate like that. This is Sylvia's decision to make, not Kian's."

"I'll have a talk with her on the way to New York. Or better yet, I'll have Arwel talk to her."

"Why Arwel?"

"Because he is sacrificing his sanity to be a Guardian. He would've been much happier in the accounting department. But he knows that his talent is crucial to the force."

"Laying the guilt. That's your recruiting strategy?"

Victor shrugged. "Whatever works. I know money will not convince her. Maybe duty will."

"I can just imagine Roni's reaction. The kid flipped when he heard she was going on the mission."

"Tell me about it. That's why he's tagging along. But I guess I might be able to use him too. Having a hacker of his caliber on call is always good."

From the corner of her eye, Bridget saw the two enter the classroom. "They are here. Let's start with the briefing." She scanned the room and counted heads.

"Hello, everyone."

Julian, who was sitting in the front row between Yamanu and Arwel, gave her the thumbs up.

"Is everyone clear on their flight assignments?" Bridget lifted her tablet in case someone had a question, but it seemed everyone knew where they were going.

Some were flying in the clan's two jets, and the rest were on commercial flights. They all should be arriving at about the same time.

Lifting his clipboard, Turner took over. "Ragnar has reserved four floors for us, including the executive lounge, which will serve as our command center. A tour bus is going to transport us from the airport to the hotel. Ragnar bought five used vans for our use. Any questions so far?"

Peter asked, "What about the equipment?"

"Taken care of already. We put everything on a truck three days ago. Everything will be ready for us when we get there."

After Turner answered several more questions, Bridget verified that every Guardian knew where and when he was flying out. Roni and Sylvia were going with Turner on the smaller of the clan's jets.

He followed her to her office, closed the door behind him, and locked it. "We have about an hour before I head out to the airstrip. I thought to put it to good use."

Smirking, Bridget leaned against her desk and crossed her arms over her chest. "Don't you have some last-minute details to take care of?"

Walking up to her, he put his hands on her waist and lifted her to sit on the desk. "Nope. Everything is done, except for this." He cupped the back of her neck and kissed her.

She arched a brow. "Here?"

"I locked the door."

10

VIVIAN

"What's the game about?" Magnus sat next to Parker on the coffee table.

"It's a shooting game. Want to give it a try?"

"Sure."

Parker paused the game and rose to his feet. "I need to get another controller for you. I'll be back in a sec." He rushed into the bedroom.

"It's nice of you to play with him," Vivian mumbled from the couch.

She was so tired after the sleepless night she'd spent talking with Magnus, holding on for as long as she could, but after dinner, it had become a losing battle.

Magnus turned around. "I've wanted to learn how to do it for some time. My roommates are game programmers, and I can barely understand what they are talking about."

"Your ex-roommates."

He wasn't going back to his old place. Once they moved to the village, it would be into a brand new house together.

"Right."

Parker came back with a controller, paired it with the system, and then handed it to Magnus.

Watching them together and listening to their conversation, Vivian enjoyed the sounds of their voices and the ease with which they interacted. It took less than sixty seconds for her eyelids to start drooping, and another two for her to fall asleep.

"Mom, wake up." Parker nudged her shoulder. "Go to sleep in your own bed."

Vivian lifted up, rubbed her eyes, and then shifted to a sitting position on the couch. "How long was I asleep?"

"More than three hours. It's after eleven."

"Where is Magnus?"

"In his room. After you fell asleep, I taught him how to use the controller and how to play the game. He was clumsy for about ten minutes, but then he got the hang of it and almost beat me. Immortals learn fast."

"They do? I thought it was only languages."

Parker shrugged. "Magnus didn't say anything about it. I just figured that he was so good because of his super reflexes. But maybe it's his soldier training. Like the shooting games made me good in the real shooting range, it worked the other way around for him."

"Thanks for keeping him company." She yawned and stretched.

"No problem. I like hanging out with Magnus. He's not like other older guys."

"How so?"

"He's easy-going, and he is not condescending at all. You know, because I'm a kid and he's a grownup. He doesn't do that, doesn't talk down to me. He treats me with respect. I like it."

Vivian liked it too. "I couldn't ask you before because we

didn't have a chance to be alone, but how are you taking all of this?"

"The immortal part, or the Mom loves Magnus part?"

"Both."

He shrugged. "The immortal part is the coolest thing ever. I feel like the luckiest kid in the world who just won the biggest lottery. All of us did. You and me and Ella. Because what can be better than discovering that you can be immortal with super-powers, right? But then I feel guilty for feeling lucky or happy because of Ella. I shouldn't be happy while she's miserable."

Vivian rose to her feet and pulled her son in for a hug. "I know exactly what you mean. It's hard to allow yourself to rejoice in your good fortune when someone you love is suffering."

Parker pulled out of her arms. "The way I explain it to myself is that Ella is lucky too. She will just have to wait a little longer to have all that. Immortality and a great new dad." He glanced at Vivian with a pair of guilt-ridden eyes. "Is that okay to be happy about Magnus wanting to be my dad? I really like him, and I don't remember my real father. I know he was awesome and everything, but it would be cool to have Magnus around. There is so much he can teach me."

Vivian's eyes misted with tears. "It's more than okay, sweetie. As long as you keep the memory of Joshua Takala in your heart, you can enjoy having Magnus as your father and even love him guilt free. In fact, it would make me very happy."

She turned to discreetly wipe the tears away. "I need coffee."

"Why? Don't you want to go to sleep?"

She shook her head. "After such a long nap, I doubt I'd be able to. Besides, I feel bad about not spending time with Magnus."

"You kind of did. You were right here on the couch while we played."

"Did I snore?"

"Just a little. But I turned the volume up so Magnus wouldn't hear."

"Did you forget about his enhanced immortal senses? He heard."

Parker shrugged. "If he wants to marry you, he should know that you snore." He flipped the two big couch cushions to the floor. "I'm unfolding the couch, so you can't invite him to sit here. You need to go to his room." He pulled the bed out.

"I'll help you with the bedding." She tucked in the sheet and fluffed up the pillows.

"You know, Mom, it would be much more comfortable for everyone if you and Magnus moved in here, and I moved into Magnus's room. I hate the pullout bed, and I hate having to go through your bedroom to get to the bathroom when you sleep."

Vivian felt her cheeks catch on fire. This was so awkward. "You've slept on the couch without pulling the bed out, you can keep doing it, and I can leave the door open."

Parker rolled his eyes. "I know what you're doing. You're changing the subject because you think I'm too young to understand, or something like that. I'm not. You and Magnus love each other, and you are going to get married." He scratched his head. "What I'm trying to say is that it's okay with me if you want to sleep together. I mean, I know that you want to, and that you are not doing it only because of me. It makes me feel bad."

Again, she'd underestimated her son's maturity, and by doing so had hurt his feelings. Maybe she could salvage the situation by implying a different reason.

"I don't want you to be alone in the apartment. Not because I think that you are not safe here, or because I don't trust you to be alone." She waved a hand around. "I wouldn't want to be by myself in here. It would creep me out. This place is nicely decorated, but we both know that it's just a fancy dungeon, with no windows and a door that can probably withstand one heck of an explosion."

"I don't mind. I think that's super cool, and I know how to open the door with the phone. So if you leave it with me, I'll be fine."

Vivian narrowed her eyes at him. "Is this about you wanting me out of here so you can play all night?"

His sheepish expression confirmed her suspicion. "That too, but it's the weekend, and you said that I can play as much as I want. It would be fun to have this entire place to myself, though. It's soundproof, and I can blast music as loudly as I want, and jump on the couch and on the bed. Please, just go." He made the puppy face he knew she couldn't resist.

"Fine. But I need to check with Magnus first. What if he doesn't want me to sleep in his room?"

Parker snorted. "Really, Mom? I'm not five. Of course he wants you there."

Ignoring the last comment, Vivian picked the phone up and sent out a text.

Parker is kicking me out of here. Can I spend the night at your place?

The answer was immediate. *I'm coming over to move your things.*

Smiling, Vivian quickly typed another text. *Not so fast. I'm going to grab a nightshirt and a toothbrush. We will figure out logistics tomorrow. Start the coffeemaker.*

Yes, ma'am.

They'd found the thing in the cabinet under the sink, tucked all the way in the back corner. Not that Magnus had made much use of it. He either got coffee at the vending machines upstairs or at her place.

In the bedroom, Vivian put her nightshirt and a few toiletries in the paper bag Amanda had brought the wig in. Perhaps she should take it too?

Nah, they could have fun with the wig some other time.

Tonight, she was going to experience the real Magnus for the first time and actually get to remember it, including the fangs and the biting and everything else that was different about having sex with an immortal male. She should stay real as well.

She'd taken a shower in the morning, but maybe she should have another one?

On second thought, she could shower at Magnus's suite. Hey, they could shower together. Now that she was going to spend the night, they had time to indulge.

Vivian smiled. With the rooms being soundproof, they could do all kinds of naughty things in there.

Though nothing was more naughty than having sex with a vampire-like lover. Talk about fantasies coming true.

Except, getting bitten for real was scary.

While brushing her teeth, Vivian's eyes gravitated toward the reflection of her neck in the mirror. There was no way it wasn't going to hurt like hell, at least for several seconds until the venom numbed the pain and turned it into pleasure. And in those seconds, Magnus would have to hold her head still to prevent her from jerking away and tearing her skin.

When he'd explained all of that last night, she'd found it both arousing and frightening. The wicked-looking fangs that were going to end up in her neck were scary enough, but the temporary immobilization was even more so.

Then again, Vivian trusted Magnus not to hurt her. The only difference between this time and those that came before was that she was going to remember everything about it.

11

MAGNUS

Vivian was coming to spend the night with him.

Magnus felt like going over there and giving Parker a big hug, but that was highly inappropriate, and so was a twelve-year-old kid telling his mother to go sleep with her lover.

Future husband.

That made it a little better.

The coffeemaker finished brewing at the same time Vivian walked in.

"Oh, good. I'm in desperate need of coffee."

He pulled her into his arms. "And I'm in desperate need of a kiss."

Vivian smiled. "Kiss, then coffee. I can live with that." She puckered her lips.

He would've gladly skipped the coffee and carried her to bed, but the lady always got what the lady wanted, at least as long as it was within his power to fulfill her wishes.

With an effort, Magnus let her out of his arms. "What exactly happened with Parker?" he asked while pouring coffee into two mugs. "I assume he didn't really kick you out. Because if he did, I need to have words with him." He handed Vivian a cup and sat next to her on the couch.

Vivian patted his bicep. "Of course not. My son is a respectful young man. He would never do that." She made a sad face. "Before today, I would've said that he's my sweet little boy."

"Parker is a sweet boy, just not so little anymore."

She took a long sip of the coffee and sighed. "I know. He's so mature. He said that it would be much more comfortable for everyone if you moved in with me into the bigger suite, and he moved into your room. It was his way of telling me that he's okay with us sharing a bed. I think he knows we were sneaking around, but he's too polite to say it."

Magnus put his mug down on the coffee table. "I'm surprised he's taking it so well. We've been together for such a short time. How did he react to your other boyfriends?"

Vivian arched a brow. "All two of them?"

"Yes. You said that you dated each one for several months. Did Parker interact with them?"

"Mostly, he ignored them. I didn't encourage anything because I didn't want him to get attached to a guy until I was sure he was the one."

Magnus couldn't hide the smirk. "If memory serves me right, you didn't try to discourage Parker from spending time with me. Did you already know then that I was the one?"

"I didn't, but you were so good with him, and he needed a distraction. I wasn't about to interfere with that." She finished the last of her coffee and handed him the mug for a refill. "I think all three of us have bonded so quickly because of how intense everything was. Still is."

Magnus poured the rest of the coffee from the carafe into

Vivian's mug, stirred in a little creamer, and handed it to her. "Or, we might have bonded because it was meant to be."

Cradling the mug between her palms, Vivian nodded. "Or maybe both." She looked up at him with a sly smile on her beautiful face. "Now that I'm properly caffeinated, I feel like taking a shower. I took one this morning, but that was a long time ago. Would you care to join me?"

Given the hitch in Vivian's breath, his eyes must've started glowing. He ran his tongue over his fangs, but those hadn't elongated yet.

Cupping her cheek, he asked, "What's the matter? Are my eyes glowing?"

She nodded.

"That's because I'm aroused thinking of you naked with me in the shower. Are they freaking you out?"

She shook her head.

"Then what's the problem?"

She pointed at his mouth.

"Not yet." He flashed her a broad smile, showing his teeth.

Vivian let out a breath. "I don't know why it freaked me out. I've already seen them, but then you told me that they were only slightly elongated. I'm scared of seeing them at their full length."

"Then we should turn the lights off."

"In the shower?"

"Why not? I can see in almost complete darkness. I'll wash you."

The sly smirk returned. "I guess I'll have to trust you. I'll be at your mercy."

Quickly, Magnus closed his mouth. If Vivian didn't want to see his fangs, he'd better get her into the bathroom using immortal speed and turn the lights off.

Lifting her up into his arms, he leaped into the bathroom and kicked the door closed.

The only source of light was the charge indicator on his shaver, a small blue dot that was enough for him to see by, but not for Vivian. She was completely helpless.

"I can't see a thing." She clung to him, her arms wrapped around his neck.

"I got you. Don't worry about a thing." He stepped into the shower. "I'm going to lower you onto the bench, and then I'm going to undress you."

"Okay."

When she was seated, he knelt on the tiled floor in front of her. "I'll start with your shirt. Lift your arms."

With a chuckle, Vivian did as he asked. "Your eyes are like small flashlights. I can see exactly where you're looking because they mark the spot."

"You should close your eyes, then."

"Why? Are there any more secrets you don't want me to see?"

"There aren't. But when the eyes are deprived of sensory import, the other senses go into overdrive. You'll feel everything more acutely."

Vivian nodded and closed her eyes.

Pulling the shirt over her head, he tossed it outside the shower. The bra he was saving for later.

"Lift up for me." He pulled her pants and panties down, flinging them in the same direction the shirt went.

Lastly, he reached behind her and unclasped her bra. "I must have a little taste before I turn the water on." He took one ripe berry into his mouth and swirled his tongue around it.

Vivian arched into his mouth, her hands finding his head

and holding it to her breast. She moaned when he switched to the other one.

Magnus would've loved to continue showering attention on Vivian's sensitive nipples, but judging by the goosebumps rising on her arms, she was getting cold.

"I need to warm you up." He stepped out of the shower and leaned inside to turn the water on.

When the temperature was right, Magnus shucked off his clothes and stepped into the shower, closing the glass door behind him.

12

VIVIAN

By the sounds coming from outside the shower, Magnus was taking his clothes off. Imagining his magnificent body, Vivian opened her eyes and tried to catch a glimpse. Except, straining to see in the dark was pointless. It was better to just keep her eyes closed.

Instead, she listened.

He was moving fast, the garments hitting the floor at an incredible speed. Then he was stepping in and closing the door behind him. A moment later, as his large hands gripped her waist, she switched from listening to feeling.

Magnus lifted her, and then sat on the bench with her on his lap, her back to his front.

"Do you want me to wash your hair, love?"

She debated for a moment and then shook her head. "It will take too long."

"Unless you're tired, we have all the time we need."

"I'm not tired."

"Then it would be my pleasure. Is there anything I need to

know? I've never washed a woman's hair before." He ran his fingers through her long tresses.

"Shampoo twice, but try not to get it all tangled up, or we'll end up spending half the night combing out the knots. I'd rather be doing other things." In case her meaning wasn't clear, Vivian rubbed her bottom against his hard length.

"Got it." He groaned. "No knots. What else?"

"After rinsing the shampoo off, cover it with a generous amount of conditioner and let it sit for several minutes. You have conditioner here, right?"

"I do. But I don't know how good it is."

Vivian lifted up and turned around, kneeling on the bench between Magnus's spread thighs. "How about we skip the hair washing?" She wrapped her arms around his neck and opened her eyes.

Up close, the glow he was emitting reflected from her pale skin and cast a barely-there soft light on his face. It was enough for her to find his lips without banging his forehead.

"Careful." His hand shot to the back of her neck, cupping it and holding her a fraction of an inch away from his mouth. "My fangs might scrape you."

"Can I see them?"

"Isn't it too dark for you?"

"The glow from your eyes reflects off my skin and casts a tiny bit of light back on your face."

He tilted his head, the glow from his eyes moving to a different spot. "Are you sure you're up for it before the bite? Maybe it's better to wait for after."

"After the bite, they will go back to their regular length. I want to see." She tapped a finger on his lips. "Open wide for me."

It was something she'd said countless times over the years

to numerous clients, but given what she was about to see, it sounded like a joke.

Her breath caught when Magnus parted his lips. His fangs were long, at least an inch and a half. And he was going to sink those monsters into her?

Vivian shook her head. "I don't think I can do that. I mean the bite. Those will feel like double daggers stabbing into me. I'm not into pain."

He smoothed his hand over her back, his touch gentle. "My saliva contains a mild analgesic, so I can mitigate most of the pain. I've bitten many women, and none of them did more than whimper for a second. I don't think it's that bad."

Vivian really didn't like the reminder of his prior partners, or that he was more than a couple of centuries old, which meant there had been a lot of them.

"Grrr, Magnus. Did you have to spoil the mood like that? I don't want to hear about your other conquests when I'm naked in the shower with you and getting all sexed up."

It was hard to see his expression in the dark, but his luminous eyes had gotten sad. "I'm sorry. We should've talked about it before getting naked." He put his hands on her waist and turned her around again. "Close your eyes and let me wash you. Don't think about the fangs. Just enjoy my touch."

Easier said than done since his slurred speech was painting a vivid image of those fangs in her head. Unless Magnus's hands could do magic and make her forget the knife-like long monstrosities, she was not going to relax.

Rubbing soap on his hands, he cupped her breasts while kissing the spot where her neck met her shoulder. "This is where I'm going to bite you." He licked the spot, then kissed it again. "You'll have the best orgasm of your life, I promise."

Somehow, what he was doing with his hands made his slurred speech sound sexy. Maybe they were magical after all.

Vivian let her head drop back, resting it against his shoulder, then turned it sideways. "Kiss me, Magnus."

He took her lips gently, applying hardly any pressure at all before slipping his tongue inside her mouth. But even so, she was keenly aware of his fangs.

Perhaps the best way to overcome fear was to face it.

Lifting her arm, she wrapped it around his neck and brought him closer to her. "Let me kiss you, Magnus. I know now why you never let me do that before. I'll be careful."

When he retracted his tongue, she followed with hers. Hesitantly seeking entry, she slipped it in between his fangs, hoping the sides weren't sharp. They shouldn't be, but then nothing about this was normal.

Discovering the sides were smooth, Vivian got bold and licked along the length of one. When Magnus groaned, and his shaft twitched under her bottom, she licked along the other one. The effect was the same.

Apparently, an immortal male's fangs were an erogenous zone. Who would have thought?

Fascinating.

But even though it was obviously immensely pleasurable to him, Magnus wasn't the kind of man who was happy to be on the receiving end. Cupping the back of her head, he pulled away. "Let me rinse you."

Impatient man. "You didn't do my back yet," she teased.

"You can get on your hands and knees right here on the shower floor, and I'll do your back while I do you, or I can rinse you, towel dry you, and take you to bed. Your choice."

Getting on all fours in the shower wasn't something she'd

done before, but perhaps she could give it a try some other time. Enough new sensations coming her way tonight.

"Take me to bed."

"I thought so."

It took him less than a minute to get her out of the shower, wrap her in a soft towel, and carry her to bed.

Gently, Magnus put her down on her back, but Vivian had other ideas. Rolling out of the towel, she got on all fours and looked behind her shoulder. All she could see were his glowing eyes, but that was good enough.

"I liked your idea, just not on the shower floor." She wiggled her bottom.

The other time Vivian had assumed that pose, she'd been comfortable thinking that he couldn't see her with all her lady parts on full display. Now that she knew that he could, she no longer minded.

There were no more secrets between them, and baring their souls to each other had required more courage than baring their bodies.

Besides, in this pose, she wouldn't see the bite coming.

Climbing behind her, he cupped her hot center. "Don't be afraid. I won't accidentally scrape you while having a taste."

A moment later his hot breath fanned over her moist folds. "Spread wider for me." His hand rested on her left buttock.

She moved her knees a little further apart.

"More."

Any more than that and she was going to fall on her face.

As Vivian moved her knees another couple of inches apart, Magnus rewarded her with a soft lick, then probed her opening with his finger, just rimming it for a couple of seconds before pushing it slowly inside her.

Impatient for more, Vivian moaned.

How the hell was he able to take his time with her? He'd already been close to the edge in the shower.

But that was Magnus. Her pleasure always came before his. Except, this time he didn't bring her to a climax first.

When he'd gotten her wound up so tight the coil was about to snap free, Magnus removed his fingers and his tongue. She wanted to scream in frustration, but then she heard the night-stand drawer open and close, and then the unmistakable sound of a wrapper being torn.

A moment later he gripped her hips and plunged into her, filling her up with one powerful thrust and then holding still for a couple of seconds to let her adjust to his girth.

When she pushed back, he surged forward, then back, again and again, and soon his gentle thrusts turned into powerful pounding, tightening the coil inside her to a breaking point.

As it sprung free, she yelled out his name, her eyes rolling back in her head.

Magnus draped himself over her, his big body enveloping hers as he licked the spot where he was going to bite her.

She tensed for a moment, expecting him to sink those fangs into her neck all at once, but again, Magnus surprised her. When he broke the skin, it was only with the very tips. It felt as if he'd just scraped her. There was a moment of pain, but it was tolerable, and the venom itself felt cold, not hot.

Then the euphoria hit, washing away any remnants of pain and inducing another powerful orgasm, and then another.

Shuddering and twitching from the onslaught of pleasure, Vivian collapsed on the mattress, and when another orgasm rocked her, she felt as if her body was weightless and soaring on a cloud of bliss.

13

ELLA

Ella dipped her hand in the water and then cranked the hot water faucet all the way up. The tub was the biggest Jacuzzi she'd ever seen, so big that she suspected Dimitri had had it custom built.

Or maybe he'd installed an outdoor model indoors.

Four people could get comfortable in it, and she wondered if Dimitri had entertained several female guests in there at once.

She couldn't care less about the hookers he'd most likely had delivered to the estate, or even volunteers. All she cared about was whether he'd used protection. Getting a disease from him would just be the poisoned cherry on top.

Then again, he wasn't stupid or ignorant, so she had to assume that he'd been careful.

When another dip confirmed that the water temperature was just right, Ella shrugged off the bathrobe and climbed into the tub.

It felt heavenly, an oasis of tranquility in hell.

Not that her day had been hellish. Far from it. Dimitri had

left for Moscow early in the morning, and he wasn't coming back until tomorrow.

Ella had spent the day horseback riding with Misha and visiting two more villages. They'd had lunch in the first one, and dinner in the second, which was a tavern that served beer and vodka along with the food. A band had played Russian country music as well as popular stuff, and she'd even gotten to dance with Misha, or rather she'd danced while he stood in place, swaying from foot to foot.

It had been a good day, and since Dimitri wasn't coming back until the next evening, she was going to have a wonderful night and most of the day tomorrow as well.

Looking at the bottle of wine she'd brought into the bathroom, Ella debated between drinking straight from the bottle or pouring it into a glass. On the one hand, she didn't like drinking from a bottle, but on the other hand, it would feel very satisfying to treat Dimitri's super expensive wine with such disregard.

Any act of rebellion, no matter how small, was so satisfying. If she had a phone, she would've taken a selfie while holding the bottle up and then showed it to Dimitri. After all, he encouraged her to develop a taste for wine. He hadn't specified that she had to use a glass.

Leaning forward, Ella snatched the bottle and then lay back, resting her head on the inflatable pillow that was part of the tub.

Since it was still early, it was a good time to open a channel to her mom. They could talk for hours. No one was going to intrude on her while she was soaking in the bathtub.

Hey, Mom, are you busy?

Not at all. I'm so relieved to hear your voice in my head. I was starting to worry. What's going on?

Nothing much. I'm sorry I didn't talk to you before. I was either asleep or surrounded by people. Right now, I'm soaking in the bathtub with a bottle of wine, and no one is going to disturb me. We can talk as much as we want.

Her mother chuckled. *I'm not going to pretend that I didn't hear the word wine mentioned. But under the circumstances, I guess it's okay. Where is Gorchenco?*

He's on a business trip to Moscow, and he's not coming back until tomorrow evening. But I don't want to talk about him. That's all we've been talking about. I want to talk about you and Parker and what's going on with you, and especially about the witchy ritual. Did it lift the curse?

Since we have time, give me a moment to get comfortable. I've just brewed some coffee and was about to have my first cup.

Isn't it a bit late for your first coffee?

It's Sunday. I can sleep in. Besides, I don't have much to do here. Parker started a homeschooling program, so from time to time I help him with that, and Magnus takes us to the gym, so there is that. Oh, and they have a pool here. We went swimming the other day.

Sounds like you're having fun.

Through the mental connection, a wave of guilt floated toward Ella, preceding her mother's voice in her head, *As much as we can while worrying about you.*

Don't feel guilty about that, Mom. I had a great day today. I went horseback riding with Misha, my bodyguard, and we visited two villages. It's not like I'm being tormented every moment of the day. Now tell me about the ritual. Did it work?

I can't be sure, but I think so. It felt powerful.

What did you do? Can you tell me, or is it a secret?

Her mother chuckled nervously. *You won't believe it, but thirteen ladies, fourteen including me, danced naked in a circle and chanted a prayer to the goddess. We did it for so long that at some point I fainted. When I woke up, I felt like a weight was lifted off my chest. I felt strong, hopeful, and optimistic. It's probably all in my head, but the lady who organized the whole thing said that maybe my belief in the curse was inviting negative energies. So if I want it gone, I should stop believing in it.*

There was something to that. All the self-help gurus claimed that positive thinking and believing in yourself was crucial to success. And if that was true, then the opposite of that was true as well.

That sounds reasonable. So how are you going to test it?

Ella had a feeling she already knew the answer to that. Her mom had a thing for Magnus. The question was whether she had the guts to do anything about it.

I need to tell you something, Vivian began.

I knew it! You and Magnus, right?

We are in love.

Oh, Mom, I'm so happy for you. And a little envious. *Does Parker know?*

Yes, and he's okay with it. He likes Magnus a lot. When Magnus told him that he wants us to be a family, Parker actually hugged him. He wasn't like that with my two other boyfriends.

Ella hadn't been crazy about them either, but she'd kept her opinion to herself because her mother had finally been dating.

It wasn't nice to think ill of the dead, but the contractor guy had been a tightwad who'd rarely taken Vivian out to nice restaurants or shows, and it hadn't been for lack of means. The accountant had been nice but awkward, and Ella had suspected him of being a mama's boy. She didn't know anything about Magnus, but her little brother liked him, and that was good enough for her.

After what happened with Romeo, I trust Parker's judgment. If he likes Magnus, then the guy is okay.

I can't wait for you to meet him. I'm sure you're going to like him too.

Hopefully, it will be sooner rather later, Ella said before realizing she'd voiced her thought.

She'd had no intentions of telling her mom about the latest development. Vivian would flip if she heard that Dimitri wanted to get her daughter pregnant.

Usually, Ella was good at channeling only what she wanted to say to her mother and keeping the rest locked away. But sometimes slips happened.

What's going on? Talk to me, Ella.

Great, now she had her mom worried. *Nothing new, Mom. I just want my life back. That's all.*

14

BRIDGET

"Thank you so much for coming to see Parker." Vivian offered Bridget her hand.

"I feel bad about dragging you out here on a Sunday," Magnus said. "It's just that we are eager to find out if Parker is ready to attempt transition."

"It's my pleasure." Bridget shook Vivian's offered hand. "It's natural. And anyway, Dormants are a big deal for us. We are all ready to jump through hoops for you." She followed Vivian into the tiny apartment.

Parker pushed to his feet and offered her his sweaty palm. "Hi, Doctor Bridget."

"Hello, Parker." She smiled at him.

At twelve and a half, the boy was about her height, which was average for his age, so they were eye to eye.

"Would you like some coffee?" Vivian asked.

"Sure."

It would give her time to chat a little with Parker before taking him to the clinic for a checkup. The questions and checks she needed to perform would be embarrassing for him, so it was a good idea to get him comfortable with her first.

"Come sit with me, Parker." She walked over to the couch. "I want to talk with you a little."

Gingerly, he sat on the very edge of the sofa. "Are you going to ask me questions about, you know, puberty stuff?" He glanced nervously at his mother.

"Later, when we are alone in my clinic. Right now I want to talk to you about the transition and what's involved. By the way, I wanted to tell you that it was very brave of you to volunteer to go first."

Parker sat up a bit straighter, his shoulders no longer slumping forward. "Thank you. But I just thought that this was the best way to go. Mom has to wait until Ella is back, and I'm almost thirteen."

"When did Magnus tell you about us?"

"Yesterday."

This was the first time a Dormant this young had been found, and Bridget was curious to learn the differences in reaction between kids and grownups. The clan boys grew up knowing that they were going to transition at thirteen, so it wasn't a surprise for them and it wasn't scary.

Well, not terrifying was more accurate. Getting wrestled down by an older, transitioned boy must've been a little scary for most of them. She still remembered Julian's transition and how nervous he'd been before the ceremony.

"Did you believe him right away?" Bridget asked.

"I saw him swim."

She arched a brow. "And that convinced you that he's immortal?"

"I love superheroes, and Magnus can swim like Aquaman.

But that was just half of it. When he showed me his cute little dragon illusion, that was enough for me." Parker smirked.

"It wasn't cute," Magnus grumbled. "Just small. I didn't want to frighten the kid."

"Or me." Vivian handed Bridget a coffee mug and another one to Magnus. "He'd used the same illusion to convince me first. I asked for a dragon, and Magnus showed me one that wasn't threatening. I thought it was very considerate of him."

The looks the two were exchanging were so full of mutual adoration that it was almost too sweet.

Had she and Turner looked like that at the start of their relationship?

Hopefully, they had been more restrained with their show of affection. Two mature adults shouldn't act like love-sick puppies, at least not in public.

Taking another sip of coffee, Bridget stifled a chuckle. Evidently, the saying about partners growing more alike over time was true. She was starting to think like Turner.

Putting the mug down, she asked, "Do you know what's involved in turning a dormant boy into an immortal?"

With a serious expression on his face, Parker nodded. "Magnus told me it involves getting bitten. I wanted him to do it, but he said he can't get aggressive with me because he likes me too much."

"Can you suggest someone?" Magnus asked.

They didn't have any boys Parker's age in the village. The youngest guys were the troika of Jackson, Gordon, and Vlad. Gordon was away in college, and Vlad would probably scare the kid, which left Jackson. Roni, who was about the troika's age, was on a plane to New York, and he wasn't as nice of a guy as Jackson.

"Jackson. He's nineteen, but that's the youngest we have."

Parker shifted uncomfortably. "I hope he's not an asshole."

Vivian cast Bridget an apologetic glance and then frowned at her son. "Parker, please watch your language."

Ignoring the exchange, Bridget lifted the mug and took another sip of coffee. "Jackson is very nice. I'm sure you're going to like him. He and his buddies have a rock n' roll band."

As the boy's eyes sparkled with excitement, Bridget knew she'd said the right thing.

"Awesome. When can I meet him?"

"First, let's have that checkup to determine if you're ready." Bridget put her empty cup down on the coffee table and got up. "Ready?"

Parker glanced at his mother.

"Do you want your mom to come along? It's fine if you do."

He shook his head. "No, that's okay."

Wrapping her arm around his shoulders, she walked him out. "It shouldn't take long," Bridget said for the adults' benefit. "We'll be back in less than half an hour."

Parker walked with as much enthusiasm as if he was on his way to the principal's office. Shuffling his feet, he avoided her eyes.

As they entered the elevator, he cleared his throat. "What are you going to check, Doctor Bridget?"

"You have nothing to be embarrassed about. I have a son, you know. And besides, you are about to become an immortal, and we are not very bashful about our bodies."

His eyes widened. "Really?"

"Yes, really. We take pride in them. That doesn't mean that it's okay to stroll around naked, but it's not a big deal if someone happens to see you walk out of the shower."

"Even girls?"

"Yes. Even girls." Bridget opened the door to her old clinic.

He followed her into the exam room. "But it's not a sure thing that I'm a Dormant."

"It is not. But I have a good feeling about you." She motioned for him to hop on the exam table. "Take your shirt off."

She went through the motions of listening to his lungs, and then feeling for his glands, just to have him get used to her touch. "Lift up your arms."

"You have armpit hair. That's a good sign. Did you notice any changes in the size of your penis and testicles?"

Blushing profusely, Parker nodded.

"A lot of change, or just a little."

"I think it's a lot."

"Would you mind if I check?"

He shrugged.

When she was done, he sat up and quickly zipped up his pants. "So what do you think, am I ready?"

"You certainly are. You can come down and put your shirt on. We're done."

He hopped off the table. "Is it going to hurt? I mean the bite."

"Yes. But only for a few seconds. Once the venom enters your system, the pain will go away, and you'll feel euphoric."

"Does it feel like taking drugs?"

"I wouldn't know." She guided him out the door. "I've never tried any. Not even when I gave birth to Julian, and he was a big baby."

"Why didn't you? It's okay to take them for pain, right?"

"Yes, but I didn't want to. I was afraid to miss out on the experience. One of the downsides of immortality is a very low birth rate. I'll probably not have another child. Very few of us get more than one. Most don't get even that."

"Yeah, Magnus told me how lonely and hopeless everyone was until you started finding Dormants. I hope you find many more." He looked down. "You said that there are no boys my age in the village. Are there any girls?"

She shook her head.

"So if I transition and become an immortal, I will have to find a Dormant too."

Bridget chuckled. "When you are immortal, age becomes irrelevant. Once you're fully grown and ready to date, you might catch the eye of an older girl or even several of them. Since you're not related to us, you'll have many to choose from and it won't matter that they are older than you." She leaned closer. "I'm many decades older than Turner."

His eyes widened. "How old are you?"

"That, my dear Parker, is not a question a gentleman asks a lady."

15

VIVIAN

"We have twenty minutes," Magnus whispered in Vivian's ear as Bridget left with Parker.

Putting his hands on her waist, he drew her to him and kissed her softly. "You're tense," he said.

"I'm anxious. I should've gone with him."

"He's safe with Bridget."

"I know. I meant for moral support."

He lifted a brow. "Yours or his? Because the kind of questions Bridget is going to ask him are not what a boy his age wants to answer in front of his mother."

"Like what? That he's growing pubic hair? He told me that."

"Did he also tell you that he started masturbating?"

Vivian waved a dismissive hand. "Parker is too young for that."

"Not really."

Given his superior sense of smell and hearing, Magnus might have noticed something she'd missed. "Do you know that for a fact?"

He shrugged. "I know that I did it at his age. A lot."

She had a feeling Magnus knew more than he was admitting to, probably out of a sense of loyalty to Parker. Would Josh have done the same thing?

They'd had no secrets from each other. If he had suspected Parker had started doing it, he would've told her.

But maybe that was the prerogative of a father as opposed to a future stepparent, who had to prove himself to the kids over and over again. Gaining a stepchild's approval was hard, and losing it was easy.

She pulled out of his arms. "I'm going to brew fresh coffee."

The carafe was still half full, but it would give her something to do.

Magnus followed her to the bar area. "Do you want to go out for lunch later?"

"Let's hear what Bridget has to say first."

"Right. Maybe she'll give us a reason to celebrate. That will determine the kind of restaurant we choose to go to."

Vivian nodded even though she wasn't sure what result she was hoping for.

Everything was happening too fast. Magnus had assured her that boys' transition was easy, and that nothing bad was going to happen to her son. Nevertheless, it was a big deal, and it was scary, and she would've appreciated more time to mentally prepare.

"I hear them coming," Magnus said.

A moment later Parker rushed inside, his big grin telling her all she needed to know.

"I'm ready."

A few seconds later, Bridget followed him inside. "He was so excited to tell you that he ran all the way from the elevator."

Parker was jumping up and down. "When can I do it? And

where? Is Jackson going to come here, or do I go to him? How does it work?"

"There is a ceremony involved." Bridget sat on the couch. "Come sit with me, and I'll tell you all about it."

"I'll get coffee." Vivian walked over to the coffeemaker.

"We have a ceremony to celebrate a Dormant's transition. Close relatives and friends gather to watch the fight, which usually happens in the gym. Then Kian says a few words about the young man and his readiness to attempt the transformation. Two people vouch for the boy's readiness. In your case, Magnus and I will vouch for you."

"What about the mother?" Vivian handed Bridget a mug of fresh coffee.

"Not considered objective." Bridget took a sip and turned back to Parker. "After that, the initiator is chosen. Naturally, he gets chosen beforehand, but for the ritual's sake, Kian asks for a volunteer. When the initiator steps forward, he will ask you whether you accept him. If you do, you also pledge to honor him with your friendship and your respect from now on."

"But I don't know the dude who's going to do that. How can I promise that? What if Jackson is a douchebag?"

Vivian gasped. "Parker! Language."

Bridget lifted a hand. "That's okay. He's right. Normally, the boys know each other. Perhaps we should arrange for Parker to meet Jackson before the ceremony. But first, I need to ask Jackson if he is willing."

Vivian frowned. "Is there a chance he'll refuse?"

"It's considered an honor. I'm sure he'll accept."

Parker grinned. "I can't wait. I'm so excited."

"Don't forget that it's not going to be fun for you," Vivian said. "You're going to get beat up or wrestled down, and then you'll get bitten. And it's going to happen in front of people."

Parker shrugged. "It's so worth it. I'm going to get lots of money."

Bridget arched a brow. "What are you talking about?"

Vivian shook her head. Parker was a glutton for presents. Every birthday, he nagged her to invite all the kids in his grade, not just his class, so he could get more presents. Gift cards were his favorite.

"It's a thirteenth birthday celebration, right? It's like a bar mitzvah. My friend Nick is a little older than me, he had a huge party and got close to ten grand in presents."

Magnus chuckled. "Dream on. We don't celebrate birthdays."

"I don't get it. There is no party after the ceremony?" Parker asked. "Like with food and music and people dancing and presents?"

Bridget glanced at Magnus. "No, but that's not a bad idea. We should have a party."

"Awesome." Parker rubbed his hands.

"Don't expect money," Magnus said.

Parker didn't look happy. "So what do you usually bring people on their birthdays?"

"Since we don't celebrate them, nothing."

Parker's shoulders slumped. "Bummer."

"We can start a new tradition and tell everyone to bring presents." Bridget patted his knee. "But the best one is going to be your immortality. Is there a better present than that?"

"You're right. Magnus said that I might get a superpower."

Bridget arched a brow. "Really? Because that's news to me. What kind of superpower are we talking about?"

When Parker cast Magnus an accusing look, Magnus shrugged. "With his mother and sister being telepathic, I figured Parker would at some point develop the ability as well. Or maybe something else."

Bridget looked doubtful. "Most immortals don't have any special abilities other than thralling and shrouding. Very few have additional gifts. I don't have any."

"I don't either," Magnus said. "But I know several people who do. Arwel said that his telepathic ability started manifesting only in his twenties, and Yamanu told me that his incredible thralling ability increased gradually. He wasn't always as powerful. So you never know."

Bridget nodded. "True. Still, it's rare, and I don't want Parker to have false expectations." She turned to him. "Immortality comes with a lot of bonuses. You'll be stronger, faster, your senses will be much sharper. I think that's super enough."

"But what happens if I don't transition?"

"We will have to erase the memory of us from your mind, and the same goes for your mother. Because if you're not a Dormant then neither is she."

Parker looked at Magnus. "I don't want to forget you."

As tears pricked at the corners of Vivian's eyes, she looked away, staring at the cabinet above the wet bar. Would fate be that cruel to her and her children?

Magnus got up and went to sit next to Parker. "I know in my gut that you will transition."

"Do I have to give the presents back if I don't?"

Magnus laughed. "You'll get to keep them no matter what."

16

MAGNUS

"I'm going to call Kian and get the ball rolling," Magnus said after Bridget left.

Vivian took the empty mugs to the sink. "Everything feels so rushed."

Scarlet, who'd been napping the entire time Bridget was there, got up and nudged his leg.

"I need to take her out. If you don't mind, I'll call Kian while walking her."

Now that the cards were on the table, Magnus had no reason to have a private conversation with the boss. Even if Kian asked him about Vivian, he could deflect and mention that Parker was there. But it was something to do while Scarlet took her time sniffing every tree on the way.

"That's okay. You can tell me about it later."

"How about going out for lunch when I come back?"

"Sounds like a plan."

Before leaving, Magnus kissed Vivian's cheek and high-fived Parker. When he was out of the building, he dialed Kian's number.

The phone rang for a few seconds before the boss picked it up. "What's up?"

"Sorry to bother you on a Sunday, but we have a very interesting development. Bridget gave Parker a checkup, and she says he is well enough into his puberty to attempt transition. When he does, it would confirm that Vivian and Ella are Dormants as well, and they can all move into the village."

"That's brilliant. Whose idea was it?"

"The kid's. After I talked with you, Vivian and I decided that we would move to the village, and that she would attempt transition as soon as Ella was back. That way if she wasn't a Dormant, we would have to erase only weeks from her memory, not months. But when we told Parker the plan, he offered to go first. I hadn't thought of him because he's not thirteen yet, but according to Bridget he's ready."

"Congrats and good luck."

Magnus rubbed the back of his neck. "Who usually makes arrangements for the ceremony? Sari's secretary does it in Scotland. I don't know who's in charge here."

"Shai can make the arrangements, and I will preside. It's not a big deal. We can do it in the keep's gym. Are you going to initiate him?"

"Parker is like a son to me. I can't summon aggression toward him. Bridget suggested Jackson. She's going to ask him if he's willing."

"Good choice."

"Parker wants a party."

Kian chuckled. "A chance at immortality is not enough for the kid?"

"He wants a celebration like his friend's bar mitzvah, with food and music, and most importantly, lots of presents."

"That's a first." Kian laughed. "I have to meet that kid. But anyways, if you want a party, talk to Amanda. That's her specialty."

"I'll do that."

"Let me know when's the ceremony. I'll have to reshuffle things to make time for it, but initiating a Dormant is a priority."

"Thank you."

Magnus clicked the call off and scrolled for Amanda's contact.

When he told her what this was about, she squealed so loudly his ear went deaf for several minutes.

"Don't worry about a thing, darling. I'll have everything ready by tonight. Tell Parker to take a good nap so he'll have the energy for a midnight ceremony."

That was a surprise Vivian wasn't going to like. She already felt rushed. Having the ceremony tonight was going to send her into panic mode.

"We are not in that big of a hurry. Can't we do it tomorrow, or Tuesday?"

"Sorry, but I can only pull it off today. I work during the week. Right now I have nothing to do, and I love organizing a party."

He tried a different tactic. "Parker wants presents. How are people going to buy him stuff on such short notice?"

"I'll tell everyone to either give him cash or print out gift cards. You don't have to go to the store for them anymore. Besides, you said he was envious of his friend getting lots of money for his bar mitzvah. Parker is going to prefer cash."

That was true.

"I don't know if Bridget asked Jackson yet."

"Hold the line. I'm going to call him and get back to you. Great choice, by the way."

The woman sure worked fast. Less than two minutes later she was back on the line. "Jackson said that he would love to do it."

"Hold on. Parker and Jackson should meet first. Parker will be less anxious if he gets to talk to his initiator before the fight."

"That might not be the best idea, darling. If Jackson likes Parker, which I'm sure he will, then it will be difficult for him to summon aggression toward the kid. Parker is much smaller and younger than Jackson. But, I can send you a picture you can show Parker. Jackson is very photogenic."

"Thank you. I hope it will help."

"I'm going to mobilize the two Odus to make the food, and anyone else that I can rope into volunteering to help with the decorations and the tables and chairs. If you want it to be a surprise for Parker, keep him away from the gym level."

"When do you think you and your army of helpers are going to be here?"

"I need to plan a menu, figure out which ingredients are needed to make the dishes, buy them, and then drop Okidu and Onidu at the big kitchen in the keep. So my best guess is that they're going to be there in about an hour and a half. The decorations and the tables and chairs can go in much later. I'm thinking around ten at night should be fine. Two hours is plenty of time to get everything ready."

"Let me know if you need my help."

She chuckled. "I'm sure I'll have plenty of volunteers."

Impressive.

Despite her diva persona and princess status, Amanda was a can-do, hands-on type of woman. Well, not her hands, but organizing others so quickly to lend theirs was no less admirable.

17

ELLA

"Hello, beautiful," a male voice said.

Ella popped her eyes open and screamed. She was staring into Logan's dark eyes. Except, they weren't really dark because they were glowing. A reddish, demonic glow.

He was lying on his side in her bed, his head propped on his hand, leering at her.

Only that was impossible. She was in Dimitri's impenetrable estate in Russia, and there was no way he would've allowed Logan in there while he was gone.

It was a dream. "Go away," she told the specter.

Logan frowned. "Ella!" He shook her shoulder. "What's wrong?"

"Get out of my head!"

"Ella! It's me, Misha. Wake up!"

As she opened her eyes for real this time, it wasn't Logan's too handsome face and evil smile she was looking at, but her bodyguard's ugly one.

The most beautiful and welcome sight ever.

"What happened?" Misha asked.

"I had a bad dream. How did you know to come in?"

He took a step back and let out a breath. "I heard you scream. I thought someone was here."

"But that's impossible. No one can come into Dimitri's estate uninvited, right?"

"It is impossible, yes. But maybe it is. You scream, I come. That is my job."

"Thank you. But I'm okay now. You can go back to sleep."

"You sure? I can lie down on the sofa and watch you."

As much as she liked Misha, she didn't want him staring at her while she slept. It sounded creepy. "No, it's okay, Misha. Good night."

"Good night. Call for me if you have bad dream again."

"I will."

When he finally left, Ella took in a deep breath and stared at the ceiling. Going back to sleep wasn't happening. For some reason, Logan was lurking around her mind, waiting for opportunities to haunt her dreams.

Why the hell was she so scared of him? And why did he seem so familiar when she'd never met him before Dimitri had introduced them?

Familiar wasn't the right term, though.

Ella knew she had never seen Logan's face before that lunch with Dimitri, in person or in a picture. He was too striking to forget. The sense she'd gotten was of like recognizing like. And maybe that was what had frightened her the most.

Because Logan was bad. Ella felt it in her gut, and she'd learned the hard way not to ignore those subtle whispers. They'd been there with Romeo, she'd just chosen to ignore them because she wanted the fairytale to be real.

Was she bad too? She hadn't done anything malicious in her

life. The trouble she'd brought upon herself and her family was the result of stupidity and naivety, not malice.

Her mother had mentioned something about negative energy. Perhaps that was what it was. Just like her mother, subconsciously, Ella was either a producer or attracter of bad vibes.

With that unpleasant thought running through her brain's synapses, she got out of bed, put on a night robe, and padded over to the wine cooler. Pulling out another one of Dimitri's expensive wine bottles, she uncorked it, and then took it with her out to the terrace.

She was turning into quite the drunkard.

The other bottle was still in the bathroom, half full, or half empty, depending on how she wanted to look at it. In the morning, Ella was going to pour what was left down the toilet. It was such a sweet waste. She would've offered it to Misha, but he didn't like wine, preferring something more potent like vodka.

Or maybe he just didn't want to touch the boss's prized wines, either out of fear or out of respect. Probably both.

It was evident that Dimitri's people were loyal to him because they respected him, and as long as everyone did exactly what he demanded from them, they were also treated well.

He was the king of the castle, the absolute ruler, for better and for worse, holding their lives and those of their families in the palm of his hand so to speak.

Ella could understand the appeal of a safe and predictable life, but she wanted no part in it. Heck, with her bad juju doing its thing, Dimitri's empire might just crumble and fall.

That would serve him right.

For a moment, Ella allowed herself to enjoy the imaginary

power of that juju, fantasizing about Dimitri's downfall. Except, with him gone, some other oligarch would move in and take over, one who was worse.

Her negative energy would then affect everyone under Dimitri's control.

Lying on the chaise lounge, she brought the wine bottle to her mouth and took a long swig. The taste was growing on her. Except, if something was good, shouldn't it taste wonderful from the start?

She took another swig.

Getting used to living in all that luxury and drinking thousands of dollars' worth of wine was easy. She might even get used to Dimitri.

Right, she could barely tolerate him.

She pretended to be okay with him because she had to. Not only as a way to lull him into trusting her more, but also as a coping mechanism. It was her way of keeping herself together until her rescue arrived. Falling apart was not going to do her any good. She needed to remain strong.

But if Dimitri got her pregnant, she was going to hate him forever. Not the child, hopefully, but the father for sure.

What if the rescue never came through, though?

What if she was stuck with Dimitri forever?

To survive living with him, she would have to deaden most of who she was. What little was left of her spirit would be snuffed out.

Maybe she would be better off dead. That would serve him right. Dimitri would be crushed. Losing his dream girl for the second time around would devastate him.

Ella lifted the bottle, took a long gulp, and then frowned. Something about that overly dramatic thought pricked her mind. A thread of a solution. If she were dead, Dimitri would have no reason to search for her or her family.

What if the rescue team could fake her death?

Perhaps they could time the fire for when Dimitri was away. They could make it look as if she died from smoke inhalation. Burning to a crisp would be better, but faking it would probably be too dangerous. The whole house could catch fire, and many people might get hurt. Yeah, suffocating on the smoke would be easier to fake. Maybe she could even start the fire.

There were several problems with her brilliant idea, though.

First was Misha, who was always around. He would play the hero and rush to rescue her. But that could be solved by someone knocking him out with something nonlethal. She should tell her mother that Misha was not to be harmed.

Then there was the hospital she would supposedly be taken to and the morgue. Dimitri would search for her there. Maybe the ambulance could suffer an accident and land in a lake or a river? Or maybe catch fire, so there were no bodies to identify? But that would look suspicious too.

And most importantly, would the people helping her mom agree to go to all that trouble just because she didn't want Dimitri to die?

It wasn't that she was a softie. Ella wouldn't have minded Stefano going to hell together with Romeo. But that was because she'd witnessed first-hand the evil they had done. With Dimitri, she was aware of it, but she didn't know the what, or how, or who he was harming, only that he surely did.

The mafia, by definition, was not a charitable organization.

Without bearing witness to his crimes, though, she shouldn't be the one to put him on trial and then sentence him to death without even giving him a chance to defend himself. Dimitri should get punished for the crimes he'd perpetrated against her, but they didn't deserve the death penalty.

Besides, that gut feeling or intuition that she was learning to tune in to was telling her that it wasn't Dimitri Gorchenco's time to die. He still had an important part to play in the grand scheme of things.

Whatever that grand scheme was, she had no idea. It was a vague sense of some cosmic order she was dimly aware existed. Or maybe it was just her imagination.

Taking another swig, she opened a channel to her mother.

Mom.

Hi, sweetheart. What are you doing awake at three o'clock in the morning?

Thinking. What if Magnus's people can fake my death? If Dimitri thinks that I died in the fire, he will have no reason to search for you or for me. Case closed. We are all free.

That's not a bad idea, but pulling it off is much more complicated than killing him. Not that I know it for a fact, but it makes sense.

You said that they were going to stage a fire, right? Maybe I can die from smoke inhalation. Talk with Magnus's boss. See what he thinks about it.

I will.

Can you do it now? I can stay awake and contact you in an hour.

Why don't you just leave the channel open?

I want to do some more thinking, and I'm so used to keeping it closed that it requires too much concentration keeping it open.

I see. I'll check with Turner and wait for you to contact me.

18

VIVIAN

Vivian opened her eyes and let out a breath.

"Were you talking to Ella?" Magnus asked. "Your eyes glazed over and you just stared into the distance. When you closed them, I thought you were tired, but then you started emitting an anxious scent."

"That's an interesting observation. I didn't know I was being so obvious."

"It's only obvious to someone who knows that you can do it. Everyone else would assume that you're just zoning out."

She shook her head. "If it looks suspicious, Ella is right to restrict her communication with me to when she's alone. It's better not to give anyone reason to wonder what she's doing."

"True. So what did she say that made you anxious?"

Vivian pushed off the couch, walked over to the bar, and pulled out a bottle of soda from the fridge. "She came up with the idea of faking her own death during the rescue. Smoke inhalation, or something of that nature. If Gorchenco thinks she's dead, he'll have no reason to come after her or us."

Magnus rubbed the back of his neck. "She must be suffering

from a bad case of Stockholm syndrome. I don't understand why it's so important to her to keep the guy alive."

"She's just a girl, Magnus." Vivian sighed. "She doesn't want anyone to die, and especially not on her account. The guilt would eat her alive. Can we call Turner and ask his opinion?"

"Let me text him first. I don't want to call at a bad time." Magnus pulled out his phone.

"I'm going to the bathroom to take this off." She tugged on her wig. "My scalp is itchy."

"I'll wait for you to come out before making the call."

"Thanks."

In the bathroom, Vivian stood in front of the mirror and reached for the pins holding her wig in place. After being cooped up in the underground for so long, going out to a restaurant for lunch had felt stressful, and not because she was afraid of being recognized by surveillance cameras despite her and Parker's disguises.

She'd been relieved when the meal was done, but then Magnus suggested they stop at a sports clothing store and get Parker an outfit for the ceremony.

More stress.

The tension had started to ease only when they'd headed back.

Sitting on the couch in Magnus's room, on the other hand, felt like home.

Vivian understood now why released prisoners had trouble adjusting to the outside world. Apparently, habits and routines had a stronger hold on people than she'd assumed.

They also formed incredibly fast.

Was Parker as affected?

Kids adjusted more easily to changes in their environment. Except, if he transitioned tonight, he'd have a much bigger adjustment to make than just moving out of the windowless underground and into the open air village.

When all the pins were out, she combed out her hair, hung the wig on a hook, and opened the door.

"Ready?" Magnus asked.

Vivian nodded.

While the phone rang, he activated the speaker.

"What's up, Magnus?" Turner's slight southern accent gave his tone a misleading softness.

There was nothing soft about that man.

"Ella came up with the idea of faking her death during the rescue. Can it be done?"

"It's doable, of course, but complicated. On the other hand, doing it that way will close the case without further complications, which I like. The Russian mafia will not be an issue. The question is how to pull it off. I need time to think it through."

Vivian leaned forward to get closer to the speaker. "Ella said it would be best to stage the fire while Gorchenco is away from the estate."

"That would be ideal. But we can't plan for that. We have a small window of opportunity while he is at his New York estate, and we need to use it regardless of whether he's there or not."

"What should I tell Ella?"

"Tell her that I'm working on it. If I come up with a reasonable plan of action, we will do it her way. Otherwise, it's back to plan one."

"Got it. Thank you."

"You're welcome."

After Turner ended the call, Vivian checked the time. She still had half an hour before Ella contacted her again. "I'm going to check up on Parker. He should wake up and start getting ready."

Magnus caught her hand and pulled her back down. "Let the kid sleep a little longer. The ceremony is at midnight. There is plenty of time. The more rested he is, the better."

"When you're right, you're right." She leaned against him and put her head against his bicep. "I'm just stressed."

"You have nothing to worry about. Parker is going to be fine."

"What if it doesn't work?"

He kissed the top of her head. "There's no point in ifs. There are so many of them that you can always find something to worry about."

"I wish I knew how not to do that."

Hooking a finger under her chin, Magnus turned her toward him. "I know how to take your mind off things."

He dipped his head and kissed her, softly at first, but when she responded by moving over and straddling his hips, he cupped the back of her head to hold her for some serious plundering.

They were still kissing when Ella's voice sounded in her head.

Mom.

Vivian pushed away from the hard chest she'd been plastered against and gave Magnus one last soft kiss before moving over.

"Ella?" he asked.

She nodded.

Hi, sweetheart. We called Turner, and he said he's going to give it some thought.

Does that mean that he is really trying to come up with a plan, or is it just a brush-off?

He's taking it seriously. He said that if it's doable, it's a better solution all around. But he also said that he couldn't plan for Gorchenco not to be there while they stage the fire.

That's not true. During the time I've been with him, he leaves for hours at a time. It's just a question of timing, and I can let you know exactly when he leaves and when he's planning on coming back. He tells me whether I should wait to eat dinner with him or not. And if he's running late, he calls.

Vivian shook her head. It seemed Gorchenco was acting like a devoted boyfriend. No wonder Ella had a problem with him dying despite everything he'd done to her. She wondered if the pervert really cared or was just pretending. Not that it mattered to her. If it were up to Vivian, she would've pulled the trigger herself.

I'll pass it on to Turner.

Thank you. And another thing. I don't want them to kill my bodyguard either. Misha is a really nice guy.

And how would they know who he is?

First of all, as soon as the alarm sounds, he will rush to save me, so they will find us together, and I can tell them not to harm him. I know that they will have to take him out, I'm just asking that they don't kill him. He's a big guy, around six three or six four, with muscles like a pro-wrestler, and an ugly face.

Sounds like a charmer.

He is a good guy and my only friend here, Mom. What's on the inside doesn't match what's on the outside.

19

MAGNUS

When Magnus walked into the keep's kitchen, the place was humming with activity. He'd expected to see only the two Odus, but working side by side with them were also Callie, Ruth, Wonder, and Carol.

"I see that Amanda managed to rope you into cooking for Parker's party. Thank you for helping out."

Callie waved a spatula. "She didn't have to work hard at it. We volunteered. Parker is going to get one hell of a party."

The big island taking up most of the industrial kitchen's floor space was covered with two long rows of disposable trays. Most of them were already full. "I can see that. How many people are coming?"

"I put a note on the clan's bulletin board," Carol said. "Everyone is invited, but I don't think they will all come on such short notice."

"I hope not. Parker is going to freak out."

Wonder cast him an amused glance. "The more people come, the more money he'll get. I think a large turnout is going to make him very happy."

"I hope you're right. I'd better see if the guys need my help organizing the tables."

"See you later."

As Magnus entered the gym, he hardly recognized the place. All the machines had been pushed flat against the walls and hidden behind a partially done wall of balloons.

The center was roped off like a boxing ring, and about a dozen or so Guardians were arranging tables and chairs around it as if it was a dance floor.

In one corner, Anandur was sitting with a big-ass helium tank and inflating one balloon after another, while Ingrid and Sylvia were tying and adding them to the ever-growing wall hiding the equipment.

Above it all, Amanda stood on a chair and was issuing commands. "That's too close, Liam, you need to leave more space between the tables so people can push their chairs back."

Magnus walked up to her and looked up. "You're unbelievable. I don't know anyone who could've pulled off a party this size in one afternoon."

She smiled and executed a theatrical bow. "Thank you. By the way, Jackson and Tessa are here. Do you want to talk to him?"

"Sure. Where is he?"

Amanda looked around. "They are over there." She pointed somewhere behind the tables. "You can't see them because they are on the floor, unpacking the tablecloths. That's their assignment."

"Do you need me to do anything?"

"Once the buffet tables are set up, you can help carry things from the kitchen."

"Yes, ma'am." He saluted before heading to where she'd indicated Jackson was.

He knew the guy, but not well. Jackson was running around trying to grow his pastry business. Last Magnus had heard, the kid had rented a large bakery, hired several bakers, and was supplying a bunch of coffee shops with pastries.

Not bad for a nineteen-year-old.

He found the young couple unpacking boxes and organizing piles of paper tablecloths in several colors, or rather shades. White, and several shades of blue.

As Magnus approached, Jackson lifted his head. "Are you going to tell me to take it easy on the kid?"

"How did you know?"

He pushed to his feet and offered Magnus his hand. "Because I would have done the same if he were my kid."

"Parker is not mine, but you're right. I feel as if he is."

"If you want to worry about something, it should be about me being able to get aggressive with a twelve-year-old. I hope he's big for his age."

"Not really. He's a scrawny computer nerd. But when we move to the village, I'm going to work on that."

"Good luck." Jackson smirked. "I can't get Roni to move his ass. I need him on the drums, and they require stamina. He gets winded way before the rest of us are ready to call it a day."

"Who is us? Is Gordon back?"

"No, but Tessa joined the band. She sings." Jackson looked at his mate with adoring eyes. "Like an angel."

Hopefully, she could really sing, and Jackson wasn't listening with his heart rather than his ears.

"That's great. When are we going to see you guys perform?"

"When Roni gets his shit together, and we are actually ready to go in front of an audience."

"Do you want me to tell Parker anything before you guys meet at the ring?"

"Tell him not to be scared. If he can come up with something to annoy me, that could be helpful."

Magnus laughed. "I can give him a few pointers."

Jackson narrowed his eyes at him. "Oh, yeah? Like what?"

"It's going to be more effective when you're not ready for it."

"Yeah, I guess you're right. But now I'll just keep thinking what it could be."

On the floor, Tessa chuckled. "Jackson thinks he's perfect."

"Why? Do you have any complaints?"

She shook her head. "None. You are truly perfect."

"So why did you say that I only think I am?"

Magnus left the young couple to their teasing and headed back to the dungeon level.

Both doors were open, but Vivian was back in the larger suite, looking amazing in the dress he'd gotten for her.

"Getting ready already?" He pulled her in for a kiss. "I love how this dress hugs your curves."

"What curves?"

"Stop it." He slapped her butt lightly. "I don't want you to talk or think like that. You are beautiful and sexy, and I'm one lucky guy to have snagged you."

Vivian smiled and lifted on her toes to kiss him back. "In your eyes, maybe. But I'm going to meet a lot of new people today. I want to leave a good impression."

"Oh, you will." He gave her a smoldering look over. "Starting tonight, every guy in the village is going to cast me envious glances."

"You're sweet."

"No, I'm not. It's exactly what's going to happen. Is Parker up?"

"He's in the shower. Why?"

"I have a few pointers to give him before the fight. I just spoke to Jackson. He needs Parker to annoy him so he can get aggressive."

"How is he going to do that?"

"He can start by calling Jackson a pretty boy. The guy is truly blessed in that regard."

She arched a brow. "More than you? Impossible."

"Sadly, it is true."

"What else can he say to aggravate Jackson?"

"Well, anything that would be offensive to his mate, but that's a big no-no."

"He is mated at nineteen?"

Magnus pulled Vivian close against his chest. "Jackson is very fortunate. He didn't have to wait long for his one and only. And so am I. Kian had to wait almost two thousand years for Syssi."

"Wow, that's a really long time."

20

VIVIAN

As Magnus put his hand on the gym's door, Vivian lifted a hand to stop him. "Give me a second." Looking down, she twisted her dress a little, making sure that the side seams were perfectly aligned. Next was the hemline that was supposed to reach only a couple of inches above her knees but had a tendency to ride up her thighs. The dress wasn't tight, only form-fitting, but still, it wasn't the same as wearing a pair of leggings and a T-shirt and forgetting all about it.

"You look gorgeous."

She glanced at Parker, whom she trusted more to tell her the truth. "Do I look okay?"

"You look awesome. Except for the lipstick you got smeared on your teeth."

Horrified, she reached with her finger but then remembered she hadn't put any on. "You!" She laughed, wagging her finger at him.

"Made you laugh."

"Are we ready?" Magnus asked.

Vivian nodded.

Parker pushed the door open and walked in as if he owned the place.

When cheers and claps erupted, her son lifted his arms and kept walking as if he was the boxing champion of the world and the crowd's favorite.

"Thank you all for coming to my ceremony," he called out.

"Not shy, is he?" Magnus whispered in her ear.

"I had no idea he had a showman in him. He loves the attention."

"Apparently."

Amanda walked up to Parker and gave him a hug. "Does that meet with your approval, Master Parker?"

He looked around, his eyes taking in the balloons and the other decorations and the tables with people sitting around them. There must have been close to two hundred immortals there, all smiling at Vivian's son.

"Oh, yeah. I like it a lot. Thank you for organizing it."

Amanda beamed. "You're welcome, my darling."

"Is there going to be a DJ?"

Vivian wanted the floor to split open and swallow her. Parker was acting like a spoiled brat. What had gotten into him? Was it the impending immortality?

"No DJ." A huge redheaded guy approached and ruffled Parker's hair. "Live music. We have bagpipes, and smallpipes, and several excellent dancers for your entertainment."

Parker eyed the big man suspiciously. "You're joking, right?"

"Nope." He offered his hand. "I'm Anandur, Magnus's partner."

From behind him, a beautiful man with long blond hair stepped forward. "I'm Brundar. Anandur's brother." He didn't offer his hand, but he dipped his head.

"It's nice to meet you," Parker said with a smile.

Shaking Anandur's hand, Vivian nodded at Brundar. Some people were germaphobes and didn't like shaking hands. That was okay with her.

The greetings and introductions continued until Amanda put a stop to the procession. "Okay, people, that's enough. Everyone, please get back to your seats."

She took Vivian's hand on one side and Parker's on the other. "This is Vivian." She lifted their conjoined hands. "And this is Parker, her son, and the star of tonight's event. Please give him a round of applause as a welcome to our clan."

The clapping that followed was deafening, but Parker was grinning from ear to ear, eating up the attention. Who knew that her computer prodigy, as he liked to refer to himself, was a stage animal?

Suddenly, the clapping stopped, and everyone's eyes shifted from Parker to whoever had just opened the gym's doors.

Vivian turned on her heel and lost her balance. Luckily, Magnus caught her elbow to stabilize her.

"My apologies for the late arrival." The most stunning man she'd ever seen strode toward her.

With her eyes riveted on the guy, Vivian noticed Syssi only in her peripheral vision. It took her confused brain a split second to put what she was seeing together.

So that was Kian. Syssi's husband. The big boss. Amanda's brother. The goddess's son.

He certainly looked like a god.

"Holy Batman," Parker murmured.

Kian's intense gaze shifted from Vivian to Parker, and a big smile brightened his severe expression. "Young man." He offered Parker his hand. "I assure you that I'm not Batman."

Parker shook what he was offered with a raised brow. "You

don't get out much, do you? Holy Batman is an expression. It's like holy moly."

Vivian felt faint. She and Parker needed to have a talk about boundaries, and what was appropriate to say to whom and when.

"Who is moly?" Kian asked.

Syssi patted his bicep. "It's the same as wow."

"Oh, now I get it." Kian didn't seem bothered by his pop culture ignorance. Still smiling, he turned to Vivian and offered her his hand. "It's my pleasure to welcome you and your children into my clan."

"Thank you."

She didn't want to mention that their welcome wasn't a sure thing. If Parker didn't transition, Kian and his clan would be erased from her and her son's memory.

Amanda clapped her hands to get their attention. "Let me show you to your table. As the guests of honor, you are sitting right here up front."

Vivian looked at the roped-off arena and swallowed hard. "When is the fight supposed to happen?"

"After we eat." She winked at Parker. "And after this boy gets his presents, so he's in a good mood."

Parker's eyes sparkled. "I get to open my presents now?"

"No, darling. But you see that big box with your name on it? It's full of envelopes. And guess what's inside those envelopes."

"Money?"

"You got it."

Parker threw his arms around Amanda's waist and gave her a hug. "Thank you."

Her eyes widening, Amanda teetered on her spiky heels, but recovered quickly and hugged him back. "Aren't you just precious." She kissed the top of his head.

As Vivian took her place at the head table next to Syssi and Kian, she felt like a celebrity. But since the food was served buffet style, she didn't get to sit down for long.

Following the crowd to the buffet, she shook hands and accepted words of welcome, as many more clan members introduced themselves. Eventually, though, she gave up on trying to remember everyone's names.

All along, Magnus stood protectively by her side, and then carried both their plates to the table. There were many advantages to having an old fashioned fiancé.

Wow, he was her fiancé, wasn't he? In so many words, Magnus had proposed. Except, he hadn't really asked her. Not that it was important. She kind of liked it that he'd taken it for granted that if she loved him, she wished to marry him. That too was old fashioned but nice.

"Are you okay?" he whispered as they sat down.

"My feet hurt from standing in these gorgeous shoes you've gotten me, and my face hurts from smiling too much, but other than that and the upcoming fight, I feel incredible. Your clan is so warm and welcoming."

"They are like candy. A small serving is great, but too much can make you nauseous. Wait until you move into the village. I can just imagine all the visitors you'll get."

"About that. Where exactly are we going to live, did you check availability?"

"Not yet." He turned to Kian. "We need a three-bedroom house. I guess the only ones available are in the new phase, true?"

Kian nodded.

"Are we going to be the first ones to move in there?"

"Second. Merlin arrived yesterday, and he didn't want to

share a house with anyone, so we had to rush the opening of the second phase."

"Merlin moved here? I didn't know he had such plans."

"Who's Merlin?" Vivian asked.

"He is a doctor from the Scottish arm of the clan. A fascinating fellow."

"In what way?"

Magnus waved a dismissive hand. "Describing him is going to take away from the effect. When you meet him, you'll understand what I mean." He switched his attention to the food on his plate.

As Vivian tried to imagine them living together in a brand new house, the image wavered and refused to solidify. The truth was that everyone was acting as if Parker had already transitioned, and making plans for a future that wasn't guaranteed.

But maybe that was the right attitude. She often mulled over what Amanda had said in regards to negative energies inviting negative experiences. Perhaps focusing on the positive outcome created a positive energy that would help it manifest?

21

MAGNUS

After the meal was done, Anandur together with several Guardians put on a short sword dance performance, and then it was Kian's turn.

As he rose to his feet, Magnus wrapped his arm around Parker's shoulders and whispered in his ear, "Here comes the ritual speech."

When the room quieted down, Kian began, "First of all, I want to thank Amanda for organizing this event." He waited for the claps and cheers to subside. "I also want to thank the Guardians for the entertainment portion of the evening."

As the dance team stood up and took a bow, more cheers and clapping ensued.

They'd done a fine job, but a sword dance wasn't the same without kilts and the actual swords. Then again, it had been an impromptu performance.

When Kian lifted a hand for everyone to hush down, his serious expression heralded the ceremonial part of the event. "We are gathered here to present this fine young man to his elders. Parker is ready to attempt his transition even though he is not thirteen yet. I applaud his courage for volunteering to go first and prove that he, as well as his mother and sister, are Dormants, enabling them to join our community while still in the dormant state."

As Kian clapped his hands, signaling for everyone to join him, Parker seemed to grow a couple of inches taller, straightening his spine and squaring his shoulders.

Magnus had planned on giving the kid a little pep talk right before the fight, but it seemed that after Kian's speech it wasn't necessary.

Kian lifted his hand, and the clapping stopped. "Vouching for Parker's maturity and readiness to attempt his transition are Guardian Magnus and Doctor Bridget. Who volunteers to take on the burden of initiating Parker into his immortality?"

Jackson stood up and lifted his hand. "I do."

Kian nodded and turned to Parker. "Parker, do you accept Jackson as your initiator?"

"I do," Parker said.

"Do you accept him as your mentor and protector, to honor him with your friendship, your respect, and your loyalty from now on?"

Parker turned to look at Jackson, then shifted his eyes to Bridget who smiled and gave him the thumbs up.

"I don't know Jackson personally, but if Doctor Bridget says he's okay, then he must be. I accept."

As another round of applause erupted, Kian waited until it was done, then continued with the ceremonial words. "Does anyone have any objections to Parker becoming Jackson's protégé?" He glanced around and waited for a couple of seconds. "As everyone here agrees that this is a good match, let's seal it with a toast." He lifted his wine glass. "To Parker and Jackson."

Parker reached for the wine glass in front of him. "Am I supposed to drink it too?"

Magnus lifted his. "This is the one exception when you're allowed."

They clinked glasses, then Parker clinked his with Vivian's. Another round of clinking included Kian and Syssi, and then it was done.

Kian put down his glass. "Parker and Jackson, please come forward."

Magnus got up together with Parker and escorted him to the roped-off matting.

As Parker bent down to go under the rope, Magnus caught his elbow and whispered in his ear, "You need to spur Jackson's aggression, but you only need to last a few seconds. Can you do it?"

Parker smirked. "Don't worry, I know how to fight."

Magnus sincerely doubted it, but he admired the kid's confidence.

In the center of the ring, Parker was jumping up and down like a boxer as he waited for Jackson to get in.

Smiling, either to reassure Parker or because he found the boxing warmup routine funny, Jackson stepped over the rope and approached Parker with his usual confident swagger.

Catching everyone by surprise, Parker leaped forward and head-butted Jackson in the stomach.

Not expecting the sudden attack, Jackson lost his balance and stumbled backward.

Not missing a beat, Parker kept going and kicked him in the shin.

"Ow, that hurt!" Jackson's eyes started glowing, and his fangs punched out.

Magnus couldn't have been prouder. The boy had guts.

The moment Jackson's fangs made an appearance, though, Parker's bravado evaporated and he turned on his heel, leaping for the rope on the other side.

Parker had healthy survival instincts. Magnus had to give him that. When outmatched, it was always better to run.

Except, there was no outrunning an immortal. In one leap, Jackson was on Parker, toppling him face down on the mat and then straddling his legs.

As Vivian gasped, Magnus reached for her hand and clasped it, but not wanting to disturb Jackson's concentration, he didn't say anything to reassure her. The quicker the bite was done, the better for Parker.

Jackson hissed, struck, and eighteen seconds later retracted his fangs and licked the puncture wounds closed.

"Can I go to him now?" Vivian whispered.

"Let's go." He helped her up.

Jackson was still kneeling over Parker as they entered the roped-off arena.

As he lifted his head and smiled at Vivian, Magnus was relieved that Jackson's fangs were back to their normal size, and that there was no blood on them. "Your son is a fighter," he said. "I like him, and I'm looking forward to many years of friendship with him."

"Thank you." Vivian knelt next to Parker and smoothed her hand over his hair. "Look at that smile. He looks happy."

Jackson chuckled. "He's flying high."

"How long is he going to be out?"

Kneeling next to her, Magnus gently turned Parker to lie on his back. "Minutes."

"I remember not wanting to wake up," Jackson said.

"I just hope you gave him enough. Eighteen seconds is on the short side."

Jackson shrugged. "That's what Doctor Bridget told me to do. She said a minimum of fifteen and a maximum of thirty. Since Parker is skinny, I thought it was safer to stay on the lower end, and I counted."

"My presents?" Sounding dopey, Parker asked, "How much did I get?"

Vivian let out a long breath. "Jackson was referring to counting seconds, not how much money you got."

The laughter and clapping started at the tables nearest the arena and then spread throughout, until all the immortals in the room were on their feet and cheering.

Opening his eyes, Parker looked at the wall of smiling faces. "Why are they clapping? Did I transition?"

"Not yet. It doesn't happen right away." Magnus took Parker's hand and threaded his arm around the kid's back, helping him up to a sitting position. "But you gave them one hell of a show. No one expected you to launch an attack and head-butt Jackson."

"You told me to get him going. So I did."

"Good job, kid." Jackson patted Parker's shoulder. "See you on the other side."

"What now?" Vivian asked.

"He needs to rest," Bridget said from behind them and then crouched in front of Parker. "You'll feel a little loopy and might develop a low fever. That's normal and nothing to worry about. Don't eat for the next couple of hours. Your stomach might get queasy."

"How will I know that anything is happening?"

Bridget smiled. "When you feel like you want to eat an entire steakhouse, that's a clue that your body needs fuel for the transformation. The next clues are swollen gums, a toothache, and a throat ache, not necessarily in that order. I'll get you painkillers for that."

"Thanks, doctor."

"Do you want me to carry you back?" Magnus asked.

Parker cast him an incredulous look. "With all these people watching? No way. I'm walking."

"I'll give you a hand." Magnus got up.

When Parker shook his head, Magnus knelt back down. "The venom makes you loopy. No one gets up and just walks away. Every boy who's ever transitioned needed help getting up and walking home. You can lean on me."

"Are you sure no one ever did it? What about Kian?"

Magnus rolled his eyes. It seemed Parker had found a new superhero to worship. "Kian didn't have to transition because he was born immortal."

"How come?"

"I'll explain later. Now let me help you up. Your new idol is waiting to shake your hand."

22

ELLA

"I went over the list of courses you sent me, and I can't decide between psychology and philosophy." Ella forked another piece of beef and put it in her mouth. It practically melted on her tongue.

Dimitri's chef's cooking was the one thing she was going to miss when this was over. Well, she was going to miss the horses too. And maybe having a bidet. But other than that, nothing. Well, maybe Misha too. A little.

Dimitri laughed. "Do you know what my father used to call such fields of study?"

"What?"

"Blah-blah, as in useless talking about nothing. The only subjects of study he acknowledged were medicine and engineering."

The conversation Ella had started about choosing a subject to study was meant to make Dimitri believe she was content staying with him, and maybe get him talking about their next destination, but she couldn't help being curious about what had shaped him to become who he was.

"Was your father an educated man?"

"He was an electrical engineer, but he spent very little time working as one."

"Did you get along with him?"

Dimitri laughed. "The way to get along with my father was to say yes sir to everything demanded of me. But I can't complain. He was a good father, and I know he wanted the best for me."

"Did you love him?"

"Of course."

"How about your mother?"

He lifted his wine glass and smiled. "Naturally, I loved her too. She was my mother. What has prompted all these questions?"

Ella shrugged and lifted her own glass. "I just want to get to know you better. Part of this is finding out what made you who you are. Who were the people who shaped you."

He narrowed his eyes at her. "Who do you think I am?"

"A very powerful man. That's all I know because you don't tell me much."

"There isn't much to tell. I had a legacy to follow, and I did it to the best of my ability."

"Which is quite formidable."

That comment seemed to please him. "Indeed. My father would've been proud."

"I'm sure."

Dimitri put his wine glass down and pulled a small tablet out of his jacket pocket. "I have a surprise for you."

"What is it?"

"You wanted an electronic reader. Here is a tablet with thousands of books already downloaded. Also, it's loaded with a Rosetta Stone Russian course."

Clapping her hands, Ella pretended to be overjoyed. With a happy squeal, she jumped out of her chair, kissed Dimitri's cheek, and snatched the tablet from his hands. "Thank you. This is the best present ever."

She activated the device and started scrolling through the book selection. It was enormous. "So many books to choose from. You even got me romance novels. Awesome!"

Dimitri looked very pleased with himself, which was precisely how she wanted him to feel.

"I bought the tablet and gave it to the minister's secretary to load with whatever she thought would interest a young woman. I'm glad her choices are to your liking."

"They are. If you see her again, tell her a big thank you from me."

He nodded. "I will. Now you'll have something to do on long flights."

Hoping she wasn't overdoing it, Ella leaned and put her hand over Dimitri's. "You're so considerate. When is our next flight?"

"Wednesday."

That was in two days. Nervous butterflies flapping their wings in her stomach, Ella tried to keep the excitement at bay. "Is it going to be a long one?"

"About six hours."

So it wasn't New York.

Bummer.

"Where are we going?"

"Dubai."

"Ugh. Will I have to cover myself from head to toe?"

He laughed. "No, sweetheart. Anything you choose from the wardrobe I got for you is fine. All that's required is modest attire, no public displays of affection, no profanity, and no insults against their religion, not even as a joke. Also, don't open doors or offer anything with your left hand. It's considered unclean."

"Got it. Can I stay on the plane? It's probably very hot there, and I don't like hot places. How long are we going to be there?"

"I thought to stay two nights and spend a day sightseeing with you. But if you prefer, I can be done with my meetings in one day, and we can leave the next night."

"It depends where we're going next." It was hard to keep breathing normally and not hold it in.

"After that, it's back to New York."

Ella's heart almost jumped out of her ribcage, but she forced herself to make a face. "In that case, I'll take you up on your offer to do some sightseeing in Dubai."

The rescue team would probably need the extra day to get ready. Ella didn't want to undermine the operation just because she had no desire to go sightseeing in a place that was hotter than hell.

"I see that you're not happy about going back to New York. Where would you like to go?"

"Paris." She said the first thing that came to her mind while praying he wouldn't want to indulge her.

"Regrettably, I don't have any business there at the moment. But perhaps I can make a detour when we leave for Belgium after New York."

Keeping her face neutral, she asked, "Do you have an estate in Belgium too?"

"I have a house in Brussels, but it's not an estate. Besides, if we want to continue to Paris, it's better to stay on the plane."

"Cool. How long is the flight from Brussels to Paris?"

"About an hour."

Ella leaned back in her chair. "I can't wait to see it. I've heard it's a beautiful city."

"It is."

As Dimitri told her about Paris and the many places he could take her to see, Ella pretended to listen while waiting for him to be done so she could contact her mother and tell her the amazingly good news. It was crucial to keep her cool, though. If Dimitri got suspicious, he might change his plans, or leave her behind.

It was another hour before he excused himself to go make some phone calls, and Ella was finally alone.

"I'm going to read in bed," she told Misha.

"Okay. I walk you upstairs."

She knew there was no point arguing that she knew the way. Besides, his room was down the hall from the master bedroom, so he was never far even though there was no danger lurking in the house for her or Dimitri.

"Good night," she said at the door.

"Good night."

"*Dobroy nochi.*" He winked. "You want to learn Russian, eh?"

"I do. *Dobroy nochi*, Misha."

Closing her door behind her, Ella walked over to the couch, kicked off her high heels, and lay down with her new tablet. If Dimitri came in, she could pretend to be absorbed in a book.

On the other hand, the thing had a camera, so it could be watching her. She'd read somewhere that phones and tablets could do that even when turned off. Just to be on the safe side, she tucked it under her pillow.

Mom, are you up yet?

I'm up. Good morning, sweetheart. Or rather good evening, right?

Right. I have great news. Dimitri told me we are going to Dubai and from there to New York. I'm too excited to make the time differ-

ence calculations, so you'll have to do it. We are leaving Wednesday, and we are going to stay two nights in Dubai and from there straight to New York. I'll contact you again before we leave Dubai.

That is the best news I could hope for. I thought we would have to wait for weeks.

Me too. Did you talk to the team leader? Does he have a plan?

Not yet.

Well, what is he waiting for? The clock is ticking.

23

VIVIAN

"Mom, I'm hungry," Parker called out from the couch.

"Scoot." She sat next to him. "How are you feeling?"

"I told you, I'm hungry."

"Other than that." She put her hand on his forehead. "Do you feel feverish?"

"No."

"Does your throat hurt?" She patted his neck.

"Nothing hurts except for my stomach. It feels like I have a vacuum there. Forget that. It's a black hole."

Bridget had said that the first sign would be hunger. So maybe Parker was transitioning. Except, it wasn't the first time he'd woken up starving.

"Go brush your teeth, and I'll make you something to eat."

"Do I have to? Can't I get a one-day pass as a reward for my brave performance last night?"

"Nice try. Go brush."

Grimacing, he got up and padded to the bathroom.

Vivian opened the fridge and pulled out a pack of cold cuts, mayo, and a bag of buns. Other than sandwiches or cereal, there wasn't much else she could make without a stove.

When she was done preparing two overstuffed sandwiches, the front door opened, and Magnus walked in with Scarlet trotting behind him.

"Is she still mad at you?"

After her stay with the guys at the guard station last night, the dog was behaving like a kid who was resentful after being left with a babysitter for the first time. Ever since Magnus had picked Scarlet up, she'd been casting him sad sidelong glances and keeping her tail tucked between her legs.

Except, taking her into the gym had been out of the question. Even restrained, she would've tried to protect Parker and barked at Jackson, which would've broken his concentration.

"We had a talk and reached an understanding."

"Oh, yeah?"

"Every time I have to leave her behind, I'll later reward her with a treat, and she'll forgive me."

"What did you give her?"

"All the bologna from my sandwich."

As soon as Parker opened the bedroom door, the dog's tail started wagging, and her tongue lolling as she gave him a doggie smile. It seemed Scarlet was mad only at Magnus.

"Here is my girl." Parker crouched down and let her lick his face.

"Your sandwiches are on the table."

"Thanks, Mom."

"Wash your hands."

Rolling his eyes, Parker went over to the bar sink and did as she asked before picking up a sandwich from the plate.

"I have great news," Vivian said. "Ella contacted me earlier.

Gorchenco's next stop is Dubai, and after that New York. We need to tell Turner."

Magnus didn't seem excited by the news. In fact, he looked doubtful. "And he just told her that? After keeping her in the dark about everything?"

"Apparently, her plan is working."

"I wasn't aware that she had one."

Vivian glanced at Parker. What went on between Gorchenco and Ella was not really appropriate for his young ears, but on the other hand, he'd earned the right to be included in grownup conversations.

"She's pretending to like him and makes him believe that she wants a life with him. It seems that he's falling for it."

Magnus shook his head. "I doubt an eighteen-year-old girl can fool someone like him. Nevertheless, we need to call Turner. Let's do it from my place."

"Are you okay here with Scarlet?" What Vivian had actually meant was whether Parker felt offended by not being included.

"Yeah, I'm fine. I'm going to finish my breakfast and then go back to bed and watch anime. No schoolwork for me today, right?"

"You've earned a pass."

Parker's eyes widened. "I totally forgot! Where is the box with all my presents?"

"On the floor in the closet."

He looked at the half eaten sandwich in his hand, then at the bedroom door, and then back at the sandwich again. "I'll eat first and then count my money."

"Good choice." She gave him the thumbs up.

Wanting to watch over Parker, Vivian hadn't spent last night in Magnus's room. She'd offered to sleep on the couch and let Parker have the bed, but he'd plopped on the couch and gone to sleep right away. She'd put a pillow under his head, covered him with a blanket, and then left the door to the bedroom open in case he needed her. He hadn't, but just in case, she'd gotten up several times during the night to check on him.

"I'll brew us some coffee first," Magnus said as they entered his room.

"Yeah, I need it. I didn't get much sleep last night."

"I figured. Any signs of transition?"

"He woke up starving. But that's all."

"It's a good start."

When the coffee was ready, Magnus handed Vivian a mug and sat next to her on the couch with his.

"Let's make that call." He pulled out his phone and dialed Turner's number.

"Magnus. What do you have for me?"

"Ella contacted Vivian. She and Gorchenco are leaving for Dubai Wednesday, and two days later they're going to New York. What I find suspicious about this, however, is that he's suddenly confiding in her."

"He's probably softening up toward the girl," Turner said. "There is no way he can suspect that she can communicate telepathically."

Vivian let out a breath. Magnus had her worried with his suspicions, but if Turner, who was the expert and supposedly quite paranoid, didn't think there was a cause for worry, then she trusted that he was right.

"Ella asks if you came up with a plan to fake her death."

"Faking it is only half the problem. The real challenge is having her body disappear in a way that will not cause suspicion. Julian has a crazy idea we are checking out."

"What is it?"

"A story about Ella donating her body to research and it being sent to some remote university. The idea is for the paperwork to get messed up, so no one knows where the body ended up being delivered. He says he remembers a case like that when he was in medical school. I'm having my people look into it. It is paramount that the story withstand the most careful scrutiny. She is important to Gorchenco. He will leave no stone unturned until he's convinced that she's really dead."

24

TURNER

"A Russian restaurant." Yamanu shook his head. "What do they serve there? I've never had Russian food before. Is it any good?"

"Who cares?" Arwel said. "We are going there to test your thralling powers on Russians, not to enjoy the food."

"Can't we do both?"

As the two Guardians kept going back and forth about this or that ethnic food, Turner glanced at Julian who was sitting shotgun next to him in the van. "How is it going? Any luck?"

The doctor was busy texting old friends from medical school about cadavers, the procedures for obtaining them, and whether anyone had heard about losing a cadaver.

"Everyone is happy to share information about all the necessary procedures for submitting a request for a cadaver for research, but no one is fessing up to losing one."

"What are you telling them about why you need the info?"

Julian lifted his head from the screen and cast Turner an amused sidelong glance. "My cover story is that I'm writing a suspense novel about organ smuggling and missing cadavers."

"Smart."

Hopefully, Julian would get some information because Turner's people had come up with nothing. If cadavers were misplaced in university research centers, the information was being covered up so no one would find out and sue the facility. It seemed that the only way to find out was to get insider information, which was what Julian was trying to do.

The other issue they had to figure out was whether Russians were genetically more resistant to thralling or was it just a cultural thing—a tendency to be overly suspicious and defensive.

If it was just a behavioral issue then Yamanu would have no problem thralling the vast majority of Gorchenco's personnel because they wouldn't see it coming. But if they were genetically resistant, then even Yamanu's incredible ability to blanket thrall large areas from afar wouldn't fool enough people to believe there was a fire happening.

They would have to stage a real one, using Sylvia to cause an electrical short in a sensitive spot.

Julian had suggested a Russian restaurant as a good place for the test. The question was whether they would find real Russians in a Russian restaurant. Their other option was the Russian consulate, but that was much more tricky.

"You rock the rapper look, Yamanu," Julian said as they got out of the van.

"I do, don't I." Yamanu bent from his considerable height to examine his reflection in the van's side-view mirror.

For the outing, he'd braided his long black hair into several thin braids, and put on a pair of dark sunglasses to cover his pale blue eyes.

Julian waited on the sidewalk. "If you can use this disguise whenever you want, why do you prefer staying in the village?"

Flashing him a big smile, Yamanu flipped his long braids back. "Because I get too much attention from the ladies. I don't want to cause riots."

It was a joke. Even Turner had heard the rumors about the guy's self-imposed celibacy. Yamanu was a walking contradiction, and as such he fascinated Turner. The guy was friendly and outgoing, and yet he acted like a recluse. He was very good-looking, and yet he stayed away from women.

He wasn't gay either.

Turner hadn't caught him looking appreciatively at members of either sex.

And although he liked to joke and tell stories about old battles and the shenanigans he and his fellow Guardians had pulled, Yamanu never revealed anything personal.

"How many?" the hostess asked.

"Four," Julian said.

She smiled at him, then pulled out four menus and sauntered over to a table. "Is this one okay?"

"Perfect." Yamanu flashed her one of his smiles.

She gave him a thorough look over.

The restaurant was almost full, and the good news was that everyone around them was speaking Russian.

"She wants you," Arwel said after the hostess had left.

Yamanu grinned. "I know. They all do." He lifted the menu. "What should I order? Do you know what's good?"

The interesting thing was that Turner had smelled the woman's arousal, and even Arwel had emitted a little of his own. Yamanu hadn't emitted even a whiff, and neither had Julian.

Julian was obsessed with a picture of a pretty face and paid attention to no other, but what was Yamanu's excuse?

Turner knew some humans who were asexual. But this was

the first immortal he had encountered that seemed not to be interested at all.

"Try the Tashkent salad," he suggested. "My grandmother used to make something similar. I remember it being tasty."

"White radish and beef topped with yogurt and onions," Yamanu read from the menu. "I'll try it."

"Your grandmother was Russian?" Arwel asked.

"Her mother was."

"Maybe we should look for Dormants in Russia."

"It was my paternal grandmother."

"Oh."

When they were done with the main course, Turner ordered coffee and cake for everyone.

"I can't eat another bite." Yamanu rubbed his flat stomach.

Turner leaned toward him and whispered, "We need the cake for the 'Happy Birthday' song."

"Whose birthday is it?" Arwel asked.

"No one's. I want Yamanu to thrall everyone to sing 'Happy Birthday' to Victor. We will see who is singing and who's not."

Yamanu nodded.

"Good idea," Julian said in a hushed tone. "No one would get suspicious about singing 'Happy Birthday'."

Turner smiled and leaned back in his chair. "Precisely."

Yamanu waited for the cake and coffee to be served, then cast his thrall. "It's on."

Several people started singing, while others looked at them and frowned since there was no cake with a candle on any of the tables. As the waiters came rushing in to see if they'd missed something, some were singing, and some were not.

"Happy birthday, Victor," Yamanu said out loud.

Relieved to find out who the birthday customer was, the waiters congregated around their tables and sang. Some of the reluctant audience joined in, but others went back to eating their dinner.

"It must be genetic," Turner said after the waiters had left. "Otherwise they wouldn't have resisted the thrall. There was no reason to."

"I agree," Yamanu said. "I used full power. I won't be surprised if people on the street are singing 'Happy Birthday' to Victor."

Arwel rubbed his jaw. "Maybe that's why you're immune, or were as a human. You have Russian blood in you."

Turner crossed his arms over his chest. "I was told that it was my superior intelligence that made me immune." He was only half joking.

Yamanu offered a compromise. "Maybe it's the combination of both. But in any case, we have proof of your hypothesis.'

Turner nodded. "Regrettably. Things would have been much simpler if you could fool everyone on that estate."

25

MAGNUS

The sitting and waiting and doing nothing was driving Magnus nuts. Especially since he had his dream woman sitting right next to him and the most he could do was wrap his arm around her shoulders or give her a platonic kiss.

Parker was sprawled on the couch in Vivian's suite, so it was either sitting on the uncomfortable dining chairs over there, or on the sofa in Magnus's room. They'd opted for the second one, leaving both doors open.

Regrettably, with how anxious Vivian felt, necking was out of the question, so the two of them had watched a Netflix movie, and after that Vivian had started reading a book.

Unfortunately, Magnus wasn't much of a reader. He'd already read all the interesting articles on his news application, checked the clan's virtual bulletin board, and had even considered sending his mother a text.

Not a good idea for several reasons. First of all, she hated texting, and he would get berated for not calling. And secondly, he wanted to delay telling her about Vivian until after Parker's transition. Ideally, he would've preferred to wait for Vivian to transition herself, but by then the rumor would have traveled all the way to Scotland, and his mother would be mad that he hadn't told her anything.

Pushing off the couch, Magnus stretched. "I'm going to check on Parker and see if he is in the mood for going out to dinner."

Vivian looked up from the book she'd been reading on her phone. "I checked on him less than an hour ago, and he was fine, but still, I think we should order takeout. Bridget said to take it easy and watch him. What if he starts feeling sick in the restaurant?"

"You're right. I'll just go and see how he's doing."

Bored and restless, Magnus could've used an invigorating swim in the pool, or alternatively pumping some iron in the gym, but he didn't feel like leaving Vivian and Parker alone, more for moral support than anything practical.

If the kid started feeling sick, Vivian could call Bridget just as well as he could.

"Hi, kiddo. How are you feeling?" Magnus said as he stepped in.

"Good." Parker didn't even spare him a glance and kept on playing.

Scarlet lifted her head and gave him one of her sad looks, as if saying, "You abandoned me, and I'm not going to forget it anytime soon even if you give me all of your bologna."

"Oh, come on, girl. Get over it." He scratched behind her ears, which produced a little tail wagging.

Pathetic. But it was progress.

She scooted to make room as Magnus sat on the couch next to Parker. He watched him play for several moments. "Don't you get bored doing this all day long?"

"There is nothing better to do. Mom said that I don't have to study today because of the transition."

"You can read a book."

"I do. Mom forces me to read three chapters every day."

"You don't like reading?"

Parker shrugged. "It's boring. Too slow and no visuals. Mom says that I need to see what's happening in the book in my head, but I don't." He cast Magnus a sidelong glance. "Do you? I mean can you picture in your head what you're reading? Like a movie?"

"When the story is really interesting, then yeah. But I'm not much of a reader either. I like doing things and making stuff."

Parker shot the last of the villains in the virtual warehouse, paused the game, and pulled the blanket up to his chin. "For me, gaming is like that. I feel like I'm inside the game, and I'm doing things. Also, not all the games are about shooting bad guys, it's just what I'm in the mood for lately. I have one where I build houses and villages and whole environments. So that covers the making stuff. The only difference between you and me is that you do it in the real world, and I do it in the virtual one."

It was an intriguing way of looking at it. Parker reminded Magnus of his roommates.

"You know, my roommates in the village are like you. They are both programmers, and they sit in their rooms all day, creating games. They live like vampires, and I don't think it's healthy. I don't mean physically because immortal bodies are very resilient, but mentally it can't be good for them. People, humans and immortals, need to move around, breathe fresh air, and socialize."

Parker narrowed his eyes at him. "What's the speech for? Are you trying on the dad role?"

Should he be offended?

Had he sounded preachy?

Maybe a little. It hadn't been his intention at all, but apparently Parker was not ready to accept him as a father figure yet.

They'd bonded quickly over the two intense weeks they'd spent together, but that was just the beginning of the process. It would take a long time for all of them to become a family for real.

But it was okay. Magnus wasn't in a hurry, and he wasn't going to push Parker or Ella into accepting him. To start with, he was only going to be someone they would feel comfortable being around. The rest would come with time.

"I told my roommates the same thing, as a friend. You can take my advice or leave it. "

Parker let out a breath. "I'm sorry. I didn't mean to sound like a brat. I'm just stressed. Nothing is happening."

"That's what I came to check. So nothing hurts? No fever?"

Parker shook his head. "Nada. Maybe I'm not transitioning."

"Let me check. Open your mouth." Magnus patted the gums above Parker's canines. "They seem to be a little swollen. Let me feel your throat." He searched for a swelling where the new venom glands should start growing. "I can't feel them yet, but that doesn't mean a thing. They might be very small at this stage."

Vivian entered the room. "Well? Anything?"

Magnus turned to her. "I think his gums are swollen."

"Let me see." She did the same thing he had. "I think you're imagining it."

"There is another test we can try, but I prefer for Bridget to do that."

"What is it?"

"She can make a little incision and check how quickly the bleeding stops and the skin knits itself back together."

"You mean she's going to cut me?" Parker asked.

"It's just a tiny cut on the palm of your hand."

"The palm? No way. I need my hands for gaming. Can't she check something else? I mean, if there is no other way, then fine. But what if I'm not transitioning yet and get stuck with a bleeding cut?"

"Bridget will not leave it bleeding. She'll bandage it."

"But it will hurt."

Magnus pulled out his phone. "I'm calling Bridget. We'll let her decide which test to run."

Vivian nodded. "I feel bad about dragging her out here, but I can't stand the uncertainty. Maybe you should text her instead of calling? It's not like anything has happened and it's an emergency. Give her the option to decline."

Good point. With Julian gone, Bridget was probably extremely busy. Merlin had just arrived, and the guy would take his time getting settled before he showed up in the clinic.

Unless someone was in excruciating pain and needed immediate medical assistance, or a human under his care was dying, Merlin was never in a rush to do anything.

After spending a couple of moments thinking how to phrase his request politely, but at the same time encourage Bridget to come, Magnus read the text out loud. "Vivian and I are wondering if you have time to come check on Parker. As you can imagine, all three of us are anxious to find out whether he's transitioning or not. I'm ordering dinner, and I would love for you to join us. Let me know what is a good time for you."

"Excellent," Vivian approved. "Send it."

A moment later his phone pinged with a return text. *I can be there in an hour.*

26

VIVIAN

As Magnus opened the door for Bridget, Vivian rushed to welcome the doctor, pulling her in for a quick hug. "I'm sorry for dragging you out here. I'm sure you have your plate full. But speaking of plates, dinner is getting cold. We should sit down to eat."

Bridget smiled. "I'm actually glad for the invitation. Turner and Julian are in New York, all the preparations are done, and with Yamanu there to help them, I'm not as worried as I would've been otherwise. I actually had nothing to do."

"Who's Yamanu?" Vivian asked.

With a smirk, Magnus wrapped his arm around her shoulders. "Let's sit down to eat, and I'll tell you all about our secret weapon."

"The secret weapon is a guy?" Parker asked.

He was already at the table, a napkin tucked inside his shirt collar, the fork and knife ready for some steak action.

"Yup." Magnus pulled out two chairs, one for Bridget and the other one for Vivian. "I got you the only vegetarian dish they offered. Mushroom risotto."

"Thank you for remembering." Bridget sat down.

"Of course."

"Bon appetit, everyone," Vivian said.

As Parker attacked his steak, Bridget grinned. "Judging by his appetite, he's transitioning."

Vivian wished it was true. "That's nothing unusual. Parker loves steaks. But he woke up very hungry this morning, which is a little unusual."

"I'll check him after dinner."

"Thank you. Now, who wants to tell me about Yamanu?" She looked at Magnus.

He finished chewing and wiped his mouth with a napkin. "Yamanu is a master thraller. He can thrall large groups of people at once, and his thralls are very realistic. Smell, touch, texture, a human can't distinguish between illusion and reality. He can also shroud a big area, hiding it from humans, including all sights, sounds, and smells."

"What an incredible asset he must be to your people."

Magnus reached for her hand. "Our people. You belong with us."

"Provided we are Dormants."

"I'm sure you are." Magnus squeezed her hand. "Anyway, Yamanu is going to create the illusion of fire. Ella, being still human, is going to be as affected by it as everyone else on the estate. That's why we asked you to warn her, but before I spilled the beans about us, we couldn't tell you about the illusion. That's why we said we were going to use pyrotechnics."

"So there isn't going to be any fire whatsoever."

"Correct."

Bridget cleared her throat. "I don't want to worry you unnecessarily, but Turner thinks that many Russians are immune to thralling. It's probably genetic. So it's not going to be an easy in and out. They will have to stage a real fire, and there will be some fighting. But humans don't stand a chance against our Guardians. I'm sure they are going to get Ella out without a problem."

Vivian lost her appetite.

Real fire was dangerous, it could spread out of control, and fighting meant bullets flying. The immortals would be wearing protective suiting, and even if they got hurt, their bodies would repair the damage. Ella didn't have any protection. She was a vulnerable human girl.

"Don't worry, sweetheart. We know what we're doing, and Turner is the best in the field in hostage retrieval, which is how he is handling Ella's situation. It's no longer a simple trafficking rescue mission."

Bridget put down her knife and fork. "Let's take care of at least one variable. Parker, are you ready?"

He stuffed the last piece of steak into his mouth and pushed to his feet. "I'm going to brush my teeth, and I'll be right back."

"Good idea," Vivian said. "And don't forget to floss."

Bridget walked over to the coffee table where she'd left her doctor's bag and pulled a tongue depressor and a slim flashlight out. "I'm ready."

"I'll start the coffee." Vivian got up and got busy with the coffeemaker.

Her entire life and that of her family depended on the result of Bridget's checkup. The next several minutes were going to be nerve-wracking.

When Parker came back, Bridget motioned for him to sit on the couch. "Open wide."

He let out a breath. "I'm glad you're not going to cut me."

Bridget turned to look at Magnus. "You told him that?"

"It's an option. So why not?"

"Never mind." Shaking her head, Bridget turned back to Parker. "Open wide and stick your tongue out." She used the tongue depressor and shone the flashlight down his throat. "I see them. They are still tiny, but those are definitely venom glands." She offered Parker her hand. "Congratulations, young man."

Her head spinning, Vivian collapsed into a chair. "Thank God."

A split second later she found herself in Magnus's strong arms. He crushed her against his chest. "Thank the merciful Fates." He kissed her in front of Bridget and Parker.

Vivian didn't care.

A new chapter in her life was beginning. There would be no more hiding who she was or what she could do, not for her and not for Ella.

Suddenly, she felt confident that everything was going to work out. The Guardians were going to get Ella out, and her daughter would have the life she always wanted.

"Is it normal that they are so small?" Parker asked.

Bridget ruffled his hair. "What did you expect? That they would magically appear fully grown? Nature takes time to build things."

He still wasn't convinced. "Are they the same size as the other transitioning boys'?"

The doctor pretended to ponder his question, then leaned to whisper in his ear, "I think yours are bigger. But don't tell anyone I told you that. I don't want the other guys to feel bad."

"You're messing with me."

She grinned. "Yes, I am. Your glands are the exact size they should be one day into your transition."

"Thank you, doctor." He remembered his manners.

"I'm so happy," Vivian said. "I wish I could tell Ella. In fact, I don't see why not. She won't tell anyone."

Magnus shook his head. "She'll think that you've lost your mind. It's better to wait for her to be rescued first and then show her proof."

Vivian didn't agree, but after all that the clan had done for her, she wasn't going to betray their confidence. The good news could wait.

"When can we move to the village?" Parker asked.

Magnus pulled out his phone. "I need to call Kian."

Vivian wanted to suggest that he should text first, but maybe this time a phone call was preferable. As she'd realized lately, Parker's transition was big news not only for her and her family, but for the entire clan.

"Good evening Kian, I'm putting you on speaker. Bridget is here, and she's just confirmed that Parker is transitioning."

"Congratulations, Parker. Welcome to immortality."

"Thank you. I can't wait for my fangs to come out."

"Patience, young man. I still remember how much that hurts, and I'm almost two thousand years old. I was born immortal, but they didn't come out until I was thirteen."

Parker's jaw was hanging so low, his chin was touching his chest. He looked at Vivian and mouthed, "Two thousand years old?"

She shrugged. "What did you think being immortal meant?"

"When can we move into the village?" Magnus asked.

"As soon as you want. I can send Okidu to pick you up tomorrow."

"Awesome." Parker pumped his fist in the air.

27

ELLA

Dimitri put the porcelain cup down and lifted a folded newspaper. "Will it bother you if I read, Ella?"

So polite. If she cared for him, it most certainly would have. Someday in the distant future, when she was having breakfast with someone she loved, she would want his attention on her.

In the present, however, it would be a relief to drop the cheerful expression and eat breakfast in peace.

"Not at all. Go ahead."

He reached over the table and clasped her hand. "I'm a lucky man." He brought it to his lips and kissed the back of it.

Ella forced a smile, holding it until he opened the newspaper and disappeared behind it.

With a stifled sigh, she picked up another piece of toast and buttered it.

Hopefully, Dimitri would be gone all day at meetings.

Having sex with him last night had been unavoidable, but despite the effort he'd put into pleasing her, she'd remained unaffected and remote. Ella was good at finding ways to cope, but she'd reached her limit when a possible result was an unwanted pregnancy.

At least he didn't repulse her as she'd feared in the beginning.

Dimitri was reasonably fit, and he always smelled good, mainly because of the super duper expensive colognes he used, but also because he always showered before coming to bed. Still, he wasn't a young man, and the skin on his face and on his body was sagging.

Unbidden, Logan's handsome face popped into her head, and a strange, unwanted yearning tightened her stomach.

Ella shook her head. She was really losing her mind. If Dimitri and Logan were the only men left on earth, she would've chosen Dimitri or jumped off a cliff. Both options were better than Logan.

She didn't want Logan. He scared her. And yet, there was an undeniable pull. Like a magnet, or rather a black hole, she couldn't help but feel the draw even though she knew it was a death trap.

The Sith Lord was calling to her.

Stifling a chuckle, Ella lifted her small coffee cup and took a sip. It all made sense in a twisted way. Her dark energy was drawn to the dark side.

Yeah, she was officially losing it. She should choose to study psychology. Maybe it would help her understand what was going on in her messed-up head.

Dimitri folded his newspaper and put it down on the table. "I have a surprise for you."

Instinctively, she glanced at his jacket pocket. He wasn't wearing a suit, which was unlike him. Not that he'd gone as far as putting on jeans, she doubted he even owned any, but he was wearing casual slacks with a brown turtleneck. A plaid jacket was draped over the back of the chair.

Ella had a feeling that Dimitri's surprise wasn't another gift.

"I took the rest of the day off to be with you."

Damn. She plastered a smile on her face. "Dimitri, you're spoiling me. A day with me on the estate and then another one sightseeing in Dubai? What will your business empire do without you?"

He took her hand. "It will survive. What's the point of having all this money if I can't enjoy it?"

"Don't you enjoy the wheeling and dealing?"

He smirked. "Oh, I do. But I have a beautiful, young fiancée, and I want to spend time with her."

Right. Fiancée. He hadn't even asked her if she wanted to marry him. Not that it was going to happen. In a few days, she would be free. In the meantime, though, she needed to play the part she'd set out to play.

"I'm so excited. What are we going to do?"

"Let me surprise you."

"I need to know what to wear."

He looked her over. "What you have on is fine. Wear either flats or your riding boots and take a jacket. It might be chilly by the lake."

"Ah, now I know where you're taking me."

He lifted her hand and kissed it. "You don't know the whole plan."

He had a plan. He'd actually spent time thinking and preparing a fun day for her.

Damn. Sometimes the guy made it difficult to hate him. She needed to remind herself that none of it was her choice. He'd decided he wanted to marry her and get her pregnant, not necessarily in that order, and she had no say in any of it.

She pulled her hand out of his. "I'll put my boots on and grab a jacket. Do I need anything else?"

"No, *lyubimaya*." He gave her a thorough once-over. "You're perfect."

28

MAGNUS

"Is Parker asleep?" Magnus asked hopefully as Vivian walked into his room.

"Finally. He was so excited that it was hard for him to relax. I told him that the more sleep he got, the faster his body would make the transition. That convinced him to turn the television off and close his eyes."

"Come here." He patted the spot next to him on the couch. "Are you in the mood to celebrate?"

She sauntered toward him, but instead of sitting next to him, she sat on his lap and wrapped her arms around his neck. "What do you have in mind?"

"I'm open to suggestions."

"Oh, so it's my choice?"

He nodded.

"Hmmm. What should we do? How about playing cards?"

"Strip poker?"

"You naughty boy. Unfortunately, I don't know how to play."

"And I don't have cards."

"Then we have to come up with another game. I wish I hadn't left the wig in the other room."

"Why? What would you have done with it?"

"Pretended to be someone else. Maybe a spy?"

He cupped the back of her neck and brought her mouth to his. "I don't want anyone else. I want you." He kissed her until she ran out of breath and pushed on his chest.

"Vivian the dental hygienist is not very exciting," she said.

"I beg to differ." Magnus lifted her and carried her to his bed. "Let me show you how exciting you are." He took her hand and put it over the hard bulge in his pants. "Any more excitement than that and the zipper will give out."

"I would like to see that." She grabbed the bottom of her shirt and pulled it over her head. "How is it doing now?"

"I think I hear ripping sounds."

Vivian lifted her bottom and pulled her leggings down. "How about now?"

"Barely holding. I should take my pants off before they are destroyed."

Crooking a finger, she beckoned him to her. "Let me." She unbuckled his belt and slowly lowered the zipper. "Oh, my. What do we have here?"

When she leaned forward and kissed his straining shaft over his cotton briefs, the smooth head popped out over the elastic band.

"Well, hello there." She kissed the exposed tip. "Someone is happy to see me."

This playful side of her was new, and Magnus loved it. He had a feeling that this was the real Vivian. The one he'd gotten to know up until now was the worried and stressed-out version of her.

He was looking forward to discovering all of her different facets.

Rubbing her thumb over the tip, Vivian pulled down his briefs with her other hand. "Your eyes are glowing. Do you know why I love it when they do that?"

"Because you can see better in the dark when they do?"

She laughed. "That too. But it's another indication that you desire me."

"I always desire you." He swept the hair away from her shoulder and kissed it. Her skin was so soft there, so smooth.

"Take your clothes off. I want my hands all over those incredible muscles of yours."

Popping the top button of his shirt, he chuckled. "You're in a bossy mood today." He popped another one and pulled the shirt over his head, then kicked off his shoes.

Something about his comment must have bothered her. Vivian let her arms drop by her sides and leaned back to sit on her haunches.

He hooked a finger under her chin. "What's the matter, lass?"

She hesitated for a moment, then let out a breath. "I wanted to show you that I desire you just as much as you desire me, but I like it better when you're the one being bossy. It turns me on."

Her blush matched the slight scent of embarrassment she was emitting.

Magnus leaned and took her lips in a quick kiss. "I'm glad you like it because being bossy comes naturally to me. I was trying to be all progressive and let you lead. I thought you were enjoying yourself."

"I was, but it is not easy for me to act assertive and to initiate. It doesn't come naturally to me."

"Then we are perfectly matched."

Vivian smiled. "I'm glad we have it all straightened out." She wiped away imaginary sweat from her forehead.

As Magnus pushed his pants and briefs all the way down and stepped out of them, he was glad he hadn't bothered with socks. Those were the most awkward items of clothing to remove while stripping for a lady.

His lady, who was eating him with her eyes as if he was her favorite treat.

Zeroing in on his straining shaft, Vivian lifted up on her knees and licked her lips, sending a bolt of fire straight to his groin.

But as much as he craved those lush lips of hers around it, he had a different game in mind, and she was still wearing too many clothes.

When he reached behind her and unclasped her bra, and then pulled the straps down her shoulders, she didn't shy away or try to cover her small breasts as she usually did.

Magnus's heart swelled. It meant the world to him that she was finally confident in his desire for her.

Hooking his fingers in the elastic of her panties, he pulled down. "Lift your knee." He pulled the panties further down. "And now the other one."

When she was nude in front of him, he reached for her nipples and clasped them gently between the thumb and forefinger of each hand. As he rolled and tugged, Vivian arched her back and let her head drop back. He pinched them lightly, eliciting a strangled moan.

"No need to keep quiet, love. No one can hear you but me."

She lifted her head and opened her eyes. "Kiss me."

He did, cupping a breast with one hand and her hot center with the other.

"Spread your legs a little wider, love."

When she inched her knees apart, he ran a finger along her wet folds. "You're mine."

It was a caveman thing to say, but Magnus couldn't help the powerful possessiveness that had washed over him. This incredible woman was his, and he would have her for eternity. It was almost too good to be true.

What had he done to earn such a boon?

"I'm yours, and you're mine," she whispered. "Forever."

"Yes." He hooked his arm around her waist, pulling her closer to him as he pushed a finger inside her, and then another.

Throwing her arms around his neck, she pulled him down to her parted lips.

He slid his tongue inside her mouth, his fingers thrusting in and out of her in sync with his plundering.

Her juices pouring over his fingers and whetting his appetite for a taste of her, Vivian moaned into his mouth.

Tightening his arm around her waist, he lifted her, put her down on her back, and dove between her spread thighs.

29

VIVIAN

A few flicks of Magnus's expert tongue were enough to catapult Vivian over the edge. As she arched her back and cried out, he covered her with his body and effortlessly slid into her.

She orgasmed again.

He rode her slowly, waiting for her to come down from her high.

Orgasming had been something Vivian had only enjoyed sporadically, even with Josh. She'd loved sex regardless. For her, it had been more about intimacy than explosive climaxes. She hadn't minded not coming every time she had sex.

Now she was orgasming more than once every single time. The chemistry between her and Magnus was off the charts.

Was it because he was such a skillful lover? Or was it her being more comfortable in her own skin with him?

Probably both.

Without a doubt, though, Magnus knew precisely which buttons to push and how to beautifully balance tenderness and care with dominance.

When she opened her eyes and smiled at him, he kissed her softly and pulled out. Wrapping his arms around her, he flipped them around.

That was unexpected.

"I didn't put a condom on." He reached for the nightstand drawer, opened it, and pulled a packet out. "Do you want to put it on me?"

At least one of them was still thinking straight. Vivian couldn't believe she'd overlooked such a crucial detail. Without the protection, she could go into transition prematurely, and that would be a disaster.

"I've never done that before. What if I rip it?"

He tore the packet and handed her the rolled up rubber. "I have plenty."

Gripping his hard length in her hand, she put it on him. "Did I do it right?"

"Perfect." He lifted her up and positioned his covered shaft at her entrance.

Magnus wanted her on top? Vivian wasn't sure how she felt about it. Was she supposed to ride him now?

Except, she should have known Magnus would take the lead even in that position. His hands wrapped around her waist, he pulled her forward and back, thrusting up into her with increasing force.

But even though he was doing most of the work, pretty soon her thighs started shaking from the effort of trying to match his thrusts.

As always, she didn't have to say anything for him to figure out this wasn't working for her. With a hand on her back, he guided her to lie on his chest. Holding her to him, he bucked into her for a few moments longer, and then flipped them around once more.

Vivian smiled. "That's better."

She liked him on top of her, especially now that the room wasn't entirely dark and he didn't demand that she keep her eyes closed. He was such a handsome man, and watching his expression while he was gripped in the throes of passion was a major turn-on despite the glowing eyes and the long fangs.

Or maybe because of them.

She found his alienness erotic rather than scary.

Maybe all those vampire and shifter romances Vivian had read over the years had something to do with how easy it had been for her to accept him the way he was.

Nah, it was who he was on the inside. That was who she loved, and she would've loved him with or without fangs, and with or without muscles. Although both were a definite bonus.

"I love the way you look at me," he said, sounding a little slurred.

"And how is that?"

"As if you adore me."

"That's because I do."

He thrust harder, wresting a gasp out of her. "I can't get enough of you." Another hard thrust. "And I can't believe how lucky I am to have found you."

When he started moving faster, talking became impossible. She wrapped her arms around him and held on tightly as he climbed toward his climax, taking her along for the ride.

His shaft thickening inside her, he growled, the animalistic sound both frightening and arousing.

She knew what was coming next.

Scared and yet curious, Vivian forced her eyes to remain open, but as he lifted his head and bared his fangs, her courage left her, and she turned her face, offering him her neck.

When he bit her, Magnus wasn't as gentle as he had been

the other time, but then again, she didn't need him to be. This time around, she was ready for it and knew bliss would follow in a matter of seconds.

In the absence of fear, the momentary pain was erotic rather than stressful, bringing on another orgasm even before the euphoria-inducing venom entered her system.

She felt his hot seed jettison into the condom at the same time as the first drop of his cool venom slid into her vein.

Vivian climaxed. Once, twice, three times, the powerful shockwaves rocketing her into space, and the euphoria that followed keeping her floating on a cloud of bliss.

Sometime later, she floated back to earth and found herself wrapped in Magnus's strong arms.

Had it been seconds? Minutes?

"Am I going to black out every time you bite me?" she murmured into his chest.

"Does it bother you?"

Thinking it over for a moment, she realized that it didn't because Magnus was there, keeping her safe. She could float for as long as she wanted. The question was, how long was it? While soaring on the clouds, she had no sense of time.

"I don't mind the floating. It's awesome. But I lose sense of time. How long was I out?"

"Only a few moments. It seems that the blackouts get shorter with each consecutive bite. Apparently, your body grows accustomed to the venom."

"Hmm, so it's like a drug. The more you use it, the less effective it becomes."

Magnus chuckled. "Don't worry. The orgasms are not going to diminish in quantity or quality. But I guess that at some point, you're just not going to black out anymore."

"I hope so."

He hugged her closer and kissed the top of her head. "Once you're immortal, you will have the stamina for much more."

Vivian faked a worried expression. "We are never going to get out of bed."

"It's a risk I'm willing to take."

30

ELLA

As they walked toward the pier, Dimitri held Ella's hand, a romantic gesture that was wrong on so many levels. First of all because what they had wasn't a romance, and secondly because of the bodyguards surrounding them at a not so discreet distance.

Apparently, Dimitri's estate wasn't as impenetrable as he'd led her to believe.

"Why are you taking so many bodyguards with you? Don't you feel safe on your own estate?"

He smiled indulgently. "I never assume that I'm safe. The moment I do, I'll be proven wrong. Many people live inside the borders of my estate. Delivery trucks come and go. An assassin could find a way to sneak in despite all the guards and the sophisticated monitoring equipment I employ."

She frowned. According to her mother, Dimitri's Russian estate was a fortress that the people helping her could not penetrate. And yet Dimitri feared an assassination attempt. Perhaps it was possible for a single individual to sneak in and do the deed. But she couldn't see a way for the assassin to escape unless he killed Dimitri quietly and no one knew that their boss was gone.

Which meant at night while he slept.

With her in bed.

A shiver ran through her. "I thought I was safe here."

He squeezed her hand. "You are. There are always bodyguards around, and I sleep with a gun within reach."

She looked up at him. "I didn't know that. Where do you keep it?"

"Usually, I keep it under my pillow. But now, with you in my bed, it's in the nightstand drawer."

She could kill him so easily. Take the gun and shoot him. But to what end?

The guards would kill her on the spot. Even Misha wouldn't come to her rescue if she murdered his boss.

It was a sobering thought. Her safety was tied directly to Dimitri's. Besides, she would never do that.

"Don't worry, my love. I'll keep you safe." He kissed the top of her head. "And here is my surprise." He pointed at one of the boats tied to the pier.

"You are taking me out on the lake?"

Ella could just imagine the spectacle. The two of them sitting in the boat with a bunch of bodyguards crowding them and doing the rowing.

"Yes. And we are going to have a picnic over there." He pointed to the tiny island smack in the middle of it.

"Sounds like fun." She glanced at Misha, hoping he would be in the boat with them.

Except, her bodyguard boarded the other boat.

Dimitri got inside the one with the nice pillows and offered her a hand. "Hold on tight and step in carefully."

When she was seated, one of the guards untied the boat and

gave it a push. Dimitri took hold of the oars and started rowing.

"I can't believe it. I was sure at least some of your men were going to join us."

He smiled. "It wouldn't be much of a romantic outing with my bodyguards in the boat, now would it?"

Instead, they were using the other boats, placing themselves at strategic intervals.

Ella relaxed and leaned against the pillows. "Thank you. This is lovely." And she even meant it.

If only he were younger and not so controlling…and hadn't bought her from a trafficker.

Right. She needed to remember that when he was being so nice to her.

Except, she wasn't made from stone, and when this powerful and hard man, with very little time to spare, was lavishing her with attention and doing his best to be soft with her, she couldn't help but feel a little flattered.

It would be easy to let it go to her head and forget that this wasn't a fairytale, and that she was there against her will with a man she resented for taking away her choices.

When they reached the island, the bodyguards jumped into the water and dragged their little boat to shore, so she and Dimitri wouldn't get their feet wet.

Taking her hand again, Dimitri led her to a clearing where a blanket was strewn over the ground. On top of it, four large pillows were arranged around a picnic basket that was big enough for a family of six.

When the bodyguards left them alone, taking positions on the shore, Dimitri opened the basket and pulled out a bottle of wine and two glasses.

"I've noticed that you've been enjoying wine lately. Did you develop a better tolerance?"

Ella blushed. The truth was that she'd flushed down the toilet more than half of each bottle she'd opened. But it wasn't as if she could admit it. Her carefully crafted happy façade would show cracks.

"I drank only a little at a time. But it added up."

He smiled. "I'm glad that you share my love for good wine." He poured her a glass and handed it to her.

"Thank you."

He filled up his own glass and lifted it for a toast. "To us."

"To us." She clinked her glass to his, adding in her head, *May we part in peace with neither of us dead.*

31

MAGNUS

Even before Magnus opened his eyes in the morning, he knew Vivian wasn't there. The bed felt cold and empty without her. What a shame. Last night he'd entertained thoughts of making love to her again in the morning.

Once was not enough for an immortal, but it had been for Vivian. When she'd fallen asleep, leaving him with a hard-on, Magnus had forced the erection to deflate by thinking about nasty things.

Not the best way to fall asleep, but a man had to do what a man had to do.

Had she gone to check up on Parker?

There was no need. The kid's transition had started without a hitch, and there was nothing to check. It would take time for his growing fangs to push out his canines, and for his venom glands to develop.

Maybe Ella had contacted her with some news?

The urge to look for Vivian and check prompted Magnus to fling the comforter off and get out of bed. Besides, his phone showed it was five in the morning, which was his regular wakeup time.

As he padded to the bathroom, Magnus debated whether he should put his workout clothes on. He needed to pack, but what he had with him wouldn't take long. He would have plenty of time before Okidu showed up to take them to the village.

After showering and getting dressed, he walked over to Vivian's suite to look for her. Through the open door, he saw that Parker wasn't sleeping on the couch and neither was Scarlet.

Had he taken the dog out for a walk? But how? The elevators hadn't been programmed with Parker or Vivian's thumbprints.

Instead, he found Vivian scrubbing the counter.

"What are you doing? And where are Parker and Scarlet?"

"I'm cleaning, and Parker is asleep in the bedroom with Scarlet."

"Why are you cleaning?"

She rolled her eyes as if it was the stupidest question she'd heard. "We are moving out of here, and I'm not going to leave the place filthy. Once I'm done, this suite of rooms is going to be as spotless as it was when we got here."

Magnus chuckled. "You don't have to do that. That's Okidu's job, and I told you how he feels about someone doing it for him."

Not that Okidu felt anything, but putting it that way saved a lot of explanations.

She smirked. "That's why I'm doing it before he gets here. I've already organized our things, but I need bags to put them in. Can you get me some trash bags from upstairs?" She crinkled her nose. "Although to tell you the truth, I hate the idea of arriving at the village with a bunch of trash bags like some homeless person." She sighed. "Except, I am kind of homeless."

He walked over and pulled her into his arms. "Is that what bothers you? Do you feel displaced?"

She nodded into his chest. "I'm starting a new life, and it scares the shit out of me, which is so weird. I'm supposed to be overjoyed. It's like a dream come true. Instead, I'm stressed out."

"Would having proper luggage help?"

She chuckled. "And where are you going to find luggage at five o'clock in the morning?"

"Walmart."

He was starting to really like that store. Anandur would be happy to hear that.

Vivian smiled. "That would be great. If not for all the games and consoles Parker got, we could fit all of our things into one suitcase. But we will need two."

"That's not a problem. I'll get three."

He was about to turn on his heel and head out when she stopped him with a hand on his bicep. "Let me make you breakfast first."

"I can grab something on the way."

She shook her head. "I'm feeling guilty enough as it is for sending you out on an errand so early in the morning. Let me at least feed you first."

"But you've already cleaned the counter."

"So I'll clean it again." She pointed at the chair. "Sit."

"Yes, ma'am."

A few minutes later she put down two steaming mugs on the table and a plate with two sandwiches. "Here you go." She pushed the plate toward him.

"Aren't you going to eat?"

"I can't. My stomach is queasy. I'll eat later."

Magnus wasn't hungry yet either, but he took a sip from the coffee and a couple of bites from the sandwich because it seemed important to her.

"How is Parker doing?"

She waved a dismissive hand. "As happy as can be. Change is easier for kids. It's us grownups that have trouble with it."

"I know exactly what you're talking about. Moving here from Scotland wasn't easy, even though I came together with many of my friends, and I knew practically everyone in the village. I still don't feel completely at home here." He took her hand. "But all of that is going to change with you by my side. Home is wherever you and Parker and Ella are."

Vivian smiled. "It's so nice of you to say. I hope the two of you will get along, but that's not a given."

"I'm sure we will. She's your daughter, so she must be awesome."

Vivian's smile wilted. "She is an amazing person. I hope this ordeal hasn't affected her too much, but there is no way that it hasn't. No one can go through a thing like that and emerge unchanged by it."

He squeezed her hand. "She'll bounce back."

"Are you sure?"

"Positive. I've lived for a long time, Vivian, and I've been through some shit. I can't say that it didn't affect me, because it did. But in time I've gone back to who I was before. We each have our set happiness level. Sometimes it goes up, other times it goes down, but eventually, it returns to where it was before."

She nodded. "I know what you mean. After Josh was killed, I felt as if my life was over as well. I was so depressed. But I had two kids that needed me, and wallowing in my sorrow was not a luxury I could afford. At first, I did everything on autopilot, crying myself to sleep every night and fighting the tears all day long. And in the meantime, I also had to learn a marketable skill so I could support my family. It felt as if I was trying to climb a steep mountainside with my fingernails. And then one day, I surprised myself by laughing at a joke. It took years, but at some point the pain subsided enough for me to enjoy life once more."

She looked up at him with adoring eyes. "And the best surprise was that I've fallen in love. I thought that would never happen to me again."

"And I thought that it would never happen to me at all. Life is full of surprises, is it not?"

32

ELLA

"Put your riding clothes on," Dimitri said when they returned from the lake. "I heard that you've made good progress."

"Okay. Although after all the food you made me eat, my poor mare might collapse under me."

Ella rubbed her protruding stomach. Hopefully, it was the food and not something else. Except, this morning her belly had been as flat as ever, and pregnancies didn't progress that fast. It was the roasted duck with spring potatoes and asparagus, followed by the best strawberry shortcake ever created by human hands.

He chuckled. "I'm not worried. But if you're tired, we can skip it."

"No, I'm fine. I'll be out in a moment." She ducked into her closet and pulled out one of the riding outfits he'd commissioned for her.

The truth was that she hadn't even had to pretend to enjoy the time they'd spent together. Dimitri was not only knowledgeable about many things, but he was also very eloquent, and listening to him had been fascinating.

Ella doubted she'd ever meet someone of Dimitri's caliber again. But if she were smart, she would have taken the out he'd offered her and said that she was tired. Instead of getting to know him better, and letting her defenses down, she should be keeping an emotional distance.

It wasn't that she was falling for Dimitri. That wasn't going to happen no matter how nice he was to her, or how fascinating she found him. She didn't love him and never would. But even admiration was dangerous. He was the enemy, and she needed to remember it.

He knocked on the closet door. "Are you ready? We don't have much daylight left."

"I am." Ella opened the door.

He'd changed into riding clothes as well, and she had to admit that he looked good in them. For an old dude. The hat covered his thinning hair, and the tight pants showed off his muscular thighs.

He noticed her looking him over and smirked. "Come on, Ella. Let's see what you've got."

"Let's." For some inexplicable reason, she wanted to impress him with how quickly she'd learned to ride.

In the stables, her mare was ready for her, looking small and plain next to Dimitri's magnificent stallion. As the groom helped her onto Mariana, Dimitri mounted his horse with ease.

"What's his name?" she asked as the groom led her mare out of the stables.

"*Grom,* which means thunder."

"Is it because he's fast?"

"Yes."

"Can you show me?"

Dimitri glanced back at the five bodyguards who'd followed them out on horseback. "I'd rather not. Today is about you. I want to see your progress."

Seeing Dimitri's perfect posture and the ease with which he was handling his horse, Ella lost confidence. She was only a beginner who'd learned the basic commands and could ride a mare that didn't need to be told what to do.

"Have you been riding long?" She trotted alongside him.

"Since I was a little boy."

"It shows. You look so natural up there." His horse was much taller than hers.

"You look good too. Not bad after only two lessons."

His praise made her feel a little better. "It's easy with a horse like Mariana." She patted the mare's back. "She just knows what to do."

"That too."

For the next hour or so, they trotted at a leisurely pace, circling the mansion and then going down to the lake and following the shoreline. When it started getting dark, Dimitri signaled his bodyguards to head back to the stables.

"I hope you had a nice day." He helped her down, hugging her to him briefly before letting her boots touch the ground.

"Yes, thank you."

He took her hand. "How is your appetite? Are you ready for dinner?"

"Oh, no. I'm still stuffed. Can we eat later?"

He glanced at his watch. "There are some phone calls I need to make, and I thought of doing it after dinner, but I can do it before."

"That would be great. While you make your calls, I can take a shower. I feel sticky."

Dimitri still held her hand as they climbed the stairs to the second floor.

"Can you be done in an hour?" he asked at the door to the master bedroom.

"I think so."

He kissed her cheek. "I enjoyed spending time with you, Ella."

"Me too. I mean spending time with you. And I'm looking forward to doing so in Dubai. By the way, when are we leaving tomorrow?"

"Around three in the afternoon. Why?"

She shrugged. "I just want to know how to plan my day. Do I need to pack anything? Or is it going to be done for me? Because, frankly, I don't need to take the entire wardrobe with me wherever we go. Some of it could stay here."

He kissed her cheek again. "Everything will be taken care of. The only thing you need to do is choose the outfit you want to wear for the flight."

The first thing Ella did when she entered the bathroom was to turn the water on in the tub. The second was to open a channel to her mother.

Mom, are you awake?

Since five o'clock in the morning. How are you doing?

I'm doing great. Dimitri took me out on the lake, and he even rowed the boat. After that, we went horseback riding. He's really making an effort for this to work between us. Not that he's going to change my mind about wanting out, but I appreciate the effort. How about you? What are you doing awake so early in the morning?

I'm cleaning. Magnus is moving us to a new location, and I want to leave the place as spotless as I found it.

Ella chuckled. *Are you nervous about moving?*

How did you know?

You always go into a cleaning frenzy when you're stressed. But why the sudden move?

It's not healthy for Parker in here. We want him to breathe fresh air and be in the sun.

Ella didn't miss the *we* instead of *I*, or how excited her mother sounded.

What's going on, Mom? You sound both stressed and happy.

I have some great news. But it will have to wait for after you are rescued. I can't tell you now.

Why not?

I just can't. I wish I could, but I can't. Magnus insists on secrecy.

What could it be? Her mother had already admitted to having a relationship with Magnus. Could she be pregnant?

Are you pregnant, Mom?

What? No! Of course not. What gave you that idea?

Oh, nothing. It's just the first thing that popped into my head.

Regrettably, her mother knew her too well. *Is there something you need to tell me, Ella?*

Yes. We are leaving for Dubai tomorrow at three in the afternoon. I don't know if it's important for the rescue team to know the exact time or not, but I figured the more information I could give them, the better.

I'll let Turner know. Anything else?

No, that's it. I have to go, Mom. Dimitri is expecting me in the dining room in half an hour, and I still need to shower and change. I smell of horses.

Okay, sweetheart. Talk to me soon.

I will.

33

TURNER

In the hotel's executive lounge, Turner opened his yellow pad and wrote down his impressions from the first completed mission on the East Coast.

The operation had gone smoothly, but there had been some differences in execution due to the density of housing in Brooklyn.

First of all, they couldn't torch the place once they were done, which meant that someone else would take over soon and business would continue as usual.

There was no way to eliminate the trade, but they were doing their best to make it more difficult for it to continue in the territories they were cleaning up. Finding a new place was time-consuming and costly, which slowed things down, and often prompted the operators to move elsewhere.

He had to come up with a different strategy for making the vacated locations inoperable.

The other variation was the rescued girls.

Because Turner wasn't usually taking part in the missions, only planning them, he didn't have to deal with the victims, a task he was ill equipped for. This time had been no different in that regard, but after the rescue the victims had been brought to the hotel, which meant he'd had to be there and receive them.

Thankfully, Yamanu had stepped in and done a great job calming the frightened girls.

What an asset the guy was.

Turner had no problem with Yamanu's reluctance to actively participate in the more mundane rescue missions. His talents were needed elsewhere and should not be squandered on activities that could be handled by other Guardians.

"I spoke with Vanessa," Julian said. "The new girls arrived safely and are already settled."

"Glad to hear that."

That was another difference. They'd had to load the rescued girls onto the clan's jet and send them to California. Going through the airport with a bunch of traumatized young women would've been impossible without Yamanu and his incredible shrouding ability. Again, his help had been invaluable.

"Vanessa says she's running out of space."

Turner lifted his head. "That's an issue she should raise with Kian. I can't help her with that."

"She had an idea. Many of the girls stay on for a long time, much longer than she originally anticipated, and that's why there is no room. She doesn't want to pressure anyone to leave, but she says that those who are doing well could be moved to another location that is more self-sufficient. It should be somewhere in the city where they'll have easier access to jobs, and maybe even venture out to start socializing a little."

"Again. That's something she needs to discuss with Kian."

"I'm just thinking out loud. We can open another location in Los Angeles, but we will need to staff it. I'm trying to come up with a way to motivate more clan members to volunteer their time there. You know that money is tight."

Turner considered himself a smart man, but he was aware of his empathic deficiency. It had taken Julian's persistence to finally make him realize what this was all about.

Julian was not seeking his advice as the team's leader, or even the head of operations. He was seeking his advice as someone close to him, the same way he would've consulted his mother.

Turner had a good relationship with Julian, but it was more cordial than familiar. They weren't close. Up until this mission, they hadn't spent much time together.

Turner took the blame for that. His emotional intelligence was subpar, probably because his brain synapses specialized in analytical thinking. There was very little room left for anything else.

Nevertheless, his emotional deficiency didn't mean he couldn't offer Julian help. On the contrary. His analytical skills would be much more valuable in this case.

"The solution to this is simple. Kian needs to incentivize volunteering."

"How?"

Turner put the pad down and leaned back in his chair. "Right now every clan member receives a share in the clan's profits regardless of their contribution. They can sit on their asses, do nothing, and still live comfortably if not lavishly."

"He can't take it away. That's the way it always has been since the Clan Mother pooled everyone's resources and started acquiring income-producing assets."

Turner smiled. "I'm not talking about taking it away. I'm talking about conditioning it on a predetermined amount of volunteering."

"What about those who work for the clan or outside of it?"

"Same thing. Those who work for the clan or independently receive compensation for their work, which is usually greater than their passive share in the profits. If they want to keep receiving their share, they will need to volunteer."

"What about those that are earning low wages? Volunteering their time could impact them financially."

Turner waved a hand. "Exceptions can be dealt with on an individual basis."

"Guardians give up their vacation days when needed," Arwel said. "I don't see why other clan members can't do this as well."

Julian turned around to look at the Guardian. "So you think this might work?"

Arwel shrugged. "Not everyone is going to be happy about it, that's for sure. But after a while, they'll get used to it. And who knows? Maybe volunteering will make them feel good."

"I think it's a good idea," Yamanu said. "I wouldn't mind volunteering in a half-way house. But I'm not sure what I can do for the girls."

"You can organize a karaoke night," Arwel suggested. "You have a great singing voice."

"He'll put them all to sleep," one of the other Guardians said.

There was something to that. Yamanu's voice had a hypnotic quality to it. Whenever he spoke, it was like a blanket of calm descending on whoever was listening, and it wasn't limited to humans. The effect wasn't as strong on immortals, but even Turner could feel it.

"Sleep is good," Yamanu said. "And I can induce pleasant dreams."

"I didn't know you could do that," Julian said.

"I'm a man of many talents."

Arwel pushed to his feet and stretched. "I'll be in accounting if anyone needs me."

Ever since they'd gotten back to the hotel, Arwel's drinking had been limited to a shot or two in the evening. Apparently, whoever he was seeing in accounting had a better effect on him than booze.

"Tell us the truth, Arwel," Julian said. "Did you find a lady friend in Ragnar's accounting department?"

Looking uncomfortable, Arwel ignored the question and headed for the door.

"Oh, come on, Arwel," Julian called after him. "You can tell us."

Arwel paused with his hand on the door handle and looked over his shoulder. "There is this girl with a very tranquil mind. But there is nothing romantic going on between us. I just sit there and help her stuff envelopes."

"Why don't you ask her on a date?" Yamanu asked.

"Because we have missions scheduled every night."

"I can take your place on one," Yamanu offered. "Ask her out."

As everyone turned to look at Yamanu, Turner shook his head. "Your looks are too distinctive to blend in."

"I can braid my hair and put sunglasses on like I did for the Russian restaurant. People will think I'm a rapper or a basketball player."

Turner had to admit that it was a good cover. "What about your thralling? You said you needed to conserve your energy for the big mission."

"I'm not going to use it. In fact, I'm in the mood for some good old-fashioned ass whupping."

34

ELLA

Dimitri had been very affectionate toward her all day long, but he was outdoing himself at dinner. So much so that Ella was starting to get suspicious.

"You look beautiful tonight," he said for the third time in an hour. "Thank you for putting an effort into looking good for me."

"I'm glad you like my dress." All she'd done was wear a dress she hadn't worn before and high heels, which she'd done every evening for dinner. Did the little mascara she'd applied to her lashes make so much difference?

Ella doubted it.

"I like everything about you." Dimitri lifted her hand to his lips and kissed the back of it.

She'd lost count of how many times he'd done that too throughout the day.

"Starting with your beauty and continuing with your intelligence and your kindness. I'm a very lucky man." Dimitri smiled.

He was doing that a lot too, which frankly was freaking her

out. Gorchenco was a serious man, a mafia boss, and all those sugary smiles were making her nervous.

He'd already told her that he intended to get her pregnant. What else could he be softening her up for?

"Would you like more wine?" He lifted the bottle.

"Sure." She pushed the glass closer to him. "It's very good."

It always made him happy when she complimented his wines.

"From the ones you've tried, which one is your favorite?"

Busted. Since it wasn't important to her, she hadn't taken notes. "They are all so good that it's hard to pick one. I like them all."

He nodded. "In time, you'll learn to note the slight differences."

"I hope so. I feel bad about drinking such expensive wines and not being able to say anything intelligent about them. Is there literature on the subject?"

"There is. But that's not the way to learn." He lifted the glass and sniffed. "Take this wine for instance. It has a tobacco undertone. Can you smell it?"

She lifted the glass to her nose. Now that he mentioned it, there was a slight tobacco scent to it. "Yeah, you're right. I can smell it."

Dimitri smiled and then dove into a long lecture about the body of the wine, its crispness, its intensity, and so on.

Stifling a yawn, Ella tried to appear interested. His long tirade was achieving at least one thing. It was calming her. He only stopped when the last course was done, and the staff served coffee and dessert.

Ella waited for the girl to fill her cup, thanked her, and took a long sip, savoring the taste. It was so much better than Dimitri's expensive wines.

Leaning back in his chair, he took his porcelain cup with him. "I can see that you're tired."

"It was a long day. Lovely, but tiring."

"The day is not over yet." Dimitri reached into his suit pocket and pulled out a little box.

No way. Is he going to propose?

"While I was away, I've given it a lot of thought and decided that I want to marry you before you get pregnant. My mother, who was a devout woman, would not have approved of my child being conceived out of wedlock."

Flipping the lid open, he revealed the biggest freaking diamond Ella had ever seen. "Would you be my wife, Ella?"

God Almighty in heaven. What was she supposed to say?

She couldn't say no, but she couldn't say yes either. Instead, she gaped at the ring.

Dimitri chuckled. "I see that I've finally managed to impress you with something other than my medical degree. Makes it worth the small fortune I paid for this." He reached for her hand. "I'll take your stunned silence as a yes." He put the ring on her finger. "It looks good on you."

She wasn't going to keep it, but there was no harm in taking a better look. Lifting her hand, she examined the colossal diamond, letting the light from the chandelier hit it from this and that angle.

"Now I'm doubly glad for Misha's protection. This thing could finance a revolution."

Dimitri laughed. "I'm glad you've recovered your voice as well as your sense of humor."

She hadn't meant it as a joke.

"I've already arranged with the priest to stop by tomorrow morning. We will wed before departing for Dubai."

Ella felt her eyes bugging out. "Tomorrow?" she croaked. He'd given her a bomb as a present with the fuse already lit.

Reaching for her hand, Dimitri kissed it again. "I want to put a baby inside you as soon as possible, and I don't want to worry about us not being married yet."

"I don't have a dress." She blurted out the first thing that came to her mind. "I can't be a bride without a white dress."

Dimitri laughed, a deep belly laugh that shook his body and reverberated through her hand, which he was still holding. "Haven't you learned yet? Do you think I would forget an important detail like that? Your dress will be delivered early tomorrow morning."

"What if it needs alterations?"

"The seamstress is going to do it on the spot."

Ella pulled her hand out of his grip and crossed her arms over her chest. "I'm not ready, Dimitri. I need more time. You can't keep doing things like this without asking me."

In the blink of an eye, his relaxed expression reverted to the severe one of the mafia boss. "There is no need for more time. I know that you're the one I want. You're going to be my wife and the mother of my children. As I recall, you said that you want to be with me too. Was that a lie?"

Ella panicked. "No, of course not. I do want to be with you. It's just that a wedding is a big deal for a girl."

In her panic, she'd almost blurted that she would've liked her mother and brother to be there, but stopped herself at the last moment. Dimitri's answer would have been that it could be arranged, and that was the last thing she wanted.

He smiled indulgently. "I understand, my dear. But this is real life, not a fairytale. You need to adjust your expectations."

She nodded.

It didn't matter. A piece of paper proclaiming them man

and wife was irrelevant. She was just going to treat it as a fake. In her heart, she wouldn't be married to him.

A small voice in the back of her head whispered that there was a simple solution to this latest problem. She could easily become Gorchenco's widow. All Ella had to do was tell her mother that she was okay with her rescuers killing him.

She was just angry enough to do it.

35

VIVIAN

Looking out the limo's window, Vivian sighed. "I could've taken it easy with the cleaning and the packing."

"Didn't I tell you yesterday that Okidu was arriving in the afternoon?"

Vivian felt bad for making Magnus feel guilty. It wasn't his fault that she'd misunderstood. Turning to him, she patted his knee. "You must've assumed that you did, but no. For some reason, I thought he was arriving early. It's no biggie."

She could've sworn that Kian had said he was going to send his butler to pick them up in the morning. But maybe in her excitement, she'd heard what she wanted to hear.

"My bad," Magnus said.

"I was actually happy that he arrived later rather than earlier. I had more time to prepare."

She'd showered and styled her hair, and then put on the elegant dress and shoes Magnus had gotten for her. Vivian was going to arrive at the village in style, looking good, with her things packed in proper luggage and not plastic trash bags.

First impressions were important.

"How much longer?" Parker asked.

"We should be arriving in twenty-five minutes or less, young Master Parker."

Master? Parker mouthed.

Magnus waved a dismissive hand. "Don't let it get to your head. Okidu calls everyone master or madam. He's old school."

Vivian had a feeling it was more than that. The butler looked to be in his late forties, smiled a plastic mannequin smile, and lived in a village full of immortals. Things didn't add up. Something was wrong with him.

She would've asked Magnus, but if Okidu was an immortal who for some reason aged more rapidly than the others, he would hear her even if she whispered. It was better to wait with her questions for when they were alone.

That was going to take a while, though. Magnus had hinted there would be some sort of a welcoming reception, but he either didn't know the details or wanted to keep it a surprise.

When the limo's windows turned opaque, Vivian knew they were getting close. Magnus had told her about the village's robust security measures.

She'd loved hearing about every detail he'd explained, even those he thought were overkill. Finally, she could live above ground and still feel completely safe.

Vivian hadn't felt safe for years. Ever since Josh had been killed and the fragility of her existence had slapped her in the face. Every day had felt like she was living on borrowed time, and that feeling had only gotten reinforced with each of the tragic losses she'd suffered.

Fear had become her constant companion.

When the limo stopped, the windows turned clear again. They were in a large underground parking structure, similar to the one in the high rise that had been her home for the past week and a half. Or had it been less? They'd arrived there on Monday, and today was Tuesday.

Magnus got out and offered her his hand.

She shook her head as she took it. "I can't believe it was only eight days. It feels like we lived a lifetime in that underground complex."

"A lot has happened, making it seem much longer than it was." He put his hands on her waist and pulled her in for a quick kiss. "Today is a new start. And after we get Ella back, I hope our lives are going to be boring and uneventful."

Vivian chuckled. "Oh, so that's what you really think of me? That I'm boring?"

"Never." He kissed the top of her head.

Scarlet bounded out of the limo, her tail working overtime and her tongue lolling in a cute doggie smile.

"I think she is happy to be back home," Parker said.

"I think so too."

As Magnus took the leash from Parker's hand, the butler unloaded their luggage, struggling to arrange things in a way that would allow him to take everything by himself, which was impossible.

Three rolling suitcases, one rolling carry-on, a duffle bag, a wooden bow, and Scarlet's big pillow bed were too much for someone with only two arms to handle, no matter how strong or motivated.

"Let me get these." Magnus reached for the two suitcases. "Parker, you take the bow and Scarlet." He returned the leash to him.

That left one suitcase, the carry-on, and Scarlet's bed, which was still too much for the butler.

"I can take the carry-on." Vivian reached for the handle.

When Okidu started to protest, she said, "I insist." And that was the end of the argument.

Pulling the suitcases behind him, Magnus leaned and whispered in her ear, "Now I know the magic words. I thought it was please and thank you, but apparently, I was wrong. It's I insist."

As they walked into an elevator that was big enough for the four of them, including the dog and the luggage, Magnus pressed his thumb to the scanner, and the thing shot up.

"I hope I'm going to get access this time," Vivian said. "I'm no longer a prisoner, right?"

"You were never a prisoner. But once Ella's situation is resolved, you'll be free to come and go as you please. Right now it's still dangerous, so you'll have to suffer me tagging along."

"Will Mom get a self-driving car with windows that turn opaque?"

"Yes, she will."

A moment after the ping announced that the elevator had reached the lobby, the doors slid open, and they exited into a pavilion made mostly from glass that was immersed in greenery.

"It's beautiful here," Vivian murmured.

Scarlet bounded forward, pulling on her leash.

"Hold on, girl." Magnus bent down and unhooked it. "You're free to roam."

"Aren't you afraid of wild animals getting her?" Parker asked.

"There are none in the village. They can't enter even if they want to, which they don't." He grabbed the handles of the two suitcases and headed toward the exit.

"Why?" Parker asked. "I mean why can't they enter, and why wouldn't they if they could?"

The pavilion's sliding doors parted as they neared, and the four of them followed Scarlet out.

"We have several fences surrounding the village. The outer one delivers a mild electrical shock as a warning, the second one delivers a much stronger one, the third and fourth are solid and tall enough to keep a mountain lion out. That leaves only birds of prey, but Scarlet is already too big for them."

"Okay, so I get why animals can't get in. What about not wanting to?"

Magnus chuckled. "Survival instinct. Immortals, especially the males, are at the top of the food chain. We are the most dangerous predators, and the other animals recognize us as such."

Parker rubbed his chin. "So why is Scarlet not afraid of you or Julian?"

"First of all, because I got her as a puppy and she's gotten used to me. But I don't have a problem with other dogs either. They just like me."

Vivian threaded her arm through Magnus's. "That's because you're a sweetheart, and dogs can sense it."

36

MAGNUS

As they cleared the pavilion, Magnus was surprised that no one was waiting for them. "Do you know where we are supposed to go?" he asked Okidu.

"Yes, master. I am to take you to your new domicile."

Still expecting a welcoming party, Magnus listened carefully to the noises of the village, but it was even quieter than usual.

Carol must've closed the café early because he could hear no murmurs of conversation coming from that direction.

He leaned and whispered in Vivian's ear, "I think the welcoming committee is waiting for us at the house. Brace yourself."

"Why are you whispering? There is no one here."

"That's why I think everyone is over there."

"A party?"

"If Amanda is in charge, then it's a given."

Okidu, who'd heard the entire exchange, wasn't volunteering any information. Probably following Kian's instructions.

Pulling the carry-on behind her, Vivian trotted on her spiky heels, trying to keep pace with the butler. "It's so peaceful here. So green."

"It's too quiet," Parker said. "Where is everybody?"

Magnus shrugged. "I hope they are not all crowded together in our house."

Parker's eyes widened as he looked at him. "Are you serious? Is our house even big enough?"

"I was joking."

Vivian sighed. "I regret wearing heels. I didn't know we'd be walking so much. But at least we have rolling suitcases. Imagine having to carry trash bags all this way."

"We're almost there. The house we are getting is in phase two of the development. So it's farther away from the center than the phase one houses."

With time, the demarcation lines separating the two sections would fade, but until all the newly planted bushes and shrubs reached the size of those in phase one, it was very clear where the first one ended and the new one started.

When they crossed into the new section, it wasn't hard to guess which of the houses was theirs. Two bouquets of balloons flanked the walkway, and a big welcome home sign was attached to the front door.

As Okidu rushed ahead, the door opened, and Amanda stepped out, followed by Syssi.

"Welcome to the village." Amanda waved at them.

"And to your new home." Syssi walked out to greet them. "Let me help you with that." She reached for Vivian's carry-on.

"Thank you, but I think I can manage a few more steps, and then kick these heels off."

Syssi glanced down at Vivian's feet. "Gorgeous shoes, but I

know what you mean. Those are good for sitting in a restaurant, not for hiking."

Amanda held the door open. "I told everyone to give you a few moments to acclimatize before coming over." She looked at her watch. "You have about twenty minutes."

"Thank you," Magnus said. "I was afraid there would be a mob waiting for us here."

He wondered where everyone was if they weren't at the house. But then if Carol had closed early, there was no reason for anyone to be outside unless they were in the mood for a stroll.

Amanda gave Vivian a quick one-armed hug. "There will be in twenty minutes." She offered Parker her hand. "Do you want to see the house? I bet you want to see your room."

"Oh, yeah. Finally. I was so sick of sleeping on the couch." He followed Amanda.

"It's beautiful." Vivian turned in a circle. "Your decorator is fantastic. I love her work."

The house looked larger than the two others Magnus had shared in the village before, and it was only one story instead of two. The second-phase houses had different layouts than their first-phase counterparts.

"The living room, dining room, and kitchen are in the center," Syssi said. "There are two bedroom-bath combos on this side." She pointed to where Amanda had taken Parker. "And two over there." She pointed at the other side of the house. "I guess you can use one of the bedrooms as an office, or do some remodeling and combine the two into one large master suite. Originally, the house was designed for four people to share. It's the largest we have."

"There is no need for remodeling." Vivian waved a dismissive hand. "I'm sure the rooms are big enough."

"Let's see." Magnus left the suitcases by the door and took Vivian's hand.

"A king-sized bed, and just look at the bedding." Vivian walked over and sat on the bed. "And there are French doors to a private patio. I'm in love." She got up and walked over to the doors.

He followed her outside and sat on one of the lounge chairs. "I can imagine us having our morning coffee here."

"Hello, neighbors." A familiar face appeared above the fence.

"Merlin, what a surprise." Magnus got up and opened the gate for his old friend. "Come in and say hi to Vivian."

"Vivian, my dear. You're even more beautiful than I've been told you are." The tall doctor took Vivian's hand and brought it to his lips for a kiss. "I'm Merlin, and I'm your next-door neighbor."

"Nice to meet you." She looked him up and down.

As usual for Merlin, the guy was wearing an outfit that didn't belong in the current century, or even the one before that. And the color combination of a purple jacket with orange pants was painful to behold.

Merlin required some getting used to.

Magnus wrapped his arm around Vivian's shoulders. "Let's go back to the living room."

Merlin followed them inside. "I heard there is going to be a barbecue. Everyone is bringing something. I'm sorry I came empty-handed, but I haven't gotten around to doing grocery shopping yet, and I'm afraid that I finished everything that was left for me by the welcoming committee. My fridge is empty, as well as the cupboards." He leaned to whisper in Vivian's ear. "If you don't mind, I'm going to pilfer some of the leftovers from your party."

She smiled. "By all means."

"Provided there are leftovers," Magnus said. "Immortals have big appetites."

As Parker came out of his room, he stopped and gaped at Merlin. "Who are you?"

"I'm Merlin. And you are?" The doctor offered Parker his hand.

"I'm Parker." The kid's eyes were still peeled wide as he shook it. "Are you a magician?"

"Of course. Otherwise, why would I dress like this?"

Parker's jaw dropped even lower. "Seriously, dude?"

Merlin bent down from his considerable height, so his face was at the same level as Parker's. "Do you want me to show you some tricks?"

"Do I ever."

Straightening up, Merlin glanced around the room. "Let's go out to the yard where we can have some privacy."

When the two left, Vivian chuckled. "I'm glad you warned me about him. Merlin is quite a colorful fellow. But if the goal of immortals is not to attract attention to themselves, Merlin is doing the opposite. What's his deal?"

Magnus shrugged. "I guess he's just eccentric. He doesn't conform in any way and behaves as if the clan's rules don't apply to him. For some reason, Sari lets him get away with it."

"Sari is the head of the Scottish arm of the clan, right?"

"Yes."

"Is she as intimidating as Kian?"

Magnus rubbed his chin. "Sari's style of leadership is very different to his. She's assertive, of course. Otherwise, she wouldn't have been able to lead a bunch of opinionated immortals, but she's much more inclusive, and she doesn't attempt to do everything herself. She knows how to delegate."

Aware that he was describing Sari in a more favorable light

than Kian, Magnus qualified. "On the other hand, Kian is running the entire business conglomerate, while Sari is only managing several local enterprises. So in a way, her job is easier."

"Is she also involved in the rescue operations?"

"No. It's all done from here. That is why my fellow Guardians and I moved here. We answered Bridget's call to come and serve a most worthy cause."

"Who has taken your place defending Sari's place?"

"No one had to. All the Guardians who came here were retired, including me. I wasn't on active duty."

She shook her head. "There is still so much I don't know about you."

He kissed the top of her head. "We have all the time in the world to learn everything there is about each other."

37

ELLA

At nine in the morning the seamstress arrived with the wedding dress, and less than an hour later, the alterations were done.

There was also a veil and a pair of white low-heeled pumps.

It wasn't the kind of dress Ella would've chosen for herself. It was big and fluffy, with tons of petticoats, and it covered her from neck to toe. As far as modesty went it was appropriate for an Amish wedding, but the pearls sewn into it and the intricate lacework were not.

It wasn't gaudy, but it was definitely ostentatious.

As the seamstress oohed and aahed in Russian, clasping her hands in front of her and sighing dramatically, Ella made an effort to smile for the old woman.

It wasn't Olga's fault that the wedding was a sham. She'd probably worked all night to have it ready by morning and deserved at least a smile for her efforts.

Dimitri was going to get only a scowl. And if he had a problem with that, she'd say that she was still in a state of shock.

Let him try and argue with that.

There was a knock on the door. "Can I come in?" Misha asked.

"Yes."

As he entered, the big guy gasped like an excited girl and put a hand over his heart. "You are the most beautiful bride I ever see."

Jumping at the opportunity for a translator, the seamstress started talking and waving her hands, to which Misha replied with the occasional *Da.*

"She ask if you like the dress."

"It's beautiful."

When Misha translated, Olga grinned and asked him a new question.

"She ask if it is too tight or too loose."

"No, it's fine."

After that got translated, Olga said something and lifted her arms.

"She ask that you put your arms up and check if it is comfortable to do."

Ella rolled her eyes but did as the woman asked. "Everything is perfect. Please thank her for me and tell her that she's free to go."

After Misha translated, Olga nodded and said something that sounded like congratulations to Ella.

"She say many happy years of marriage."

"*Spaseeba,*" Ella said.

Olga grinned and dipped her head. "*Pazhalusta.*" She collected her stuff, waved goodbye with a big smile, and left the room.

Ella let out a long breath. "This thing is so heavy. I need to take it off." Lifting the petticoats, she started toward the walk-in closet.

"The wedding is at twelve. You sure you want to take big dress off and then put on in an hour and half?"

Ella swallowed. The noose was closing around her neck, and there was nothing she could do to escape it. In less than two hours, she was going to walk down the aisle in Dimitri's private chapel, with all of his staff in attendance. He was making sure there were plenty of witnesses.

"Definitely. I'm going to take a bath and do my hair and makeup."

She contemplated using everything in her makeup bag and making herself look like a painted doll. Walking down the aisle, she would smile like a demented clown, so everyone would know the wedding was a joke.

What could Dimitri do? Send her back to wash her face?

Yeah, that was probably what he would do. King of his castle and all that. The priest and whoever was going to attend would wait until the master's wishes were fulfilled.

"Boss said Pavel is coming to do that for you."

Ella perked up. This was the best news she'd gotten in a long while. "Really?" Dimitri didn't tell me anything."

Misha grimaced. "I didn't know boss wanted to make it a surprise."

Yeah, that probably had been the idea. Dimitri liked to surprise her. Mostly, she dreaded his surprises, but not this one. "When is he coming?"

Misha glanced at his watch. "Ten or fifteen minutes. Pavel cross the second gate one hour ago."

Ella debated whether to remove the dress or wait for Pavel to get there so he could see it. Not because she wanted his opinion, but because she knew he would want to. She could just imagine the face he would make. Pavel's taste in clothing was much more refined than Dimitri's.

Except, the monstrosity was not meant for anything other than walking down the aisle in. She would have to stand until he got there because sitting with it on would require some major maneuvering.

Reaching back, she made sure she could unzip it without help and started to lower the zipper.

"What you doing?" Misha sounded horrified.

"Don't worry. I'm not going to take it off in front of you. I was just making sure that I can reach the zipper."

"Oh." He let out a relieved breath. "Boss kill me if I see you without clothes."

That was probably an exaggeration. Dimitri was strict, but he wasn't insane.

She waved a dismissive hand and headed into the closet. Pulling the zipper all the way down, she removed the sleeves first and then stepped out of the dress. The thing didn't even fall over and remained standing like a lace statue. After hanging it up, Ella put on a pair of leggings and an oversized sweater, and opened the door.

"Do you want some wine?" She headed for the wine cooler.

"No, thank you."

She glanced at Misha over her shoulder. "You really don't like it? Because if you're worried about the boss finding out, don't. I can never finish the bottle, and it just goes to waste."

Misha rubbed a hand over his square jaw. "Maybe I take a taste. But wine is for girls."

Ella chuckled. "Don't let Dimitri hear you say that. He loves his wines."

"I know. I keep my big mouth shut."

Ella smirked as she uncorked the wine and poured it into

two glasses. Unwittingly, Misha had confirmed for her that the master bedroom wasn't under surveillance. The bodyguard would have never dared to talk like that if there was a chance the boss would find out. Up until now, she'd thought the room was bugged but the equipment was turned off whenever Dimitri was there. Apparently, though, it wasn't bugged at all.

Awesome.

Every little bit of freedom was precious.

That was why when a knock sounded at the door, she rushed over, threw it open, and flung herself into Pavel's arms. "I'm so happy to see you!" she squealed.

Dislodging her arms from around his neck, he gave her a slight push. "Let me look at you, Ella girl." He gave her a thorough once over and then nodded. "Excellent. The country air has done wonders for you. Rosy cheeks, shining eyes, you look healthy."

She waved a dismissive hand. "That's the wine, not the air. Come in, and I'll pour you some of Dimitri's best."

"Don't mind if I do." Pulling a carry-on behind him, Pavel followed her inside.

Misha got up and the two exchanged back slaps like a couple of bros.

"You make Ella look good for the wedding," Misha said.

Pavel arched a perfectly shaped brow. "I'm going to make her the most beautiful bride to ever walk into a chapel."

She poured wine into another glass and handed it to Pavel. "Can you give me away too? Because it's going to be awkward to walk alone."

He batted his long eyelashes and put a hand over his heart. "I'd be honored. But the boss needs to give his okay first."

"Do you have a tux?"

Pavel humphed. "Do I have a tux? Of course I do."

"What about me?" Misha grumbled.

Pavel put a hand on his hip and struck a pose. "Well, if you wanted me to bring you a tux, you should have said so. I can't snap my fingers and conjure one from thin air."

"I don't ask about what to wear. I ask why not me walk Ella down the aisle."

Oh, damn. She should've known he would be offended. "Maybe the two of you could do that together? Or maybe Misha could be my groomsman since I don't have bridesmaids?"

Pavel laughed. "I don't think the boss is that progressive."

Ella's smile wilted. Dimitri's sham of a wedding was probably going to be very traditional. The question was whether it was going to be registered somewhere official.

Not that it mattered. If her rescuers were going to fake her death, the marriage contract would be dissolved. She would just assume a new identity, and it would be as if she'd never been married.

The other option was letting them kill Dimitri, which was still on the table.

One of the reasons Ella hadn't talked with her mother since he'd told her about the wedding was that she was still undecided. She couldn't keep changing her mind. She either left things as they were, or okayed Dimitri's execution.

It wasn't an easy decision to make.

Heck, it wasn't the kind of decision that should be left up to her at all. Maybe she should just tell them to do what was more convenient?

Except, that was a cowardly way out. For them, the choice would be easy. Kill Gorchenco, and frame her with his death, then change her identity and have her in hiding for the rest of her life.

Not that it would be any different if they faked her death, but at least she wouldn't have Dimitri's death on her conscience.

The third option of refusing to marry him was not really an option at all. If she did that, it would backfire big time and ruin her rescue. Dimitri would get angry and leave her behind in Russia, or take her with him but put her under heavier guard.

She wasn't going to risk it because of a meaningless piece of paper.

38

VIVIAN

As Vivian waited for Magnus to be done in the shower, she gazed at the landscape Dalhu had brought them as a house-warming gift. It was hanging on the wall across from their bed, where she could look at it as soon as she opened her eyes in the morning.

The painting was special, but she had a hard time putting her finger on what made it so. There were the vivid greens of the treetops that were highlighted by swathes of yellow light penetrating the dense canopy, and then there were the wildflowers blooming in the clearing the sunlight was shining on. Seemingly, it was a simple landscape, but for some reason, the overall effect inspired a sense of calm and hope.

Or maybe it was the effect of the warm welcome and the wonderful party Amanda had thrown together.

The second one in a row.

Vivian owed a debt of gratitude to Kian's sister that she had no idea how to repay. First, Amanda had organized the ritual to lift the curse, then she'd organized Parker's transition ceremony and party, and lastly the house-warming and welcome party.

All the ladies from the witchy ritual had come, and those who had partners had brought them along.

Brundar had bought a whole cow's worth of steaks, and together with Anandur, they'd gotten the outdoor grill going. Callie and Wonder had made salads, and Syssi had made her signature vegan lasagna. Others had taken care of the drinks and the desserts. Even Kian had taken a break from his busy schedule to come over and personally welcome Vivian and Parker to the village.

When the last of their guests had departed, it had been after ten o'clock at night. But although exhausted, Vivian wasn't done celebrating yet.

When Magnus came out of the bathroom, a towel wrapped around his hips and the skin on his muscular chest glistening, she was tempted to lick him all over. But before she did that, there was a question about Dalhu's landscape that had been bothering her.

"Do you recognize the spot in Dalhu's painting?

Magnus glanced at the picture and shook his head. "I think this one came from his imagination. Either that or he combined elements from different locations. I walked all over the place with Scarlet, and I didn't see anything that looked exactly like this."

"That's what I thought."

Her impression of Dalhu was that he wasn't much of a talker, but that he expressed himself through his art. That was why he was such a perfectionist about it. Amanda had said that the gift was a big deal since Dalhu deemed most of his landscapes inadequate and was refusing to sell them. But he was happy with this one.

Vivian understood.

The calm and hope the landscape inspired had come from his heart. This was what life in the village felt like to him.

Magnus arched a brow. "Is there some hidden meaning in it that I'm missing? I'm not an expert on art."

Vivian pushed up on the pillows and let the blanket slide down and reveal her breasts. "It evokes peaceful and hopeful feelings, and I love looking at it, but I love looking at you even more. How about you drop that towel and let me feast my eyes on your magnificent body."

"I thought you'd never ask." He let the towel drop and sauntered toward the bed. "You said you were tired."

Vivian chuckled. "I am, but not tired enough to postpone our private celebration."

With a wicked grin, Magnus pounced. Yanking the blanket off her on the fly, he replaced it with his body that was still warm from the shower.

Vivian shrieked, then slapped a hand over her mouth. "I forgot that we don't have soundproof doors in here," she whispered.

Parker's room was on the other side of the house, but her shriek had been loud enough for Merlin to hear all the way across the yard.

Bracing on his elbows, Magnus smiled at her. "No worries, lass. These houses are built for immortals. Everything is soundproofed. The walls, the doors, even the windows."

"So Parker can't hear us?"

"Nope, but I'd better lock the door." He jumped off the bed, locked things up, and then pounced back. Grabbing her hips, he spun her around and pulled her hips up.

Damn, she loved that pose.

Her bottom, which was her sexiest feature, was on full

display, while her breasts, which were the least sexy, at least in her opinion, were hidden under her. Not that she dared say it in front of Magnus. The last time she'd said something deprecating about her breasts, he'd threatened to spank her.

Hmm, that was something Vivian hadn't tried yet. She'd read a few romance novels that featured it as part of sex, and she'd been intrigued. As long as it was playful and not painful, she was willing to try.

Not that she was ever going to suggest it. As comfortable as she felt with Magnus, it was a line that she didn't dare cross.

But if he initiated it, she wasn't going to protest. Well, at least not too loudly or convincingly.

Imagining that, Vivian's arousal flared, and she waggled her behind, hopefully in an enticing way.

"Best ass in the universe." Magnus cupped her butt cheeks and squeezed, then spread them apart and dragged his tongue over her wet slit. "But this sweet pussy is even better."

Oh, boy, to hear Magnus say pussy was so damn erotic. He was so proper most of the time, so refined that she'd felt bad about cussing in front of him because she'd never heard him do that.

He'd also never talked dirty to her before.

"And it's mine." He licked into her.

Vivian moaned and pushed back, or tried to, but Magnus was holding on tight, and that was a turn-on too.

Lifting her bottom, he flicked his tongue over her clit, eliciting a throaty moan from her that startled her in how animalistic it sounded.

Apparently, when letting loose, Vivian was not as civilized as she'd thought herself to be. There was a wild animal inside her, and she was taking over.

Vivian had never felt as free to be herself as she was with

Magnus. There was no right or wrong, there was no embarrassment, there was only the two of them enjoying each other in every which way either of them desired.

Letting go of her butt cheeks, Magnus grunted as he pushed his tongue deeper, fucking her with it. She imagined him palming his erection and running his hand up and down the hard length as he tongued her into an orgasm.

Talk about erotic.

Vivian wished they had a mirror mounted on the sidewall, so she could see what he was doing. If she was getting so turned on from just imagining it, seeing it would be orgasmic.

When he retracted his tongue, she whimpered in protest, but then groaned as he penetrated her with two long fingers and flicked that expert tongue over her clit.

Crying out, Vivian pushed back against his fingers and tongue. With a growl that sent vibrations to the center of her desire, Magnus hooked his fingers inside her and rubbed a spot that pushed her beyond the point of no return.

On a scream, she came, thrashing and bucking as he kept milking every last drop of climax out of her.

39

MAGNUS

When Magnus was done wresting the last drops of pleasure out of Vivian, she collapsed on the bed, panting, her limbs loose.

Reaching into the nightstand drawer, he pulled out a condom and sheathed himself. He hadn't bothered unpacking most of his things yet, but the condoms had come out from his duffle bag along with the toothbrush and toothpaste.

A man had to have his priorities straight.

Vivian moaned and turned around. Her arms flopping bonelessly to her sides, she smiled. "And now for the main event of this evening's entertainment."

Climbing on top of her, he pinned her wrists to the mattress. "What about the opening act? Not important enough for you?" He nipped her lower lip.

"Very. But I ache for you to get inside of me."

Well, when put like that there was only one thing to do.

Rearing back, he pushed his hips forward, encountering little resistance as his shaft slid inside all the way to the hilt.

With a groan, Vivian's eyes rolled back in her head, and she arched up in pleasure. "Yes, that's what I need."

He pulled back and slammed home again. "This?"

"Yes, more."

Retreating almost all the way, he came back, then again, and again, slamming so hard into her that the bed frame banged against the wall with each forward thrust.

"Is that what you want, love?"

Instead of answering him, her inner muscles clamped down on his shaft, rippling over his length.

Magnus almost climaxed right there and then. Using every ounce of willpower he possessed, he held still.

Vivian smirked triumphantly, relishing the power she had over him. Or rather the power she thought she had.

Pulling out again, he hovered at her entrance and waited.

She thrashed, trying to lift her hips and impale herself on his length, but he held her pinned down with very little wiggle room.

"Please," she gasped.

If Magnus had any doubts left that Vivian enjoyed his dominance in bed, he had none now. The scent of her desire flared, and an outpouring of juices coated the tip of his shaft, making it slide forward even though that hadn't been his intention.

"Please what, love. You need to be specific."

She glared up at him. "Please fuck me."

Ooh, that was good. He'd never heard her say fuck before, and coming from those luscious lips and that angelic face it was hot as hell.

"With pleasure." He drove all the way inside her.

She spread her thighs wider, inviting a deeper penetration.

More than happy to oblige, Magnus let go of her wrists and

reached for her knees, gripping the backs and bringing them up against her chest.

Spread out before him like she'd never been spread out before, Vivian panted in anticipation.

He plunged into her, getting so deep it must've hurt, but she didn't protest. Instead, as he did that again, Vivian moaned in ecstasy.

Moving faster and faster, all games and teasing forgotten, he was aware of the lewd sounds his balls were making each time they slapped against her beautiful ass, but that only added to the ambiance of the taking.

This was a possession, primitive, uncivilized, and more satisfying than all the sex he'd had throughout his life put together.

This was his mate, his one and only, and she wanted to be taken just as much as he wanted to do the taking.

Her head thrashing from side to side as the pressure built up inside her, she was wild in her abandon. He was right there with her, climbing toward his peak with an inferno roaring in his ears and blurring his eyesight.

Hips rolling faster, his shaft pistoning in and out of her, Magnus heard himself growling. And yet, he wasn't giving in to the animal inside him.

Not yet.

As long as Vivian was still human, she could take only so much, and he couldn't allow himself to let loose.

As his shaft swelled inside her, his muscles started shaking from the effort to hold himself in check.

Vivian was going to climax again, and it was going to happen before he bit her and before his own completion robbed him of his senses.

Rubbing against her most sensitive spot with each twisting thrust, he drove into her again and again until she screamed.

Gripped by the orgasm exploding over her, her body shaking and convulsing, Vivian clung to him, her nails biting into the straining muscles of his back and triggering the inevitable.

He roared as his seed rose up like a hot geyser in his shaft and shot out, filling the condom to overflowing.

It was epic. It was all-consuming. It was the way it was meant to be between true-love mates.

The only thing he would have changed was eliminating the rubber barrier between them.

With a loud hiss, he bit her not too gently, but in her state of arousal, the pain didn't even register. She moaned as his fangs sank into her neck, her nails digging so deep she was drawing blood.

He relished the pain.

Hell, he wished she could do more and mark him permanently, proclaiming him as hers for everyone to see.

As another powerful climax rocked Vivian's body, and then another, he licked the small punctures closed and kissed her neck, waiting until the last of the shudders subsided.

"I love you," he whispered into the crook of her neck.

"I love you too," she murmured. "So much."

40

ELLA

Dimitri had arranged for a traditional Russian wedding, and nothing was going the way Ella had expected.

First of all, she'd thought he would be waiting for her at the altar. Instead he came to escort her, looking very sharp in a white tuxedo, not black.

"You are breathtaking, my Ella." He leaned and lightly kissed her cheek, careful not to smear her makeup, and then took her hand.

Pavel, who'd changed into his tux, and Misha who'd put on his ill-fitting suit, took position behind them as they walked out of the master bedroom and descended the stairs.

Up front, a horse-drawn carriage that was decorated with hundreds of white flowers and ribbons awaited them.

Dimitri put his hands on her waist, lifted her, and put her down on the bench.

Despite her gloomy mood, Ella chuckled. "It's not a good idea to show off on your wedding day. What if you throw your back out?"

It was a slight jibe reminding him that he was too old for pulling stunts like that.

He smirked. "Then I'll give myself a muscle relaxant shot. I'm only getting married once. I'm going to do it right."

Poor, delusional man. The main ingredient in his dream wedding was not the right one. He had the wrong bride.

"Who is going to walk me down the aisle? I think Pavel should do it since he's wearing an awesome tux, but I don't want to offend Misha. So maybe both of them can walk with me?"

Dimitri laughed. "This is a Russian wedding. Not American. But if you want, I can have the two of them hold the crowns."

"Crowns?"

"You'll see."

Damn him and his surprises. But whatever. She didn't care what kind of ceremony it was going to be. As far as she was concerned, they could be sitting on toilets as thrones and wear shower caps on their heads as crowns.

The carriage stopped in front of the chapel, where a priest was waiting for them at the entrance.

He blessed them in Russian and gave each of them a lit candle to hold. Another man in plain clothing came forward and said what sounded like another blessing. When he was done, the priest continued with some more mumbling that sounded like prayers.

No one bothered to translate anything for her. But then, it didn't matter. Not to her and not to Dimitri, but for different reasons. Ella viewed the wedding as a theatrical performance that meant nothing to her, and Dimitri didn't think she needed to know what was being said.

As a little boy came forward, holding a velvet cushion with the two wedding rings on top of it, the priest lifted the rings, said another prayer or blessing over them and then placed them on their fingers.

More prayers and blessing were said, but no one asked either of them if they wanted to marry the other, and they were still standing at the entry.

What a weird ceremony.

When the priest was finally done, he turned around and walked into the church in measured steps, obviously expecting them to follow.

Holding her hand, Dimitri led her in. "This was just the betrothal ceremony," he whispered in her ear. "The crowning is the actual wedding."

That explained why no one had asked them anything.

She could still say no.

Right.

The priest stopped in the center of the church. There was a piece of rose-colored fabric under his feet, and Ella wondered what it symbolized. A rosy future? A virgin bride?

Neither applied.

When they joined the priest and stood facing each other, Dimitri said something that sounded like a pledge in Russian and then repeated it in English. "I, Dimitri Gorchenco, have never been promised to another, and I am marrying Ella Takala of my own free will."

The priest looked at her, expecting her to repeat Dimitri's words.

Ella swallowed, the candle she was holding in her left hand flickering as her hand started trembling. There was no way out of this. She had to say it.

Besides, everyone in the chapel was on Dimitri's payroll and under his control. She could say that the sky was blue, and the priest would marry them anyway, and every person witnessing the ceremony would swear that she'd said the right words.

"I, Ella Takala, have never been promised to another, and I am marrying Dimitri Gorchenco of my free will."

Dimitri grinned.

Was he going to kiss her now?

Apparently not.

The priest continued with his droning for several long moments, and then Pavel and Misha approached, each carrying a pillow with a crown on top.

Lifting the crowns off the pillows, they held them over her and Dimitri's heads as the priest read some more from his prayer book.

The plain-clothed guy from before handed Dimitri a wine cup. He took a sip and then handed it to her. After Ella drank from it, the guy took the cup, and Dimitri took her hand.

She was hoping someone would take the candles away because holding hers up was becoming a struggle, but that didn't happen.

Instead, the priest wrapped his stole around their conjoined hands and led them around the Bible stand three times, with Pavel and Misha walking behind them and holding the crowns over their heads.

Weird. Why didn't they just put them on?

More prayers were said, and then it was done, which she knew because the so-called guests got up and started clapping and cheering.

Finally, the crowns were placed on their heads, and Dimitri led her out of the chapel and into the waiting carriage.

"What now?" Ella asked as the thing started moving.

Dimitri grinned. "Now, Mrs. Gorchenco, we leave for our honeymoon."

She arched a brow. "Dubai?"

Hopefully, he hadn't changed his plans and decided to take her to Paris for their honeymoon.

"Yes. We change clothes, eat lunch and head out to the airport."

She lifted the crown off her head and brought it to her lap. "Is this real gold?"

The design was simple, and it wasn't studded with precious gems. It didn't look like something Dimitri would have commissioned. Then again, she doubted he would've used commercially made crowns or fakes.

"Of course."

"When did you have it made?"

"I didn't. It is a family heirloom. They both are."

"Oh." She handed the crown to him. "Then you should put it somewhere safe."

He took it from her hands and put it back on her head. "I will. But keep it on until we get back to our room." He clasped her hand and lifted it to his lips. "My queen." He kissed the back of it.

41

VIVIAN

"I need to get up." Vivian stretched her arms over her head.

Magnus wrapped his arm around her middle and pulled her back against his warm body. "Why?"

Indeed. She would've loved to stay in bed with him and spoon some more. Maybe even have a quick romp before starting her day. One of the side effects of the venom was enhanced vigor. Vivian wasn't tired, and she wasn't sore. In fact, she felt perfect.

But she was still a mother with a son who needed to be fed. "Because I need to make breakfast for Parker." She chuckled. "He's a growing boy in more ways than one."

"There are plenty of leftovers in the fridge. He can grab something. At his age, I hunted and fished to get food."

"Right. Now I understand all those outdated outdoorsy references. Did the other kids hunt and fish?"

"Some did. Most human kids tended to sheep, though."

She turned around in his arms and lifted her head. "So you were always special."

"Oh, I don't know about that. We just didn't raise sheep, and I needed to keep busy. I wasn't particularly studious, which was very disappointing to my mother."

"I would like to meet her."

"I haven't told her about you yet."

Vivian hoped that it wasn't because he was embarrassed by her. Maybe his mother had a problem with him choosing a woman with kids?

Magnus kissed the top of her head. "I'm waiting for us to get Ella back and for you to transition. I'd rather deliver only good news and not give her any reasons for worry."

"Why? Is she the emotional type?"

He chuckled. "She's the glass-half-empty type. A pessimist."

"The opposite of you."

"In this regard yes. I'm an optimist."

"What's her name?"

"Amelia."

"It's a pretty name." Vivian untangled herself from his arms. "Come on. I need coffee."

Magnus sighed. "So I guess a morning romp is out of the question?"

She eyed his muscular chest. It looked so tempting, but it was late, and she had a son to feed. "I wish we could, but we overslept, and we really can't stay in bed any longer."

"Tomorrow, I'm waking you up at five in the morning."

"Deal." She blew him a kiss before ducking into the bathroom.

It was such a nice one, with a tub and a separate shower and a double vanity. Vivian loved everything about the house, but mostly she loved the location. They were less than an hour's drive away from the city, and yet it felt like living in the country.

The only noises outside the bathroom windows were the rustle of leaves and the chirping of birds. No car engine noises, no horns honking, but also no kids yelling or dogs barking.

Which reminded her of Scarlet. With the two of them oversleeping, the dog had probably peed in the house.

Toothbrush in hand, she cracked the door to the bedroom open. "Magnus, you need to get up. I'm sure Scarlet left you a present in the house. No one's taken her out since last night."

The way he leaped out of bed was a reminder that her man wasn't human. Except, she was no longer startled by his fits of athleticism. It was just who he was.

Sharing a shower without touching each other was an exercise in self-restraint, but they needed to be done quickly, and one little touch or kiss was sure to lead to another. Less than ten minutes after getting out of bed, they were both ready to start their day.

As Magnus opened the bedroom door, they were hit by the smell of something cooking.

They either had guests, or Parker was making himself breakfast.

Waving a spatula, her son grinned. "Good morning. I'm making eggs. Do you want some?"

Vivian gaped. Parker never expressed the slightest inclination toward cooking. A bowl of cereal or a peanut butter and jelly sandwich was the extent of his culinary skills.

"Where did you find eggs? And since when do you know how to make them?"

He shrugged. "There was a whole carton in the fridge, and I watched a YouTube video on how to make them. It's easy."

"I'll have some," Magnus said, nudging Vivian with his elbow.

"Yeah, me too. I can't wait to eat your first culinary creation."

Perhaps she shouldn't have said that. Now he would feel pressured.

But Parker seemed unperturbed. In fact, he looked smug. "By the way, I already took Scarlet out. She actually woke me up and whined by the door to be let out."

Vivian released a relieved breath. "Good. I was afraid we were going to find a puddle or two." She walked over to the coffeemaker. "There is only enough coffee left for two more rounds. We need to go grocery shopping."

"We can go after breakfast." Magnus pulled several containers with leftovers out of the fridge and put them on the kitchen counter.

"Mom, can you get the plates? The eggs are ready."

"Sure thing." She opened the top cabinet and pulled out three. "Here you go, sweetie."

They'd gotten the house fully equipped with everything a family of four needed. There were pots and pans and food storage containers, bath towels and kitchen towels, and even cleaning supplies and detergents. The interior designer hadn't omitted anything. According to Magnus, every house was delivered like this.

Nevertheless, Ingrid was added to Vivian's growing list of people she felt indebted to. Now she only needed to think of a way to repay their kindness.

Leaning against the counter, Vivian looked at her guys preparing breakfast, and her heart swelled with gratitude. The only one missing from this sweet, homey picture was Ella.

Hopefully, not for long.

When the coffee was ready, she poured it into two cups and joined the guys at the table.

"Try the eggs, Mom."

Magnus rolled his eyes in mock delight. "Best eggs I ever had."

What a sweet guy he was.

Lifting the fork, she scooped a small amount and put it in her mouth, bracing to chew and swallow even if it tasted horrible. But it didn't. The eggs were a bit too buttery but tasty nonetheless.

"Excellent. From now on you're in charge of making eggs."

Parker loved the compliment but not the assignment. "Maybe only on the weekends?"

Vivian laughed. "Good enough."

When they were done with breakfast, and the dishes were cleared, Magnus poured them another cup of coffee from the carafe. "Would you like to join me on the front porch?"

"I would love to. It reminds me of the cabin. It's almost as isolated here as it was there." She turned to Parker. "Vacation is over, sweetie. You need to unpack the laptop and do some school work."

Parker sighed. "But what if I'm not feeling well?"

"Are you?"

He hung his head. "Doctor Bridget said that my teeth are going to start bothering me. But nothing is happening yet."

"It takes time." Magnus ruffled his hair. "In a day or two, you'll be begging for painkillers."

When he headed to his room, her son seemed more excited than scared.

"There is a porch swing waiting for us outside." Magnus wrapped his arm around her shoulders.

"It's so peaceful here," she said as they sat on the swing. "Nothing but birds chirping."

"I hope Merlin keeps his windows closed."

"Why?"

"He likes to sing opera. Loudly."

"Does he have a good voice?"

"He does, but he only knows four songs. Sometimes he sings the same one over and over. I think it was the main reason that Sari didn't mind him living on his own outside the keep."

"Maybe he did it on purpose so she'd let him go?"

He glanced at her. "I never thought of that. But yeah, that might be it."

"I guess we are going to find out soon. If he still sings the same four songs here, then it's because he just knows those four."

"Right." Magnus grimaced. "I can't wait to find out."

42

MAGNUS

Vivian leaned her head against Magnus's bicep and sighed. "I just thought of something. Now that we are here in the village, you don't need to babysit Parker and me. You can go back to your regular duties."

"Are you tired of me already?"

She leaned away and slapped his arm playfully. "Don't be silly. Of course I want to be with you, spending all of our days and nights together. But that would be selfish of me. Besides, I'm sure your boss is going to realize that too."

"He might, but I'm not going to point it out to him. I want to have more time with you." He tightened his arm around her. "Let's make it our honeymoon. We can take long strolls through the village, make love all day, and in the afternoon hang out in the café."

"Sounds dreamy. Except, there is a teenage boy in the house, and we can't stay locked in the bedroom all day. Besides, a honeymoon usually comes after the wedding."

As far as he was concerned, they were mated and no ceremony was required, but Vivian was still thinking in human terms.

He kissed the top of her head. "That can be easily fixed."

"Are you proposing?"

"I thought I already did."

"You've never actually asked me. You just assumed that I wanted to. Not that you were wrong. I do, but technically you didn't ask."

"Do I need to go down on one knee?"

She laughed. "Just say the words."

"Eh, if I'm going to do the human thing, I'd better do it right."

He knelt in front of her on the porch and clasped her hand. "Would you marry me, Vivian? Would you be my mate, my partner, my one and only true love forever?" He winked. "Think carefully before you answer. Forever is a very long time for immortals."

"I don't need to think. Yes, I'll be your mate and partner, your one and only true love forever. Will you be all of that for me?"

"Yes, I will."

She cupped his cheek and leaned to kiss him. "I love you, Magnus."

He took the mug out of her hands and put it on the floor. Lifting her up, he put her on his lap and gave her a proper kiss to seal the deal.

Vivian put her head on his chest. "Normally, I would be worried about what the neighbors would think. But since we have only one and it's Merlin, the most eccentric person I know, I don't mind."

"Good. Because I love sitting like this with you. I want to do this every evening."

"Can we get married while I'm still human?"

"I don't see why not."

"I thought about it, and I don't think that I want to attempt transition right after Ella is back. She is going to be in an emotional turmoil, and she is going to need me. I can't check out, slip into a coma, and add stress to her trauma."

Regrettably, he had to agree. "You're right. I hope she'll get over her ordeal quickly. For our sakes as well as Julian's."

Vivian looked up at him. "What if she doesn't like him? He's gorgeous and sweet, but maybe he is not Ella's type? She fell for that creep Romeo. Maybe she's attracted to bad boys? If that happens, Julian is going to be devastated, and I'm going to feel awful."

"I don't think fate would've gone to all this trouble only for those two to find out that they are incompatible."

"It can happen, though."

"And a solar flare can destroy all of our electronics and plunge us into the Dark Ages, or a meteor can hit Earth and destroy most of humanity. There is no point in dwelling on the what ifs."

Vivian scowled. "Way to go, Magnus. Now you've given me all of that to worry about too."

He shifted her in his arms so he could look into her eyes. "I can go on. In the end, you'll have so many possible disasters to worry about that you'll worry about none."

She waved a dismissive hand. "Please, don't. Let's talk about more immediate problems, like what am I going to do here. I don't think I can be happy with just keeping house. I need to do more."

A wistful thought flitted through Magnus's mind. What if the two of them made a baby? That would give Vivian plenty to do. But after her transition, the chances of that would be even more minuscule than they were now.

Stifling a sigh, he asked, "What did you dream about doing when you were a girl? I'm sure it wasn't dental hygiene."

She chuckled. "I wanted to be a doctor."

"Then you can go back to school and study to become one."

"Not really. I wanted to be a doctor, but my grades were never good enough. I wouldn't have been admitted."

"Can you improve them? Is there a way to do that?"

"I don't know. But in any case, this is not a realistic goal. I wasn't a good enough student then, and I wouldn't be now. But maybe I can study to become a therapist or a counselor. I would like to help the rescued girls in any way I can. Maybe your clan's therapist can give me advice on what's the best way to go about it."

"I think it's a great idea. I'll get her number for you."

"Thank you." Vivian bent down and picked up her coffee mug. "What about you? Wouldn't you like to open a little clothing store here in the village? I was told that there are none."

"Everything can be ordered online. Being a Guardian is more important than selling clothes."

"I was afraid you were going to say that." Vivian frowned. "The truth is that I don't want you anywhere near danger. I can't lose you, Magnus. There is no guarantee that my curse is gone. It was just a silly ritual to make me feel good. Putting faith in it is too much of a leap for me."

He hugged her closer and kissed her forehead. "Humans pose no danger to me, lass. Nothing can happen to me."

"Bullshit. You told me yourself that if the injury is severe enough, even an immortal body can't repair it. A bullet to the brain can kill you. A massive explosion can kill you too."

"It would need to be one hell of a bullet to kill me."

She rolled her eyes. "Made from silver?"

"No, but a big one. As to explosives, there are none in brothels, and those are the only missions I go on."

"But there are guns."

"Yes. But these humans don't know that they need to aim for the head. The chest is a larger and easier target."

"What if they hit you in the heart?"

"Not fatal to an immortal, at least in most cases."

"But not all."

"No, not all. But you're going into the what if territory once more. We've been doing this for a while, and we haven't lost a Guardian yet. No one even got injured."

"Promise me that you'll wear a Kevlar vest under your clothes."

"Deal."

"That was easy." She narrowed her eyes at him. "Too easy. What gives?"

"Nothing. If Kevlar would ease your mind, then the discomfort of wearing it is well worth it."

She threw her arms around his neck and peppered his face with kisses. "I love you so much. Thank you for being so considerate."

"Always, love."

43

VIVIAN

"How do I look?" Vivian asked.

Going out shopping meant putting on the wig and dark glasses. She still felt weird doing that. Not in a bad way, though. Just different.

"Gorgeous." Magnus gave her a thorough once over, starting at her hair and all the way down to her feet. "But are you sure you want to wear heels to the supermarket?"

It was silly, but she couldn't pretend to be a badass spy while wearing flip-flops, in the same way that she couldn't leave her face free of makeup with the black-haired wig and sunglasses.

"I really need to buy more shoes. And clothes."

"Well, we are going out, so we might as well stop at the mall."

Vivian glanced at the bathroom mirror and smoothed a few flyaways. "Did you ask Kian if it was okay? He said that as long as I'm still human, I can't leave. And what about Gorchenco?"

"I don't have to ask. Since your son is transitioning and

about to become an immortal, we trust that you'll want to protect him and keep immortals a secret."

She turned around and leaned against the counter. "I would've never betrayed you or your people regardless of my or Parker's transition. You must know that."

He reached for her and pulled her into his arms. "Of course I know that. But those are the rules, and they are not meant for individual interpretation. I don't want to think of what would have happened if we started bending them. There is no way our existence would have remained secret."

Vivian leaned into him, absorbing his warmth and strength. "I get it. Rules are important, and it's good that you have them in place. What about Gorchenco?"

"That's what the wig and the glasses are for."

"I'm still scared."

Rubbing small circles on her back, he kissed her forehead. "If it scares you to leave the protection of the village, you can make me a list, and I'll do the shopping. I just thought that you would like to get out."

"I would. But you are right about making a list. It will make the grocery shopping more efficient, and we will be done faster."

"Good idea. But we basically need everything."

"True, but I usually make a weekly plan of what I want to cook, and then I buy groceries accordingly. Or at least I used to when I was still running a household."

Magnus frowned. "This is your home, and you'll be running it."

"Not alone, though." Vivian sat down at the kitchen counter and pulled out her phone. "Now I have a partner whose input I need to consider. What would you like me to make during this week?" She opened the notes application.

"Steaks!" Parker yelled all the way from his bedroom. "And lots of them!"

She shook her head. "We can't eat steaks all week."

Her son walked into the living room with Scarlet trotting behind him. "Why not?"

"Because it's boring. What else would you like?"

He grimaced. "No stew and no meatloaf, that's for sure. Maybe hamburgers?"

"But the meatloaf is my best recipe."

Parker was about to say something when Magnus lifted a hand. "I would love to taste your mom's meatloaf. We'll take turns. Each of us gets two days a week to decide on the menu, and on Sundays, we either eat out or bring something from a restaurant."

"I call dibs on Mondays and Wednesdays," Parker said. "Steaks on both."

"Agreed." Magnus nodded.

Vivian chuckled. "You're a good negotiator. I'm going to add Magnus The Peacemaker to your many titles."

"How many are there?" He lifted a brow. "And what are they?"

"Magnus The Protector," Vivian offered.

"Magnus The Bow Maker," Parker said.

There were some other titles Vivian would have chosen if Parker weren't there. Like Magnus the incredible lover, or Magnus of the amazing tongue.

Instead, she said, "The Famous Superhero Fancy Pants."

"Nah." Parker waved a dismissive hand. "I have a better one. Aquaman."

"Isn't that taken?" Magnus asked.

"Then you can be Aqua Immortal, or The Immortal Aquaman. Or Poseidon's Chosen."

"Ooh, I like that one." Vivian clapped her hands, but for some reason, Magnus wasn't smiling. "What's the matter? Are we embarrassing you?"

He shook his head. "Not at all. I just thought that the only titles I want are Guardian, mate, and father, and not necessarily in that order. For an immortal male, having a life partner and children is an impossible dream. I've never dared to even hope that one day those titles could be mine."

"Oh, sweetheart." Vivian leaned and kissed his cheek. "They are yours."

Parker's brows furrowed. "Is there something you guys want to tell me?"

Vivian smiled. "Magnus proposed, and I accepted."

Parker waved a dismissive hand. "Not that. I know you're going to get married. But am I getting a little brother or sister?"

Vivian tilted her head. "What has given you that idea?"

First Ella and now Parker. Were her kids trying to tell her something?

"You said that Magnus could call himself a father. So is he going to be one?"

Casting Magnus an apologetic glance, Vivian took Parker's hand. "What I meant, sweetie, was that he's going to be a father to you and Ella. But maybe that was a bit premature."

Parker looked disappointed. "So there is no baby?"

"I'm afraid not."

"Bummer. You had me all excited. I would love to have a little brother or sister, and then Magnus could call himself a dad for real. Not that I'm not happy to have him as mine, but it's not the same for him."

It wasn't. She couldn't argue with that. But as Magnus had explained, the chances of them having a child together were extremely slim.

"For me, it is," Magnus said. "If it's okay with you."

"I already told you, and I also told Mom that it is. But what I'm saying is that you probably want a kid that is yours for real."

Magnus shook his head. "For me, this is as real as it gets."

44

MAGNUS

"Can I take the wig and the glasses off?" Vivian asked as they crossed the gate into the sanctuary.

After yesterday's outing, she felt more comfortable about leaving the safety of the village. At first, she'd been casting nervous glances all around her, but after hours of shopping she'd relaxed and started to enjoy herself.

Well, except for her feet that had been so sore at the end of the day that Magnus had offered to carry her from the car to their house, or rather insisted. Vivian had been embarrassed, but he'd promised that if anyone asked, he would make it look like a romantic gesture.

"You're perfectly safe here. Everything on the inside is monitored by the clan. Just remember, the girls and the staff know nothing about immortals. As far as they are concerned, the rescues and the sanctuary are financed by several charity organizations and individual philanthropists."

"Got it." She pulled the wig off and started on the pins. "I want to meet the famous Doctor Vanessa as me, and not some glammed up version of me."

Magnus smirked. "You look just as glamorous without the wig as you do with it."

Vivian was wearing one of the new dresses he'd bought for her the day before, paired with low-heeled, comfortable pumps. She'd even put on some makeup.

With Parker staying behind and hanging out with Merlin, the outing had been their first unofficial date. It had started with a grocery run, continued in the mall where he'd gotten his way and chosen for her the kinds of outfits a beauty like Vivian should be wearing, and it had ended with dinner in one of his favorite restaurants.

She smoothed her hand over the skirt. "I'm not used to dressing up like this. I feel like I'm on a date."

He took her hand and gave it a little squeeze. "We are on a date. When it's just you and me, lass, every outing is a date."

She smiled. "I hope Parker is okay on his own."

"He is not alone. He's at Merlin's."

"Parker should be studying, and not learning card tricks from Merlin."

"Ah, but that's the beauty of homeschooling. The kid can spend the morning learning sleight of hand tricks, and then study in the afternoon when we come back home." Magnus found a spot in the sanctuary's parking lot and eased into it. "Looks like it's a busy day."

"Who do all those cars belong to?" Vivian asked as he opened the door for her.

"Vanessa used to work with humans. When she took it upon herself to run the sanctuary, she persuaded many of her colleagues to volunteer here. I guess those are their cars."

Walking through the front door holding hands, they stopped at the receptionist's desk.

She smiled up at them. "The MacBains, I presume?"

"Yes," Magnus said. "We are here to see Dr. Vanessa."

"Go right ahead. Her office is down the hall. She's expecting you."

"The MacBains?" Vivian whispered.

He shrugged. "I'm just following Vanessa's instructions. She said we needed to pretend to be a married couple. The girls are wary of men, and you wanted me to come along, so we need to pretend that I belong to you."

She arched a brow. "Pretend? You do belong to me."

"That is true. And you to me."

She sighed. "I love being with you, but normally I wouldn't be so dependent and drag you along wherever I go. I just didn't feel comfortable meeting Vanessa by myself."

He wrapped his arm around her. "I wouldn't have let you come alone even if you wanted to. Gorchenco is still out there, and I'm still your bodyguard. Onegus hasn't given me a new assignment."

"Is that the only reason?"

"You know it's not. But it's a good excuse to spend all of my time with you."

The door to Vanessa's office was open, and they walked right in.

The therapist smiled and pushed to her feet. "Hello, Vivian." She offered her hand. "I'm Vanessa."

"It's nice to meet you. Magnus told me a lot about you."

"I hope he told you only the good things." She winked.

"He said that you're the best."

"Thank you, Magnus." Vanessa shook his hand as well, closed the door, and motioned toward the two chairs in front of her desk. "Please, take a seat."

"Thank you for agreeing to see us on such short notice," Vivian said.

"I heard the word volunteer. That was all the incentive I needed to make time for you."

Vivian shifted in her chair and crossed her legs. "I'm a dental hygienist. And since my services are not needed where we live …" She looked around as if the walls had ears. "I thought that maybe I can be of service here."

"That's a lovely idea, but it would require us to purchase dental equipment. It's more economical to drive whoever needs their teeth cleaned to the city. What I need more than anything, though, are empathetic, patient women. Are you good with arts and crafts?"

"I can sew. When I was a teenager, I made new outfits out of old ones. I cut up a plain T-shirt and made something cute out of it, or added decorations."

Vanessa's eyes sparkled with excitement. "That's perfect. When can you start?"

Vivian glanced at Magnus. "Um, not right away. You're aware of the situation with my daughter, right?"

The smile melted off Vanessa's face. "I am. Once she's freed, Ella should come here. She'll need help, mine as well as the other girls'. Talking to people who've gone through a similar experience has therapeutic value. Often a victim feels isolated, like none of the *normals* understand her. The sanctuary is a good place to start the healing process."

Uncrossing her legs, Vivian leaned forward. "I agree, but Ella might be reluctant."

"Why is that?"

"When her father was killed, I took her to a therapist. The experience wasn't good. Instead of getting better, Ella got worse. Eventually, I stopped insisting that she continue seeing that therapist. Things got better on their own, and since then Ella has detested psychologists."

Vanessa nodded. "Just like in any profession, not all therapists are good."

"She came highly recommended."

"Nevertheless, she didn't know how to deal with Ella. There is no one treatment that fits all. People are complex, and each individual is unique. And yet, some therapists just follow the dogma instead of tailoring the treatment for the specific person. I can assure you that I'm not one of them."

Vivian glanced at Magnus. "I'm not sure I'll be able to convince her even to come see you."

"So don't. Tell her that she can be of help to other girls who've gone through a similar experience. She can come as your arts and crafts assistant."

Vivian looked uncomfortable. "I can't lie to her, and I don't want to."

"It's not a lie. She can come, look around, talk with some of the girls, and see if she can find solace here. That is it. And in the meantime, I'll try to get her to warm to me. If it works, great. If not, we will think of a different approach."

"Sounds reasonable enough." Vivian glanced at Magnus again. "What do you think?"

He smoothed his hand over his goatee. "I'm not an expert, so my opinion is not all that relevant. But in my personal experience, time is the best healer, especially when you're surrounded by a loving family." He cast Vanessa an apologetic look. "No offense to your profession. As I've told Vivian, I think you're doing an amazing job here. These girls don't have a support system back home, so your help and that of the volunteers is invaluable to them. But Ella has us, and also the rest of the clan to catch her if she falls."

Vanessa smiled indulgently. "The difference is that your particular trauma was shared with other Guardians. You had friends to talk to who'd gone through the same experiences. Ella, on the other hand, is going to feel isolated. I'm not belittling the healing power of her family's love, but it's not going to be enough. Not after what she's gone through."

Vivian's hand trembled as she pushed her hair back. "Ella is strong. She found a way to cope with her situation. She decided to think of it as an arranged marriage. She didn't resist."

With a heavy sigh, Vanessa leaned back in her chair. "The sad thing is that the comparison is appropriate. Those so-called arranged marriages, when a girl is coerced into marrying someone her family has chosen for her, or someone who paid the highest price, is just a sanctioned rape. Granted, in most cases it's not a violent rape, like when a woman is attacked by a stranger, beaten and then violated, but it is just as much a violation as any other sexual coercion. And in some cases it is just as bad. The fact that it's the girl's family doing it, putting pressure on her to agree or just sending her off like a sacrificial lamb, and then some cleric presides over the sacrificial ceremony, doesn't mitigate or justify the emotional and physical trauma to the girl. It blows my mind how in this day and age, entire societies still don't see it that way and continue to condone the practice."

45

ELLA

"Nice, eh?" Misha asked as he passed by Ella, holding a suitcase in each massive hand.

"Yeah, you could say so. Very impressive."

The experience of staying at the Burj Al Arab Jumeirah three-bedroom suite was not one Ella would soon forget. What made it special wasn't even the opulence or the price tag she couldn't begin to imagine. It was sharing a suite with Dimitri and five of his bodyguards. The other five were staying somewhere else.

If anything ever made it hit home that she was globetrotting with a mafia boss, that had been it. Dimitri was either super paranoid or had very dangerous enemies who wanted him dead. The ten bodyguards weren't for show.

Standing in the suite's foyer, Ella snapped several pictures with her reading tablet. Hopefully, she would be able to take it with her when the rescuers came for her.

The idea to use it as a camera had struck her the day before in the Dubai Mall. After they had arrived, Dimitri had left for his meetings with whomever, and Misha had taken her shopping in the biggest and fanciest mall in the world. With Dimitri's American Express black card in her purse, Ella could've bought whatever she wanted, but she'd been more interested in visiting the huge indoor aquarium and aquatic zoo.

Impressive didn't begin to describe it. She must've snapped a hundred pictures.

As Misha came back for more stuff, he started up the stairs but then stopped midway and turned around. "You take picture of me?" He grinned and struck a pose.

"Sure." She lifted her tablet and snapped one more for her growing collection.

Today, they'd gone sightseeing. Which meant a procession of two limousines. She, Dimitri, and four bodyguards in one, and six additional bodyguards in the second. Ella hadn't asked, but she was sure the limos were bulletproof.

Since it was hotter than hell outside, they hadn't left the vehicles much and had done most of the touring by looking out the windows.

Security had probably factored in it as well.

There were only two places where they'd had no choice but to leave the air-conditioned interior--the old Bastakia quarter and later the Jumeirah Mosque.

After that, it had been back to the hotel, a long shower to wash the sweat off, and dinner.

Holding his briefcase in one hand and his phone in the other, Dimitri came down the stairs, his army of bodyguards following behind him.

"Did you enjoy the day?" He stopped next to her.

"I did. Thank you." It was on the tip of her tongue to add that she would probably never get to see Dubai again, but Ella stifled it at the last moment.

As they walked out and headed for the elevator, two bodyguards went ahead and checked the interior before she and Dimitri stepped in. The rest of the bodyguards followed.

Dimitri turned to look at her. "I wish we didn't have to rush things and could stay another day, but I have a morning meeting scheduled in New York."

She waved a dismissive hand. "I saw all the main attractions. I doubt there would've been enough left over to fill another day."

He leaned and kissed her cheek. "I could've taken you to the mall and insisted that you spend my money. I'm very disappointed that you haven't bought anything."

"Pfft." She waved a hand. "Shopping is boring. Visiting the underwater zoo and aquarium was fun. Besides, Pavel can do a much better job than me picking out my outfits."

Wrapping his arm around her waist, Dimitri pulled her closer to him. "I thought you'd enjoy the freedom to buy things you like."

Well, that was nice of him. But as long as her freedom was restricted to purchases, it wasn't freedom at all.

"I can order things from catalogs."

"True." He walked her out of the elevator. Behind them, his cadre of bodyguards followed.

"Are we going straight to the airport?" Ella asked as they stepped out of the lobby.

"Yes. But we are only flying out at two in the morning."

"Why so late? And why are we leaving the hotel at ten if we are flying out in four hours?"

"I have my reasons. You can go to sleep on the plane. I have some work I need to do first." He kissed the top of her head. "It was a pleasure spending the entire day with you, but duty calls."

She didn't have to fake the smile she flashed him. "I understand."

If he was busy working, he wasn't going to bother her for sex. And when he came to bed, she was going to be asleep.

"I'm still a little confused with all the time zone differences," she said. "What time are we arriving at New York?"

"If we are leaving Dubai at two in the morning, we will arrive at seven in the morning at New York."

"How does that work?"

He cast her an indulgent smile. "The flight is about fourteen hours long, so when we land it's going to be four in the afternoon in Dubai. But because of the time difference, it's going to be seven in the morning in New York."

"Oh, now I get it."

"I knew you would. You're a smart girl. I try to fly overnight as much as I can, so I don't waste time. I sleep on the plane and then conduct business all day."

"Does it mean that you have meetings scheduled for the entire day in New York?" She crossed her mental fingers, hoping that he did.

The rescue operation and faking her death would be much easier with him gone. Now that she knew he slept with a gun within reach, Ella feared he would use it on her rescuers. Dimitri might be too smart to be fooled by the pretend fire. He would keep her with him and probably rush her to some safe panic room he had on the premises. Not that she knew he had one for a fact, but it made sense that someone as careful as he was would have one.

"I'm afraid so. You'll have to eat dinner without me."

Ella pulled her tablet out of her bag. "I have plenty of books to keep me busy, and I need to start on that Rosetta Stone." She smirked. "Sleeping with the tablet under the pillow didn't do the job. I still can't speak Russian."

"I can hire you a tutor." He helped her into the limousine.

"First, let me try to do it on my own. If I see that it's too hard, I'll consider a tutor." She glanced at the four bodyguards sharing the ride with them. "Misha can teach me."

The panicked expression on her bodyguard's face was comical. "I'm no good teacher."

Dimitri patted her knee. "Lesson one in doing business. Always hire professionals to do what they're trained for. The job will be done faster and better."

"I'll take your word for it."

He certainly knew a lot about doing business, but she wasn't interested in an apprenticeship.

During the drive to the airport, Ella's thoughts drifted to what she'd observed about Dimitri while she'd been with him. It seemed to her that he was mainly engaged in wheeling and dealing. She hadn't seen or heard anyone getting beat up, and the only suspicious character she'd met had been Logan. But even with him it had been all about business. Maybe not a legit one, but still.

"I want to ask you something," she said.

He arched a brow. "Yes?"

"It seems to me that most of what you do is conduct business. Why are you even mafia? Can't you make all of your businesses legitimate?"

"Most of what I do is legit, or semi-legit. Even the arms dealing. Governments contact me all the time with acquisition requests for operations they need to keep quiet. But for historical reasons, I need to provide protection to my people, the same way my father did, and that's considered mafia business."

Ella was still stuck on the first thing he'd said. "You provide weapons to governments?"

"My biggest and best-paying clients."

"Even democracies? Or just Third World countries?"

He chuckled. "All of them. Those in power—and it doesn't matter if they were elected in a democratic process, or inherited their title, or have taken it by force—do all kinds of things they don't want the public to know about. You're naive if you think that politicians care about the people they are supposed to represent. They are the biggest mafia there is. Power and money. That's their motivation. Not ideology. That's the crap they feed their citizens. It's a smokescreen. In a way, I'm better. At least I care for the people in my territory and protect them. I'm also honest about what I do."

Ella shook her head. What Dimitri was saying rang true. But she wasn't sure whether it was because he believed it or because that was indeed the reality.

"Why don't you run for president then? You say that you care about the people, and you say that you're better than the politicians. So why not? You are sure smart enough and charismatic enough for people to vote for you."

Dimitri laughed. "Running for office in Russia? I don't have a death wish. But thank you. That's the best compliment I've ever gotten."

46

VIVIAN

As Magnus pulled out of the sanctuary's parking lot, Vivian looked at her reflection in the car's window and adjusted the wig. It had been a difficult visit, mainly because of what Vanessa had said about Ella.

The road to recovery was going to be long, and she knew that her daughter was going to fight it every step of the way. Ella would act as if nothing had happened, and she was fine. She hated to appear weak, and she hated it even more when people pitied her. That was why she didn't tell anyone her father had been killed unless she had no other choice. Ella was more comfortable letting people assume that her parents were divorced.

She would never fit in with the girls in the sanctuary.

While Magnus had stayed in the office, Vanessa had taken Vivian on a tour. It had been a heart-wrenching experience even though the therapist had acted all cheerful and the girls seemed well taken care of.

The haunted look in their eyes told a different story.

The visit had convinced Vivian that she wanted to help in

any capacity, even if it was teaching girls how to create new clothes from old ones. As Vanessa had explained, creating in any shape or form helped the healing process, and most anyone could learn how to sew.

"So what did you think?" Magnus asked.

"I can do that." Vivian turned to him. "I want to do that. But the sanctuary is so far away. It's an hour and a half in each direction."

"You don't have to come every day. It can be a once a week class."

She leaned back and crossed her arms over her chest. "I'll do it. But I need something to do the rest of the week."

"Don't forget that you have to homeschool Parker until we enroll him in a regular school, and then you'll need to be there for Ella. You are underestimating how busy that will keep you."

"Yeah, you're right."

Except, knowing Ella, she would want to start working right away and push back against any attempts Vivian made to coax her into talking about what she'd been through.

Maybe creating a homey atmosphere would help. What Vanessa had said about making things being beneficial could apply to cooking. They could cook together, or even join a cooking class.

As long as Ella didn't think it was about her and her issues, she wouldn't resist.

"I can also use the time to learn how to cook better. That will make Parker happy."

"Your cooking is fine."

"And you're sweet, but you're a liar."

She knew how to make a few simple dishes, but even those sometimes didn't come out tasting good.

"Speaking of food. Can I take you out to lunch?" Magnus asked, cleverly avoiding responding to her accusation.

"Are you asking me out on a date?"

"I am."

"Then by all means. Where do you want to eat?"

"There is this place in Malibu on the beach. The food is okay, not great, but it's on our way, and the view alone is worth the inflated prices they charge."

"I'm not crazy about dining in overpriced places. But it's on the way, and I don't want to delay too long before getting back. I feel bad about imposing on Merlin. I'm sure he has better things to do than babysit my son."

"I think he enjoys Parker's company."

"Nevertheless, he didn't come all the way from Scotland to sit around in his house all day."

Magnus smoothed his hand over his goatee. "He is here to do fertility research. The idea is to find a way to improve conception rates for immortals."

Vivian got excited. "That would be awesome." She reached for his hand. "We could have a child together."

He squeezed her hand lightly. "Fates willing."

Yeah, it was way too early to start thinking about children.

First, they needed to get Ella back and help her heal. Then Vivian had to transition. The wedding could happen either before or after that. Hopefully, she would come out alive on the other side.

At the restaurant, Vivian barely touched her food, sipping on a margarita instead. Thoughts of the future that should've been uplifting were stressing her out.

Magnus eyed her plate. "You didn't eat anything."

"We can ask for a container and take it to Parker."

"Right. As if he's going to eat your salad."

"I'll add a steak to it."

"That's a good idea. Except, he is going to eat the steak and leave the salad."

"I'll take the chance."

When they pulled out of the restaurant's parking lot, Magnus asked, "What did you think about Vanessa as a therapist for Ella?"

"I like her. But I don't think the sanctuary is the right place for Ella."

"Why not?"

"It's depressing. You should've seen those girls' eyes." Vivian uncrossed her arms and hugged herself. "Ella will take one look at them and march straight out."

He nodded. "She'll need some kind of help."

"Let's cross that bridge when we get there. I don't want to make plans yet. For a professional treatment to work, she needs to approve it first."

As if summoned by the talk about her, Ella opened a channel.

Mom.

I'm here, sweetie.

I have information for the rescue team. We are on the plane, but it leaves in only two hours. Dimitri says we are going to land in New York at about seven in the morning tomorrow. He's not coming with me to the estate because he has meetings in the city all day long. The rescue should happen while he's away.

Vivian's heart skipped a beat. It was finally happening.

Can you keep the channel open? I need to talk with the team leader and get instructions from him.

I can. I'm alone in the jet's bedroom, and Dimitri is upstairs working. Until he comes to bed, I'll stay awake and keep the channel open. After that, it will be too dangerous. I might fall asleep and blurt an answer to you out loud.

I hope I will have the information for you before that, but let me know when you're about to close the channel.

I will. Talk to you later.

"Was it Ella?" Magnus asked.

"Yes. They are landing in New York tomorrow at seven in the morning, and Gorchenco is sending Ella alone to the estate. He's not going to be there the entire day. Ella says we need to strike before he comes home."

"I'm calling Kian."

As Vivian listened to Magnus relay the news to his boss, her heart felt like it was beating a thousand beats per minute.

Tomorrow Ella was going to be free.

She'd known that the operation was planned for Friday, but up until now things had never worked out the way they'd been planned, and she'd expected it to happen again.

Gorchenco could've made a detour, or he could've decided to skip New York altogether. But now it was confirmed. Ella was on her way to New York.

Well, not yet, the jet was still on the ground, so it wasn't a hundred percent sure thing. Gorchenco could always change his mind.

In some irrational part of her brain, Vivian even hoped that he would. As long as Ella was with Gorchenco, she was at least safe. The rescue operation was dangerous no matter what assurances Turner and Magnus were giving her. Anything could happen, and Ella could be caught in the line of fire, or even in the actual fire they were going to stage.

Magnus clicked the phone off. "As soon as we get back, we are going straight to Kian's office."

"I'm scared."

He clasped her trembling hand. "I know, love. But everything is going to be okay. Did you forget that we have a secret weapon?"

Right. The Guardian Yamanu who could blanket thrall the entire compound. But what if that was not enough?

Vivian shook her head. "I need to stop with all the what ifs. They are just stressing me out. So many things could go wrong."

47

KIAN

On the big screen behind Kian's desk, Turner rubbed his brows between his thumb and forefinger. "Knowing the exact timing of Ella's arrival opens new opportunities."

"Like what?"

"Instead of waiting until she gets to the estate, we can stage an accident for the car she is driven there in. Most likely it's going to be a limousine. Since Gorchenco is not going to be in there with her, I don't think he will employ as many evasive maneuvers as he usually does, with decoy limos and such like. But in any case, Ella will have to note the license plate number and give it to Vivian. The operation can be as simple as a roadblock. We can stop the vehicle, drag everyone out, and then thrall the driver and bodyguards to think that there was a fatal accident."

Kian tapped his fingers on the desk. "Could work if the driver and bodyguards are not immune to thralling. I understand that Gorchenco employs only fellow Russians."

Turner chuckled. "We can always knock them out the old-fashioned way."

"While staging Ella's death? Are you going to pretend to be assassins sent by a competitor?"

"That's a possibility. I'm just thinking out loud here. But I like having an alternative to our original plan. Staging a fire on the estate that produces enough smoke to supposedly kill Ella is tricky. Since we know not everyone can be thralled, we need to start a real fire. I pulled the house's plans from the city. Unfortunately, all the electrical wiring has been updated, so a short is not a likely cause of fire. We are still going to use it, but it's not as airtight as I would've liked it to be. Gorchenco is going to be suspicious."

"Hold on," Kian said. "I think I hear Magnus and Vivian." He walked to the door and opened it. "Come in. I have Turner on a teleconference call."

"Hello, Turner," Vivian said.

Magnus nodded in greeting.

"As I was telling Kian," Turner continued. "Ella providing us with the exact timing of her arrival opens new opportunities. I was thinking of staging a car accident. Nothing major, a roadblock or a blown tire. All we need is for them to stop. The only problem with this scenario is if the driver or the bodyguards are immune to thralling."

Vivian crossed her legs. "Don't forget that Ella asked that we don't kill her bodyguard."

Turner's usually expressionless face twisted in a grimace. "She's sure making a lot of requests. It would all have been much easier if we just came in and killed Gorchenco, making it look like she did it. Staging her death is the weakest and most complicated part of our plan."

Vivian closed her eyes for a moment, let out a breath, and

then opened them. "If you have no other choice, ignore her requests. The important thing is to get her away from Gorchenco, and for her ordeal to finally end. If she feels bad later on because of his death, we will deal with it."

Vivian was such a smart, down to earth woman. Kian approved.

Magnus, who up until now hadn't said anything, lifted his hand. "I have an idea."

On the screen, Turner leaned back in his chair and crossed his arms over his chest. "I'm open to suggestions."

"I like the idea of staging something for the limo. It's much less complicated than staging the fire, and in my experience, the more complex the operation, the more things can go wrong."

"That's true," Kian said. "But then things need to be just as complicated as they need to be. We might not have another choice."

Magnus smoothed his hand over his goatee. "What if the accident doesn't happen to the limo, but to a big rig truck that blocks the limo's way?"

"Or a gas tanker," Turner said. "That explodes when the limo stops in front of it."

Vivian gasped. "Are you insane?"

Turner lifted a hand. "Not while Ella is still in the vehicle."

Kian was trying to follow the thought thread and came up with nothing. "How are you going to take her out before the explosion? And what if the limo doesn't stop but reverses direction?"

Turner assumed that remote expression on his face, which Kian had learned to associate with the master strategist's mental gears spinning in super speed. "The accident is going to be between the gas tanker and a truck. The two vehicles are going to block the road, and the limo will have to stop."

"And what then?" Vivian asked.

"The drivers of the vehicles are going to argue and shout at each other, while pretend fire trucks and police cars will arrive and block the road behind the limo and on the other side of the accident. Because of the danger from the gas tanker, the firemen and the policemen will start to evacuate everyone to a safe distance. The first controlled explosion will happen before they are all the way out of the danger zone. It's not going to be big, just enough to send everyone to the ground. Once on the ground, we are going to knock the driver and bodyguards out, and then drag everyone a safe distance away. In the next explosion, the big one, Ella and two police officers will supposedly die."

Kian was impressed, but there were still big holes in the plan. "Isn't it better to kill the bodyguards and driver too? I mean for real? What if they remember getting knocked out by something other than the explosion?"

Turner shook his head. "We will also have ambulances at the ready. While driving to a hospital, we will attempt to thrall them. If we are lucky and they are susceptible, that's the end of the story. If not, we inject them with drugs that will do the job. And maybe none will be needed because they'll be sure that they got hit by debris flying off the truck or the tanker."

Vivian still looked doubtful. "How are you going to ensure that Ella doesn't get hurt?"

"It's not difficult to stage controlled explosions."

Kian had a different concern. "Do you have enough time to set this up? It sounds complicated."

"Not as complicated as staging a fire in a heavily guarded estate. I can make it happen."

"What about traffic? There will be a blockage, and the real police are going to arrive on the scene."

"The road leading to the estate has sparse traffic, and we can block and redirect calls to the police. Naturally, everything will have to be perfectly timed. We will agree on signs along the way for Ella to tell us exactly when the limo is passing them. That way we can calculate the time of the limo's arrival within a couple of minutes."

Wracking his brain for other possible holes in the plan, Kian started writing points on his yellow pad. "The uniforms should come from laundry services that wash police and firefighters' uniforms. We don't want anything that will look too new or not authentic. And pay attention to the shoes. Those can give you away as fake too."

Victor chuckled. "I'm not an amateur, Kian, and this is not my first rodeo. I know what I'm doing."

"Where are you going to get the police cars from?"

"Borrow them from unsuspecting officers. Thralling will come in handy."

Vivian lifted a finger. "What about the supposedly dead policemen? The police will know they didn't lose anyone. Heck, they will know that they weren't even there."

"That's where my connections will come into play," Turner said. "I'm owed several favors, and this is for a good cause my friends in high places will approve of. The police are not going to dispute the news story."

48

ELLA

Mom to Ella. Are you receiving?

Ella chuckled. *Yes, Mom, I'm receiving.*

I assume that you're still alone.

I am reading in bed. Dimitri got me a tablet with thousands of books, and if he comes in, I'll keep looking at the screen and pretending that I'm reading. I'm even flipping pages in case he's watching me through the tablet's camera. What's up? Did you talk with the team leader?

Magnus and I did. There is a whole new plan.

As long as they fake my death without killing anyone and none of them getting killed, I'm okay with anything.

Then you're going to be very happy with this one. All the deaths are going to be fake.

Ella pushed up on the pillows. *I'm all ears, or rather mental synapses.*

When her mother was done explaining the new plan, Ella rubbed her temples. *It all sounds so complicated. So many things can go wrong.*

According to Turner, this is easier to pull off than a fake fire in a heavily guarded estate that would result in your supposed death. He said that the plan wasn't tight enough for his liking.

Yeah, I thought it might be a problem to light a fire before getting inside the estate. I imagined fireworks or some other projectiles, but then the security people would've known that something is up.

I think Turner mentioned something about creating an electrical short, but I doubt it could've produced a fire big enough to cause anyone's death. That plan was good for getting the fake firefighters in, killing Gorchenco, and then making it look as if you used the confusion to do it and then escaped. But you were so adamant about wanting to keep him alive.

Her mother's mental voice was accusatory, but Ella couldn't fault her for that. From Vivian's perspective, keeping Gorchenco alive was stupid and created an unnecessary hurdle for Ella's rescuers to overcome.

In her mom's version of the story, he was the ultimate boogeyman, and his death would've solved all of their problems.

What her mother didn't know was that in the world of boogeymen, Dimitri was far from the worst. A lot of people depended on him, and if he was gone, someone else would step into his shoes, and that someone wouldn't be as good to Dimitri's people.

The villagers in his territory led a simple and peaceful life. They wanted for nothing because he didn't collect taxes from them. From what she understood, he either paid the government for them or had some other arrangement. In Russia, a lot happened under the table.

Ella chuckled. According to Dimitri, not only there. He claimed that politicians everywhere were corrupt and self-serving.

She believed him.

Her time with him had opened her eyes, and for that she was thankful. But that wasn't the reason she'd decided to spare him. That gut feeling that he had a job to do persisted. Without him around, something bad was going to happen. Maybe it wasn't something big, and all he was going to do was to keep his people protected, but that alone was reason enough to keep him alive.

It also might have been all in her head, but Ella was not going to ignore her intuition ever again. If she'd listened to it when it tried to tell her that there was something off about Romeo, she wouldn't need to be rescued now.

I know that you think I'm just making things difficult for everyone. But I need to trust my judgment. We are not ordinary people, Mom. When we have a feeling about something, you and I should listen. Like that curse of yours. I didn't believe in it, and look what happened to me. So now I know it was real.

I hope the ritual got rid of it.

Yeah, me too. I want you to have a long and happy life with Magnus. How is the new place? We haven't talked since you told me you were about to move.

Ella hadn't talked with her mom since Dimitri had dropped the wedding bomb on her, mainly because she'd been so angry that she'd been afraid to say something she would've regretted later, like telling her mom it was okay to kill him.

It's beautiful here, and we have a gorgeous house. Your new room is waiting for you, and you'll be glad to know that it has its own bathroom. No more sharing with Parker.

What do you mean by we have? Isn't it another safe house?

No, sweetie. This is where we are going to live. We can't go back to our old lives. Not with Gorchenco alive.

I'm sorry, Mom. It's all my fault.

Because of her and her stupidity, her family had to be

uprooted. And it wasn't even about her wish to spare Dimitri's life. Even if he were dead, she and her family would have to hide from the other Russian mafia bosses.

It had all started with one bad decision. She'd let Romeo lead her on.

Don't talk like that, sweetie. It's not your fault. It's just a pile of bad luck. Except, not all of it is bad. Since you've suffered so much, I hate to think about it like this, but in a way, it was a blessing. I met Magnus, and he's the real deal. He proposed, and I accepted.

Ella barely managed to stifle a happy squeal. *Oh, Mom, I'm so happy for you. Congratulations.*

Thank you. We've moved in together. This house is ours to share. I hope you're okay with that.

Of course I am. I can't wait to meet him. How is Parker taking it?

He's happy. He and Magnus get along splendidly, and he loves it here.

I think that proves that the curse is officially gone.

Vivian sighed. *I hope so, sweetie. We've had enough bad luck to last us a couple of lifetimes.*

The talk about bad luck made her think about her dark energy hypothesis, and she would've loved to discuss it with her mother, but that would have spoiled the happy mood. Besides, she would have to explain about Logan, and Ella didn't want to get into it. That disturbing episode was better forgotten.

For now, they both needed to focus on the rescue mission. *I hope that from now on everything will go our way. What are my instructions? You said something about road signs I'll need to report.*

When they tell me what those signs are, I'm going to relay the information to you. Right now, I just know that they are going to put some up and use the markers to estimate your time of arrival. The timing of creating the fake accident is crucial.

I bet. Anything else that I should know before I go to sleep?

Ella didn't want Dimitri to come in and catch her awake because he might want to have sex with her. Hopefully, she wasn't pregnant yet, and with her bad luck, it could happen tonight.

Just remember to note the license plate number on the limousine and let me know.

I will.

Good night, Ella. Soon we will be together again.

I hope so. Bye, Mom.

Pulling the blanket all the way to her chin, Ella stared at the ceiling. Could it be true?

Was tomorrow the day she was going to be finally free?

With her luck, something would come up.

First of all, she found it suspicious that Dimitri was sharing with her his exact timeline. She'd played her part well, convincing him that she was happy to be his wife, but he wasn't a trusting or sharing sort of guy. What had prompted him to suddenly start confiding in her?

Possibly because she still didn't have a way to communicate with anyone. Dimitri had even removed the phones from their hotel suite, claiming that they might've been bugged. Except, his bodyguards had checked every square inch of the suite, and they had surely taken the phones apart and checked them too. And yet, the phones hadn't returned.

Closing her eyes, she tried to imagine what her life would be like after this was over, but she couldn't. There was one crucial thing Ella had to get before she could make plans for the future.

A pregnancy test.

49

JULIAN

"I'm very disappointed," Yamanu said. "You drag me all the way out to New York, and then you tell me that my services are no longer needed."

Turner slapped the Guardian's back. "Your work here was invaluable. You helped a lot with the victims, calming them down, and you participated in a rescue mission. Don't tell me that you didn't enjoy it."

Smirking, Yamanu flipped his long hair back. "Yeah, it was fun pretending to be a rapper, but braiding my hair was a pain in the ass."

Julian chuckled. "My pain in the ass, since I was the one who did the braiding."

"Thank you, doctor." Yamanu flashed him a grin. "You did a wonderful job. I only lost one-tenth of my hair. If Arwel did it, it would've been more."

Arwel flipped him the finger.

"Besides, thanks to you we confirmed that Russians are naturally resistant to thralling," Julian said. "That was the main reason behind the change of plans. Right, Turner?"

In Julian's opinion, the new plan was riskier than the original one, but he agreed with Turner that it was tighter. If everything went well, the scenario they were going to stage was going to be nearly impossible to disprove.

Turner rubbed his hand over his jaw. "I've suspected Russians were naturally resistant to thralling for a long time, and that's why I didn't rely too heavily on Yamanu's thralling ability. But the thing that made the original plan so difficult to pull off was Ella's insistence on leaving Gorchenco alive and faking her own death. Causing a fire large enough to supposedly have her die from smoke inhalation, and at the same time not putting her in real danger, was too tricky for comfort."

Julian raked his fingers through his hair. "I was hoping she would change her mind, or that you would. But since Gorchenco is not even going to be there, that's out. I'm worried about him coming after Vivian and Parker."

"Why would he do that?" Turner asked.

The tactical mastermind had one flaw. Turner didn't account for people's emotions and expected them to behave rationally. In this case, Julian knew better. Gorchenco was going to be overcome with grief, and he would not just accept that Ella was dead without seeing her dead body with his own eyes.

"Gorchenco is a suspicious son of a bitch. Even without a body to bury, he will expect a memorial service for Ella, and he will attend it. I doubt Vivian and Parker will be able to pull off a convincing act of grieving for her, and he will know that something is up."

Turner arched a brow. "So what do you suggest? That we fake their deaths as well?"

"Why not? They are safe in the village, and we are going to

get them fake documents anyway. For all intents and purposes, to the outside world, they are as good as dead."

"Don't you think Gorchenco will get suspicious if they die the same day Ella does, and in unrelated circumstances?" Arwel asked.

Julian got to his feet and started pacing the length of the executive lounge. "It doesn't have to be the same day. No one has heard from them or seen them since Magnus picked them up at the mall. Theoretically, they could've crashed into a lake or a ditch somewhere days ago, and their bodies were just discovered. We could plant a news story about a car found with two bodies in it."

For several moments, no one said a thing, letting Turner mull over the idea.

"I need to call Vivian," Turner said. "This is not something I can decide for her."

"But do you think it's a good idea?"

Turner trained his pale blue eyes on him. "It's not absolutely necessary, but since we are going to all this trouble already, I agree that we shouldn't leave any loose ends."

As Turner pulled out his phone, Julian stayed close so he could be part of the conversation and help convince Vivian if needed.

"Hello, Turner," she answered after several rings. "Do you have more instructions for me to communicate to Ella? Because if you do, it will have to wait until she contacts me again. She's sleeping now."

"It's not about Ella. It's about you and Parker. It was actually Julian's idea. He's right here with me. I'm going to put you on speakerphone."

"Hi, Julian."

"Hi. How is Parker doing?"

Vivian had called him with the good news, but they hadn't talked since.

"He's doing well. The real rough part hasn't started yet."

Turner cleared his throat, indicating that this was not the time for polite chitchat.

"Tell Parker I'm proud of him. I'm going to let Turner continue now."

"Okay."

"We need to fake your and Parker's death as well, but retroactively. Something about your bodies found in a car wreck which was just discovered. We can plant a story about it in one of the local newspapers."

"Why?"

"Because if Ella supposedly dies in the explosion, and you two are well and alive, there will be a memorial service even if there are no remains. Gorchenco will attend for sentimental reasons and to make sure that she's really dead. He's not the type to just accept things without digging as deep as he can. But if you two are gone as well, then there will be no service. Unless you think some other family member will come forward and arrange for it."

"There is no one other than Josh's sister, and I seriously doubt she would come forward. My parents, as you probably already know, are in an assisted care facility. They both suffer from advanced Alzheimer's. And that's a problem. How am I going to visit them if I'm supposed to be dead?"

"We will find a solution."

"It's important to me, Turner. My parents don't have much longer, and I don't want to miss out on their last years even though they barely remember who I am."

"I didn't say that we will find a solution just so you'll agree to the plan. We will move them to a different facility, a private one that is closer to the village, and change their names. You will be able to visit them. I promise."

"I'll hold you to it."

"By all means."

"By the way, when you fake our deaths, you need to be aware of the message I left with the dental office. I told them that I'm traveling with a friend in her motorhome because Parker has chickenpox. I left that message when we escaped from the cabin on Monday."

"Did you mention the friend's name?"

"No. I just said a friend. A female friend."

Turner pushed his fingers through his hair. "We will need to arrange for three bodies and a motorhome. The report will state that the accident happened the day after you left the message. It will correspond with you falling off the grid."

"Sounds good to me."

When the phone call was done, Julian walked over to the windows, but he had no interest in the busy street below. Instead, he pulled out his phone and opened it. Ella's picture was now his wallpaper, so every time he used his phone, he could look at her beautiful face.

He wondered how she was doing. Was she scared? Was she excited about the rescue? Was she going to be okay?

50

VIVIAN

"Did you get any sleep at all?" Magnus padded into the kitchen, wearing nothing but loose pajama pants.

Normally, the sight of his sculpted chest would have stirred the embers of Vivian's desire, but not today.

It was three o'clock in the morning, and they were supposed to meet up with Kian and Onegus, the chief Guardian, in an hour. Not in Kian's office as she'd expected, but somewhere in the underground, in what Magnus called the war room, or mission control.

That's where they were going to stay until Ella was freed.

"Not really. I think I dozed off a couple of times, but that was it. I'm too stressed out."

He hugged her from behind, kissed her cheek, and then started massaging her shoulders. "Is that better?"

"Thank you, but it's not going to help. I won't be able to relax until this is over and Ella is home safe."

Undeterred, he massaged for a little longer.

"Let me get you some coffee." She pulled away.

Magnus sat on one of the barstools and braced his elbows on the counter. "I spoke with Callie, and she'll come over to stay with Parker. She wanted to be here as soon as we leave, but I told her that eight is good enough. He's fine by himself, and if he needs us, he can use the phone we gave him."

Vivian handed Magnus a full mug and sat on the barstool next to him holding hers. "He was disappointed about not being invited to the war room."

"I know. But I wasn't even going to ask Kian or Onegus to allow it. Civilians in general are not allowed in there, and especially not kids. For obvious reasons, you are the exception."

Vivian chuckled. "Maybe Ella and I should join the force as backup communication devices. Our telepathy works in all weather conditions, and it will withstand even electromagnetic pulses and nuclear disasters. Provided we survive, that is."

Magnus wrapped his arm around her shoulders. "I'll suggest it to Kian."

She put her head on his chest. "You will?"

"No way. I don't want either of you anywhere near danger ever again."

That was a bit hypocritical of him, but this wasn't the time to bring it up. "We should get dressed."

"Right."

"Should I make a thermos with coffee?"

"No need. I'm sure Okidu is going to be there serving coffee and food throughout."

"Kian brings his butler to the war room?"

"Why not?"

"He's a civilian."

Magnus chuckled. "I guess Okidu has a high-security clearance."

It was still dark outside as they walked toward the pavilion, and with no streetlights and the dense canopy of trees blocking the moon, Vivian could barely see where she was going. Except, with Magnus's arm around her waist, she could close her eyes and just let him lead the way.

In the pavilion, they took the elevators to one of the underground levels, which looked a lot like the ones in the keep.

It was hard to believe that they had moved into the village only two days ago. It already felt like home, while the keep seemed like something that had happened a long time ago.

Kian was waiting for them in the room that was almost an exact replica of his above ground office. With him was a blond with curly hair and a most charming smile.

"Hello, Vivian. I'm Onegus." He offered his hand.

She shook it. "Nice to meet you."

He pulled out an earpiece from his pocket. "This is for you. When the operation starts, you'll have a direct line to Turner."

"Thank you." She looked at the device, not sure how to put it on.

Magnus took it from her hand. "You pull this little hook away and wrap it around your ear." He put it on for her.

"How do I make it work?"

"I'll explain in a moment. But first, let's go over the markers the team have put in place." Onegus pointed to the oblong conference table in the center of the room. "Please, take a seat."

He waited for her and Magnus to be seated before continuing. "The first marker is obviously when they leave the airport." He clicked a remote, and a map appeared on the big screen mounted on the sidewall.

"The second marker is when they get off the highway. And the third is about five hundred feet after that. A guy will be changing a flat tire of a full-sized red van."

"Got it."

"Maybe you should write it down. It might be several hours until Ella contacts you again." Kian got up, pulled out a new yellow pad from a drawer, and brought it to her. "In a stressful situation, your memory might become fuzzy. It's better to have a list of the important things."

"Sure."

She wrote a headline and the three markers under it. "Done."

"By the way, your and Parker's deaths are in today's *San Diego Union-Tribune*. You should let Ella know in case she somehow stumbles upon it."

"That was fast. How did you manage it?"

Kian smirked. "We have excellent hackers that can plant and change official records, let alone stories in newspapers."

Vivian shook her head. "I couldn't sleep last night, so I spent a lot of time thinking about it. Without actual bodies, it's not going to withstand careful scrutiny. If Gorchenco really puts his mind to it, he will find out that it was faked. And even if you can get some mangled up cadavers from somewhere, Parker and I have dental records. It's not difficult to prove that it wasn't us."

Kian lifted his hand. "I hope he doesn't go so far. We are staging Ella's death very carefully. Our hackers had her retroactively registered as a body donor. We are going to make it look as if her body was misplaced and never arrived at the research university where it was supposed to. It should be enough."

Vivian was still uncomfortable with the whole thing. It would have been better to hold the fake memorial services for Ella. Even if her acting was not top notch, it would've been less suspicious than everyone in her family dying. Gorchenco was going to suspect something was up.

Except, it was too late. She should've voiced her reservations the day before.

On the other hand, she was just a civilian with no experience. Turner was the expert, and she should trust him to do his job.

"What will happen with my house? That's all I have."

Kian smirked. "You keep underestimating us. Our hackers had it recorded as held in trust as of two years ago. We are going to sell it for you."

"What about the sale proceeds? Money leaves traces."

"In the case of no surviving family members, the trust donates the house to a charity. Which, of course, is one of ours. You'll get your money. Don't worry about it."

"Wow, you've really thought of everything."

"Can't take credit for that. It was Bridget's idea."

Vivian nodded. "Awesome teamwork. Thank you."

Kian looked pleased. "We take care of our own, Vivian."

51

ELLA

Ella's tablet didn't have an internet connection, the function was disabled, but the clock application worked offline, which made it easy to find out what time it was anywhere in the world.

It was seven-thirty in the morning in New York, and judging by the pressure in her ears, they were about to land.

Dimitri had gone to sleep hours after her and still had woken up several hours before her, unintentionally waking her as he left the room.

After that, she couldn't go back to sleep. Dressed and ready to go, she waited impatiently to communicate with her mom.

Four-thirty was still too early, but Ella couldn't wait any longer. Her belly was full of butterflies, or rather hornets since it was aching something fierce. It hurt more than it had during her time in the auction house, which was saying a lot.

She was about to participate in a *Mission Impossible* style full-blown production, except the props were going to be real, and so were the explosions.

It was terrifying, and not only because she feared for her

life. Misha was going to be with her, and she had a feeling her rescuers wouldn't be as careful with him as they were going to be with her. No one other than her would care if the Russian bodyguard got accidentally blown up.

No one knew that under the rough exterior he was a nice guy. She was going to miss him.

Oh, well. Ella sighed and wiped the few stray tears away.

It was stress, nothing more. Misha was just doing his job, and he wasn't really her friend. She was going to leave everything about this life behind and start afresh.

Glancing at the ostentatious ring on her finger, Ella debated what to do with it. She couldn't leave it on the plane because Dimitri would suspect something, but she didn't want to take it with her either.

On second thought, though, she could donate it to the people rescuing her. Maybe they could sell it on the black market or something like that. Cutting it into smaller stones would devalue it, but selling it as it was might be too dangerous.

Dimitri was going to look for his enormous diamond.

Except, theoretically, the ring could get lost and then taken by anyone on the accident scene to be sold later.

It would be poetic justice.

Dimitri's ring would cover the expenses of her rescue, and there would probably be enough left over to finance many more.

Yeah, she was definitely keeping it.

When another ten minutes passed, and the pressure in her ears got worse, Ella opened the channel to her mother.

Mom, are you awake?

Yes, sweetie. I'm here with Magnus and his bosses. I have several instructions for you.

Shoot.

Remember what I told you about the time markers?

Yes. I'm to tell you when I see them.

The first one is when the car you're in leaves the airport. The second is when it gets off the highway.

Her mother stopped for a moment.

I just thought of something. The driver might choose an alternative route and get off somewhere else. You need to make sure that it's the exit near the estate.

Got it. I'll ask Misha, my bodyguard.

The third marker will be about five hundred feet after that. A red van with a flat tire on the side of the road, which the driver will be changing.

Got it. Exit the airport, exit to the estate, and a red van with a flat tire. Anything else?

Yes. If someone tells you that Parker and I are dead, don't panic. The organization planted a fake news article about finding our bodies burned to a crisp in a motorhome that flipped into a ditch.

What motorhome?

When we were running away from Gorchenco's goons, I left a message at the dental office that I'm not coming in because Parker has chickenpox and a friend invited us on a trip in her motorhome.

Ella chuckled quietly. *And the plot thickens.*

The tablet was in her hands the entire time she was talking with her mom, so the chuckle could be explained as something funny she'd read. She was pretty sure there was a surveillance camera hidden somewhere or a listening device. And the tablet itself was a concern too. Regrettably, she would have to leave it behind.

Right? her mother said. *After this is over, we can write a book about it.*

Yeah, but we can't have it published.

We could if Gorchenco was dead.

That's not reason enough to kill him.

But what he did to you is.

Perhaps. No, not really. Even if what he had done to her constituted rape, which she still wasn't sure it did, rape didn't carry the death penalty.

It's neither here nor there. He is not going to be with me when the rescue goes down.

Right. Keep the channel open.

I will after I'm in the limousine. Knowing Dimitri, he will want to have breakfast with me before we go our separate ways.

For good.

She was never going to see him again, except maybe in her nightmares. Still, for the next hour or so she needed to keep up the charade and pretend to like him.

There had been a short period of time when she hadn't hated Dimitri, and the truth was that she admired his sharp mind and his dedication to his father's legacy of protecting the people in his territory. But ever since he'd taken all of her choices away, she could barely tolerate his presence.

After the incredible performance that she'd managed to pull off, she should consider a career in acting. Except, as long as Dimitri lived, that door was forever closed to her. Besides, it wasn't something she enjoyed doing.

Several minutes later, Dimitri walked in. "Good. You're awake. You can join me for a quick coffee before I have to leave."

Ella smiled. "Did you have breakfast already?"

"I've been awake for hours. So yes, I've eaten. But if it pleases you, I can have a bite while you eat yours to keep you company."

So polite, so seemingly accommodating, but it was all a

sham. Dimitri Gorchenco didn't compromise on what was important to him no matter who he had to trample over in order to get it.

"I would love it." She threaded her arm through his.

Dimitri smiled, looking genuinely happy as he led her upstairs to the dining area. "I will try to conclude my dinner meeting early and have dessert with you at home."

"That would be lovely. Are you going to bring some from the city, or is the chef going to prepare something special for us?"

He pulled out a chair for her. "What would you like? Is there a dessert you favor?"

Yes, and its name was freedom.

"Zabaglione," she said instead.

Dimitri grinned. "It's my favorite too. I'll have the chef prepare it for us."

52

TURNER

As Turner looked at the fleet of six police cars lined up in the hotel's underground parking, he was once again awed by Roni's ability to hack into government data.

Instead of having to pilfer the cars, they'd collected them from the police service center for a supposed upgrade to their electronics.

The uniforms came from a laundry service, and the shoes had been bought, as had the guns, the holsters, and all other accessories needed to impersonate New York cops. The fire trucks and the firemen outfits had been ready for a while.

The gas tanker had turned out to be the hardest to get, and a team of experts had worked for ten hours straight to rig it with explosives. After that, they had been thralled to forget the job they'd done and sent home.

It had been a crazy intense sixteen hours, and Turner was buzzing with excitement. He hadn't had so much fun putting together a rescue mission in years.

"Okay, people. Line up for the last inspection."

"Again?" Arwel rolled his eyes.

"Yes." Turner pointed to the wall where the others were standing.

With a grimace, the Guardian hiked up his blue coveralls and joined the line. He'd been assigned the job of the tanker driver. Liam was going to drive the truck.

First, Turner scanned the twelve Guardians in police uniforms, inspecting them from head to toe. "You are good to go." He waved them toward the police cars.

Next were the paramedics and the firemen. Three fire trucks with three firemen each were going to show up on the scene, and they were going to actually put out the fire.

Naturally, Julian was going as one of the paramedics. Turner slapped his back. "Ready for your first mission?"

"I'm ready."

Turner leaned closer. "You don't rush out of the ambulance until you get the signal. Are we clear on that?"

"Yes, sir."

"Good." Turner slapped his back again.

"Let's go."

He was going as a paramedic as well, and riding in the ambulance with Julian, mainly to keep the kid from doing something stupid.

An hour and fifteen minutes later, everyone was in position.

He'd chosen the spot carefully. It was about a ten-minute drive from the exit and not visible from the highway. Also, there were no houses around. It was another half an hour drive to the first estate, and Dimitri's was the eighth. Which meant another ten minutes on the road.

From the exit to the accident spot, there were only two hidden cameras sending feed to Dimitri's estate. The team was parked after the first one, which Sylvia had disarmed before they'd passed it. The second camera was behind the bend in the road, which meant they were in its blind zone.

Happy he hadn't traveled to New York for nothing, Yamanu was shrouding all of their vehicles from the occasional car passing them by.

"Ella has exited the highway," Vivian said in his earpiece.

"Copy that."

Three of the police cars drove ahead to block the traffic coming from the opposite direction, with the tanker and the truck following behind them.

The fire trucks, ambulances, and remaining police cars stayed hidden and out of sight, waiting for the events to unfold.

Turner got out of the ambulance and activated the drone, flying it to where the accident was supposed to take place. It was going to be his eyes and ears on the scene.

The tanker and the truck got in position, blocking the narrow road. The dents and broken headlights from the supposed accident had been prepared ahead of time.

"Ella saw the red van," Vivian said in his earpiece.

"Copy that," he answered and got back in the ambulance.

On the drone's controller, he observed Arwel and Liam get out of the vehicles and face each other.

As Ella's limousine zipped by them, Julian stifled a gasp and turned the engine on.

"Wait. Count to sixty before activating the siren."

"Yes, sir."

When the minute was up, the fire trucks rolled out. The ambulances were next, and the three remaining police cars closed the procession.

William's voice came on the radio, reporting the fake accident in case the guys in the limo were listening to the police channel, which had been blocked off and replaced by William's fake one.

As the limo stopped, Arwel and Liam started arguing loudly.

"You fucking asshole! Where did you learn to drive?"

Behind them, smoke was starting to come out of the tanker's engine. It was fake, but it had the desired effect. The limo driver backed away and tried to turn the vehicle around, but he had to stop as the fire engines arrived blasting their horns and blocking his retreat.

Two of the firemen jumped down and rushed toward the arguing drivers. "Get away from the vehicles, the tanker is smoking!" one of them yelled.

The limo doors opened, and its two passengers spilled out. The burly bodyguard threw Ella over his shoulder, fireman style, and started sprinting with her away from the smoking tanker.

Crap. That wasn't part of the plan. They were supposed to stay in the limo and wait for the police to get them out.

53

ELLA

"Misha! What are you doing? Put me down!" Ella's head was bouncing up and down her bodyguard's back.

"It's going to blow!" Misha shouted. "I save you!"

Behind them, she could hear the firemen's boots pounding on the asphalt. As fast as Misha was running, they were closing in on him. He probably thought that they were also getting away from the tanker, but she knew that as soon as the fake firemen caught up to him, they would take him down.

Except, she was going down as well. Hanging over his shoulder like a sack of potatoes, bouncing up and down, there was little she could do to prevent the fall, or getting squashed between Misha and the fireman who was going to ram into him from behind.

Closing her eyes, Ella braced for the impact.

The sound of the explosion came first, and a split moment later they were lifted off the ground. A heavy weight crashed into them from behind, propelling them forward and down.

Everything was happening so fast, and yet she was experiencing it as if it was in slow motion.

Somehow, before landing on Misha's back, the fireman managed to grab her and toss her into the outstretched arms of his partner like she was a fifteen-pound football and not a hundred-and-thirty-pound human.

She couldn't see what happened next because the one holding her ran like the hounds of hell were on his tail, and she couldn't hear anything either because the explosion had deafened her.

Not entirely, though, because a moment later a second explosion blasted at them, propelling her and the fireman carrying her at least ten feet forward.

The man was incredibly strong, his hold on her not loosening even a little as they practically flew through the air. Landing on his feet, he kept running, clearing the two fire engines toward the open doors of an ambulance and the waiting arms of a paramedic.

The guy took her from the fireman and hugged her to his chest as if she was an injured child, but only for a moment. Still holding her in his arms, he leaped into the ambulance and placed her gently on a gurney.

She didn't know paramedics were so strong and athletic. But then he was probably not a real paramedic.

"Are you hurt?" He started examining her, so maybe he was.

"Except for my ears, I'm fine," she shouted. "What about Misha? Is he going to be okay?" Ella lifted up on the gurney and looked out the open back doors.

She saw another fireman rushing by them with Misha's lifeless body hanging over his shoulder. "Oh, my God! Is he dead?" She made a move to jump out.

A strong hand grabbed her arm. "He isn't dead. He's just

knocked out. My friends are going to take him and the limo's driver to the hospital."

"Are you sure?"

"Yes. I can hear his heartbeat."

She rolled her eyes. "Don't lie to me."

"I'm not. I'll explain later."

Now that the adrenaline was starting to abate, Ella sank back onto the gurney and looked at the paramedic.

He had the face of an angel, but before she had a chance to really take a good look at him, a short blond guy jumped into the ambulance, distracting her.

"Hello, Ella." He closed the doors behind him. "We are good to go!" he called out, then smiled at her and offered his hand. "I'm Turner."

Ella sat up and shook his hand. "Is Misha okay?"

"He is fine, as is the driver. They are being taken to the nearest hospital."

Unless they had rehearsed their answers ahead of time, Turner had confirmed what the paramedic had said.

"And I'm Julian." The paramedic with the face of an angel extended his hand.

Her eyes widened. "You are Julian? My mother's Julian?"

The guy blushed, and then cleared his throat. "I'm your mother's friend, if that's what you meant."

Turner chuckled. "You'd better tell Vivian that you're okay. She's blasting in my ear, demanding to talk to you."

He had an earpiece she hadn't noticed before.

Mom, I'm okay. Stop screaming in Turner's ear.

Thank God. Are you hurt?

Not at all. These people are like supermen. I might be still confused, but what they did seemed impossible. One moment I was flung over Misha's shoulder as he was running away with me, the next the first explosion blasted and one of the fake firemen smashed into Misha and me from the back. I was sure I was going to hit the ground like a sack of potatoes, but he grabbed me and tossed me to his friend who caught me and kept running. Unbelievable. Oh, and Julian is here. You were right. He looks like no doctor I've ever seen. Not even a TV doctor.

Her mother chuckled. *Now I know you're really okay. You're free, sweetie.*

I'm free.

"I'm free," she repeated out loud. "I'm actually free. It's over."

Turner smiled, and Julian offered her a water bottle.

"Drink this."

"Thank you."

She took several long gulps. "Can my mom hear me through your earpiece? I feel awkward about talking to her in my head with you guys looking at me."

"No, but I can call her and put her on speakerphone."

"Thank you."

She drank a little more while Turner pulled out his phone and made the call.

"Vivian, I'm putting you on speakerphone."

"Hi, Mom. So what's next? Are we riding in the ambulance all the way to California?"

"We have a private jet waiting for us," Turner said.

Ella grimaced. "I've had enough of those. I'd rather spend several days in a car than get on one."

"Don't be silly, Ella," her mother said. "I can't wait to see you."

"Fine. But this is the last time. After that, I don't want to ever get on a private jet again."

54

JULIAN

During the drive to the hotel, Turner had done most of the talking, answering Ella's many questions about the operation.

She had a quick mind like her mom, curious about how they'd managed to get everything done so quickly.

If he weren't so dumbstruck and feeling awkward, Julian could've provided the details just as well as Turner. Instead, he tried his best not to gawk, pretending to be distant.

Ella wasn't showing the slightest interest in him, while all he could think of was taking her into his arms and never letting her go.

Perhaps it was the overwhelming protectiveness he felt toward her. She was putting on a brave face, smiling at Turner and acting as if the past month hadn't been traumatic for her and she was perfectly fine.

The scents of her excitement and adrenaline rush were so strong that he couldn't sense anything else. But Julian could see the truth in her haunted eyes, and his gut twisted in knots with the need to help her and not knowing how.

At the hotel, they left the ambulance in the underground parking and went upstairs to the executive lounge.

"I'm going to change and get my things," Turner said. "You can wait in the lounge and help yourself to some refreshments."

"Thank you." She glanced at Julian. "Are you going to get changed too?"

"Obviously." The show was over, and he wanted out of the costume.

"Do you have something I can borrow? Like maybe a T-shirt?"

Looking at the elegant pantsuit she was wearing, he searched for tears or smudges, but somehow the outfit had remained intact despite the flying debris. He sniffed to check if it had absorbed any of the toxic fumes from the explosions. There was a faint residual scent, but Ella's perfume was doing a good job of masking it.

"Why do you want to change? Your clothes are clean."

She waited with her answer until the door closed behind Turner. "I don't want to take anything of his home with me. Not the clothes and not this." She took off a huge solitaire diamond and handed it to him. "Take it. This will cover the expenses of my rescue. It must've cost a fortune to arrange an operation like that. It was unbelievable."

Shaking his head, Julian lifted his hands in the air. "What you do with it is obviously your choice, but if you want to give it to someone, give it to Turner. He's the boss."

Hopefully, Turner would refuse the gift too. Even to his untrained eyes, it was obvious that the thing was worth millions.

She put the ring back on her finger. "Okay. What about the clothes?"

"I can help you with that. I have several clean shirts you can borrow."

"Great." She started walking toward the door.

"Where are you going?"

"To your room." She looked around. "I can't change in here."

"There is a bathroom over there." He pointed.

Ella smirked. "What's the matter, Julian? Is your room messy?"

He raked his fingers through his hair. "I'm afraid so."

Not true, but he couldn't tell her the real reason why her request to accompany him to his room had caught him by surprise. He'd expected her to be wary of men, but it seemed like she was doing everything to prove that the experience hadn't affected her.

Ella waved a dismissive hand. "I have a twelve-year-old brother. You haven't seen mess until you've been to his room."

"I've met Parker. He is an awesome kid."

For some reason, his comment caused the first crack in Ella's façade. A shine of tears glistening in her eyes, she nodded. "Yeah, he is. I can't wait to hold the little dweeb. I'm afraid I'll never let go."

Hell, it had been easier when she was putting up a brave face. Now he really didn't know what to do.

Planting a smile on his face, Julian pretended not to notice and opened the door to his room. "Here we are." He held it for her, letting her enter before him.

Ella recovered quickly. "You call this a mess?" She waved a hand at the rumpled bedding. "That's nothing."

"Oh, well. I usually make my bed, but this morning I just didn't have the patience for it." He lifted his duffle bag off the floor, put it on the bed, and opened it. "Everything in here is clean. Choose whatever you want."

"Thank you."

Ella took out a T-shirt and put it against her body. "This can work as a dress." She reached into the bag again and pulled out a hoodie. "Can I take this too?"

"Anything you want."

"In that case." She reached into the bag and pulled out a pair of boxer briefs. "Can I borrow these too?"

Julian arched a brow. "If it doesn't gross you out to wear my underwear, then by all means."

She brought them to her nose and sniffed. "They smell of laundry detergent. Nothing gross about that."

He thought that was it, but then she reached into the bag again and pulled out a pair of white socks. "Is that okay?"

He glanced at her elegant pumps. "I don't think socks go with those."

She waved a hand. "I told you that I don't want anything of his. That includes the shoes."

Walking like that through the airport's lobby was going to be weird, and there were no shops in the small private one they were using. Ella was going to arrive at the village looking like a hobo.

Still, it seemed extremely important to her not to bring anything of Gorchenco's with her.

Crap; he slapped a hand over his forehand. The girl was smarter than all of them put together. How come Turner hadn't thought of that? After what had happened with Vivian, it should have crossed someone's mind that Ella might be bugged.

"Are you afraid the Russian put trackers in your clothing?"

Her eyes widened. "No, I'm not. I just don't want any reminders of him. Can you check?"

As the image of him running his hands all over her popped

into his head, Julian swallowed. "Maybe you should take them off first. It will make it easier."

"Right." Ella collected the bundle of clothing she'd taken from him and ducked into the bathroom.

Pulling out his phone, Julian dialed Turner. "Can you come to my room?"

"Why?"

"We didn't check Ella's clothing for bugs, and I don't know what to look for. She's in the bathroom changing into some of mine. Can you come and check them?"

Turner chuckled. "What do you take me for, an amateur? Of course I checked her for bugs."

"When?"

"In the ambulance."

Julian was right there with him, and he hadn't seen Turner touch Ella, let alone pat her down for trackers. "How?"

"A little device that checks for transmissions. I didn't want to make her even more nervous, so I kept it in my pocket."

Letting out a breath, Julian sat on the bed. "You should've told me."

"If I told you every little detail that went into this mission, we would still be talking, and Ella would be having dinner at Gorchenco's estate."

55

VIVIAN

"Your phone is ringing," Magnus called out from the kitchen.

Vivian rushed out of the bathroom with her hands still dripping water. She wiped them on her pants before pulling the phone off the charger and glancing at the caller's ID.

"It's Julian." Vivian took the call. "What's up? Is Ella okay?"

"Everything is fine," he whispered. "We are on the plane, and I'm calling you from the bathroom so I can talk to you privately."

Vivian frowned. "Go on."

"We didn't discuss it before, but do you want me to tell Ella the whole story? Or do you want us to keep up the charade so you can fill her in when she gets to the village?"

She hadn't thought about it. The only thing occupying her mind was whether Ella was going to be okay. Other than that all Vivian wanted was to hold her daughter in her arms and never let go.

"I don't know what to tell you, Julian. Do you think she is

ready for more traumatic news? Maybe it's better to let her rest a little and tell her tomorrow. What's your impression?"

After all, he was a doctor. He should be able to assess Ella's emotional state.

"She is putting on a brave act, like she's perfectly fine, but I'm not buying it. She borrowed some of my clothes because she didn't want to keep anything Gorchenco had given her. Even the shoes. I had to take her down to the basement of the hotel so she could drop everything into the furnace. She just stood there and watched it burn."

"That doesn't sound good."

"Maybe it is. Perhaps it's her way of shedding the past. You should talk to Vanessa."

"I'll wait with that until Ella is here."

"Yeah, about that. She is wearing my T-shirt, my boxer briefs, and my socks with no shoes. Could you get her something decent to wear by the time we get there and meet us at the parking garage? I think it's important that she takes her first steps into the village with her head held high."

"You're absolutely right. Magnus and I got her some things already. We can bring them with us."

Their Wednesday stop at the mall had been mostly about buying a starter wardrobe for Ella, and a few knick-knacks for her room, so she would feel at home when she arrived.

"Good thinking. I'm glad you did."

"We are going to hitch a ride with Okidu and come get you from the airstrip. Ella can change there."

"I'm sure she will love to see you. Should I tell her, or is it a surprise?"

"That's a surprise. But about telling her the full story, I think you should at least tell her some of it. Unless she is too distraught for news of that magnitude. It's your call. I just don't want her to be lied to if it can be avoided."

"I'm going to start slow and lead her into it. If she seems reluctant, I'll stop and save the rest for later."

"I'm here if she needs me. She can contact me and ask anything she wants to know."

Magnus arched a brow and mouthed, "Anything?"

Vivian smiled and dismissed him with a wave of her hand. "At least I'll try to. I still don't know the whole story. But what I know should be enough."

"Good deal. Thank you for allowing me to do it."

"You're welcome. After all, you're the reason we have a happy ending to this story."

"It was fated," Julian murmured, sounding not at all convinced. "I'll talk to you later." He disconnected the call.

Didn't he like Ella? Was he disappointed?

Vivian shook her head. Impossible.

As Magnus had said, fate would've not orchestrated this elaborate scenario only for Julian and Ella to discover that they weren't each other's fated mates.

Except, the story already had one happily ever after. Maybe that was it?

If so, Vivian would feel forever guilty that her happiness had been earned by Ella's suffering.

"What got you so upset, love?" Magnus pulled her into his arms.

"Julian sounded off, like he was disappointed."

"No, he didn't. He sounded confused, which is a natural state for a male in the presence of a beautiful woman."

She lifted her face to look into his smiling eyes. "Really? Were you confused when you met me?"

"Completely."

"How so? You looked so confident."

"I faked it." He winked. "I'm older and more experienced than Julian. I know how to hide it well."

"So what was it? I'm curious."

He laughed. "I thought that you were beautiful and brave, but that it would be totally wrong to hit on you when you were distraught because your daughter was missing. So I decided to be supportive and offer you a shoulder to cry on. But then the fantasy continued into stroking your back, or massaging your shoulders, and then kissing you. You get the picture. I had to rein it in and appear professional, supportive, and not at all horny as hell."

"You said hell!" Parker yelled from his room.

Magnus's forehead furrowed. "Is hell a bad word?"

"Not as bad as horny," Vivian whispered. "I think his hearing is improving."

"I'm certain of it."

"We need to be careful what we say around here."

"Or make sure that his door is closed."

56

ELLA

When Turner had said private jet, Ella had imagined it would be like the Russian's.

It was so not in the same league. It was a small executive jet with eight seats and a tiny bathroom that didn't have a shower.

Julian had been in there for a long time, and she needed to pee again. But it was probably going to be so stinky in there when he got out that she decided to wait a little longer before braving it.

The door to the cockpit was open, and Yamanu, who was sitting up front, was chatting up a storm with the pilot about the latest Marvel movie and how it was the best so far.

The guy was the most handsome and at the same time the weirdest man she'd ever met. Basketball player tall, with long straight hair that reached all the way to the small of his back, and pale blue eyes that looked almost white against his dark skin.

If someone had described Yamanu to her, Ella would've imagined him as intimidating, but the opposite was true. Listening to him talk, she felt the tension that had been her constant companion ever since she'd left home gradually subside.

Was it his voice?

Or maybe the fact that he sounded cheerful and smiled a lot?

Or maybe it was the realization that she was finally free, for real, and in just a few hours, she was going to leap into her mother's outstretched arms and let her hold her for as long as she could keep those arms up.

Turner was sitting next to Yamanu, but there was nothing calm or relaxed about him. His laptop was open, he had headphones over his ears, and he looked like he was managing the world from the plane.

Ella looked away.

Although he was younger and way more handsome, Turner's stern expression, his all about business attitude, and his smart eyes reminded her too much of the Russian.

She felt bad thinking of her rescue's mastermind that way. Not only did she owe Turner her freedom, but he'd also taken the ring from her, helping her get rid of the last symbol of her captivity.

Hopefully, it was indeed the last.

A pregnancy test was needed to determine that. She was going to buy one at the first opportunity.

"Finally," she said as Julian emerged from the bathroom.

"Sorry about taking so long."

Unable to hold it in anymore, Ella rushed in, but it was not at all stinky inside. What had he been doing in there the entire time?

Probably talking to his girlfriend.

Yeah, no way the good-looking young doctor didn't have one.

For some reason, the thought upset her. It wasn't like she was interested in him. Julian was gorgeous, and he seemed like a really nice guy, but her mother's matchmaking attempt had been silly in the extreme.

They had nothing in common.

In the real world, where people met and got to know each other before getting involved, a guy like Julian wouldn't be interested in an eighteen-year-old high school graduate.

Besides, it would be a long time before she was interested in male company. Maybe never.

Was it too late to join a convent?

Except, to do that she needed to be a true believer, and she wasn't.

Done with her business, Ella washed her hands and got out without checking out her reflection in the mirror the way she used to do in her previous life. She didn't care how she looked. Her beauty was a curse. From now on she wasn't going to even comb her hair.

"Can you sit next to me?" Julian asked. "There are some things I need to tell you."

Her gut clenched uncomfortably. "What is it?"

"Nothing bad. Only good stuff."

Up front, Yamanu started humming a tune, and Ella felt her body relax in the comfortable seat. She cast Julian a reassuring smile. "Okay, shoot."

He raked his fingers through his longish hair. "You know where your mother and I met, right?"

"At the psychic convention."

"Yes. She had her reasons for being there, and I had mine. You know hers. What I'm going to reveal is why I was there."

"Go on."

He took in a big fortifying breath. "I was searching for people with paranormal talents."

Ella's gut twisted again. "Why?"

Was this whole thing another trap? This one designed to catch her mother and her?

"Because I wanted to find more people like my family and me."

Ella let out a breath. That was another thing altogether. "Are you psychic as well?"

"No. I'm immortal. And somewhat overly empathic, but only with humans."

Ella glanced at the two men sitting up front, waiting for the snorts and laughter that should've followed Julian's bad joke. But that didn't happen. Yamanu kept humming a tune, and Turner didn't lift his head from the laptop. But then he had headphones on and probably hadn't heard Julian's pathetic attempt at humor.

"You're good." She pointed her finger at him. "You can deliver a joke with a straight face. Your problem is that the joke isn't funny."

"It's not a joke. I am immortal, and so is Turner, and Yamanu, and the pilot of this plane, and every person on the rescue team."

When she glanced at Yamanu again, he smiled and nodded. "It's true. I'm over one thousand years old."

She couldn't explain it, but something in his voice convinced her that he was telling her the truth.

The guy was probably a hypnotist.

But whatever. She could let Julian explain.

"Okay. Let's pretend that I believe you. Go on."

"You can check with your mother. I was in the bathroom because I wanted to ask her permission before telling you the story. I thought she might want to be the one to tell you. She said that the sooner you know the truth, the better."

"So what you're trying to tell me is that she knew all along that your organization is made up of immortals, and she failed to mention it to me in all of our mental talks?"

"She's only found out recently, and we had asked her not to tell you. Keeping our existence secret is crucial to our survival, and you were in enemy territory so to speak. I'm sure you can understand the need for secrecy after a lifetime of hiding what you can do."

His arguments were valid, and he was so serious that she was inclined to believe him.

"So if keeping your existence a secret is so important, why are you telling me this? Why did you tell my mother?"

He smiled. "Because of what I said in the beginning about going to the psychic convention to find others like us. Some humans carry our immortal genes, but they are dormant. Some of them exhibit paranormal abilities. When we find them, we can activate those dormant genes and turn them into immortals like us."

"And you think I have those genes?"

"I know you do."

"Because I can communicate telepathically?"

"That too. But that's not proof positive. The reason I know for sure that you do is that your little brother Parker went through the transition and is on his way to becoming an immortal, which means that you as well as your mother can do that too."

Ella gaped. "No way! Parker is an immortal?"

"Almost. The transition takes a long time, but he's started the process. Which, by the way, was very brave of him. He did it to prove that you are all Dormants, and so you and your mother wouldn't have to rush into it."

"Why not? What needs to be done in order to activate our immortal genes?"

Looking embarrassed, Julian looked away. "It's a long explanation. Maybe I'll let your mother do that."

"We have plenty of time."

Julian cleared his throat. "Right. Let me start at the beginning. You know the mythical gods?"

"What about them?"

"They were real, and just as the myths tell it, they took human partners, and a race of immortals was born—"

57

MAGNUS

"Here it comes." Parker pointed at the sky.

Vivian shielded her eyes with her hand even though she was wearing sunglasses. "I can't see anything."

Magnus didn't bother to look. "I can hear it. It's coming."

Sensing the excitement, Scarlet started jumping around like a goat, her tongue lolling, and her tail wagging.

"Easy, girl." Magnus tugged on her leash. "You're going to hyperventilate."

Parker scrunched his nose. "Can dogs even do that?"

"I'm not sure. But if they can, she's going to."

"I feel naked without the wig," Vivian said. "I know this place is secure, but I still have this uneasy feeling in my stomach."

Transferring the bag with Ella's things to the hand he was holding the leash with, Magnus wrapped his arm around her shoulders. "You're just excited. I'm excited too." He leaned and kissed the top of her head. "And a little scared. I'm about to meet my future daughter for the first time. What if she doesn't like me?"

"She's gonna like you," Parker said. "And if not, I'm going to make her." He lifted his fist and made a mean face, then laughed. "Just joking."

"Now I see it," Vivian said a few moments later.

Everyone tensed as the jet aligned with the airstrip, waiting for the landing gear to touch down.

The pilot executed a perfect landing, which probably meant that Charlie was flying the jet. The guy prided himself on his soft landings.

The plane taxied for a few moments and then stopped on the runway. There was no point in taking it inside the hangar since it was refueling and going back to New York.

As the door flipped open, Vivian sucked in a breath, but the first one to emerge wasn't Ella, it was Turner, followed by Yamanu.

Ella was next and then Julian.

She practically flew down the stairs, flinging herself into her mother's arms. Parker wrapped his skinny arms around both his mother and sister, and a moment later all three were crying.

Turner waved at Magnus without lifting his head and kept going, escaping the emotional scene as quickly as he could.

Yamanu walked over and slapped Magnus on his back. "Nice family you got yourself, my friend."

"Thank you."

Magnus offered his hand to Julian. "Thank you for bringing Ella home safely."

Julian chuckled. "I wasn't that much help. Your Guardian buddies were amazing. Naturally, things didn't work out exactly per plan. Ella's bodyguard decided to play the hero, threw her over his shoulder, and started running away from the tanker. A Guardian had to tackle him to the ground. I was sure Ella was going to get bruised all over, but somehow he grabbed her and tossed her to another Guardian before falling on top of the bodyguard and knocking him out." He shook his head. "After witnessing what they can do, I gained a new appreciation for Guardians."

Magnus made a mental note to find out who the two Guardians were and thank them personally.

"Do you want me to sing to them?" Yamanu pointed with his chin at Vivian and her kids who were still huddled together and sniffling.

Everyone knew the calming power of Yamanu's singing, but this was not the time for it.

"I think they need to let it all out."

Yamanu nodded. "You might be right. It's just hard to see them cry. Breaks my heart."

"Yeah, it's hard."

"Go to them," Julian said.

"I don't want to intrude on their reunion."

Yamanu slapped Magnus's back again. "They need you."

Hesitantly, Magnus took a step forward and wrapped his long arms around his family, cocooning all three in their shelter.

If only his arms could always keep them safe.

Slowly, the crying subsided, and Ella lifted her head off her mother's shoulder. "Magnus, right?"

"I'm sorry." He let his arms fall away and took a step back.

"Don't be silly." Ella reached for his hand, pulled him back, and put it on Vivian's back, then took his other one and put it on her own. "Thanks for making my mom happy."

The end...for now...

COMING UP NEXT

THE CHILDREN OF THE GODS BOOK 26

DARK DREAM'S TEMPTATION

FOR EXCLUSIVE PEEKS AT UPCOMING RELEASES

JOIN MY *VIP CLUB* AND GAIN ACCESS TO THE **VIP** PORTAL AT

ITLUCAS.COM

CLICK HERE TO JOIN

(OR GO TO: http://eepurl.com/blMTpD)

If you're already a subscriber and forgot the password to the VIP portal, you can find it at the bottom of each of my emails. Or click **HERE** to retrieve it.

You can also email me at isabell@itlucas.com

Don't miss out on

THE CHILDREN OF THE GODS ORIGINS SERIES

1: Goddess's Choice

2: Goddess's Hope

Dear reader,

Thank you for joining me on the continuing adventures of the ***Children of the Gods***.

As an independent author, I rely on your support to spread the word. So if you enjoyed the story, please share your experience, and if it isn't too much trouble, I would greatly appreciate a brief review on Amazon.

Click here to leave a review

Love & happy reading,

Isabell

THE CHILDREN OF THE GODS SERIES

THE CHILDREN OF THE GODS ORIGINS

1: Goddess's Choice

When gods and immortals still ruled the ancient world, one young goddess risked everything for love.

2: Goddess's Hope

Hungry for power and infatuated with the beautiful Areana, Navuh plots his father's demise. After all, by getting rid of the insane god he would be doing the world a favor. Except, when gods and immortals conspire against each other, humanity pays the price.

But things are not what they seem, and prophecies should not to be trusted...

THE CHILDREN OF THE GODS

1: Dark Stranger The Dream

Syssi's paranormal foresight lands her a job at Dr. Amanda Dokani's neuroscience lab, but it fails to predict the thrilling yet terrifying turn her life will take. Syssi has no clue that her boss is an immortal who'll drag her into a secret, millennia-old battle over humanity's future. Nor does she realize that the professor's imposing brother is the mysterious stranger who's been starring in her dreams.

Since the dawn of human civilization, two warring factions of immortals—the descendants of the gods of old—have been secretly shaping its destiny. Leading the clandestine battle from his luxurious Los Angeles high-rise, Kian is surrounded by his clan, yet alone. Descending from a single goddess, clan members are forbidden to each other. And as the only other immortals are their hated enemies, Kian and his kin have been long resigned to a lonely existence of fleeting trysts with human partners. That is, until his sister makes a game-changing discovery—a mortal seeress who she believes is a dormant carrier of their genes. Ever the realist, Kian is skeptical and refuses Amanda's plea to attempt Syssi's activation. But when his enemies learn of the Dormant's existence, he's forced to rush her to the safety of his keep. Inexorably drawn to Syssi, Kian wrestles with his conscience as he is tempted to explore her budding interest in the darker shades of sensuality.

2: Dark Stranger Revealed

While sheltered in the clan's stronghold, Syssi is unaware that Kian and Amanda are not human, and neither are the supposedly religious fanatics that are after her. She feels a powerful connection to Kian, and as he introduces her to a world of pleasure she never dared imagine, his dominant sexuality is a revelation. Considering that she's completely out of her element, Syssi feels comfortable and safe letting go with him. That is, until she begins to suspect that all is not as it seems. Piecing the puzzle together, she draws a scary, yet wrong conclusion...

3: Dark Stranger Immortal

When Kian confesses his true nature, Syssi is not as much shocked by the revelation as she is wounded by what she perceives as his callous plans for her.

If she doesn't turn, he'll be forced to erase her memories and let her go. His family's safety demands secrecy – no one in the mortal world is allowed to know that immortals exist.

Resigned to the cruel reality that even if she stays on to never again leave the keep, she'll get old while Kian won't, Syssi is determined to enjoy what little time she has with him, one day at a time.

Can Kian let go of the mortal woman he loves? Will Syssi turn? And if she does, will she survive the dangerous transition?

4: Dark Enemy Taken

Dalhu can't believe his luck when he stumbles upon the beautiful immortal professor. Presented with a once in a lifetime opportunity to grab an immortal female for himself, he kidnaps her and runs. If he ever gets caught, either by her people or his, his life is forfeit. But for a chance of a loving mate and a family of his own, Dalhu is prepared to do everything in his power to win Amanda's heart, and that includes leaving the Doom brotherhood and his old life behind.

Amanda soon discovers that there is more to the handsome Doomer than his dark past and a hulking, sexy body. But succumbing to her enemy's seduction, or worse, developing feelings for a ruthless killer is out of the question. No man is worth life on the run, not even the one and only immortal male she could claim as her own...

Her clan and her research must come first...

5: Dark Enemy Captive

When the rescue team returns with Amanda and the chained Dalhu to the keep, Amanda is not as thrilled to be back as she thought she'd be. Between Kian's contempt for her and Dalhu's imprisonment, Amanda's budding relationship with Dalhu seems doomed. Things start to look up when Annani offers her help, and together with Syssi they resolve to find a way for Amanda to be with Dalhu. But will she still want him when she realizes that he is responsible for her nephew's murder? Could she? Will she take the easy way out and choose Andrew instead?

6: Dark Enemy Redeemed

Amanda suspects that something fishy is going on onboard the Anna. But when her investigation of the peculiar all-female Russian crew fails to uncover anything other than more speculation, she decides it's time to stop playing detective and face her real problem—a man she shouldn't want but can't live without.

6.5: My Dark Amazon

When Michael and Kri fight off a gang of humans, Michael gets stabbed. The injury to his immortal body recovers fast, but the one to his ego takes longer, putting a strain on his relationship with Kri.

7: Dark Warrior Mine

When Andrew is forced to retire from active duty, he believes that all he has to look forward to is a boring desk job. His glory days in special ops are over. But as it turns out, his thrill ride has just begun. Andrew discovers not only that immortals exist and have been manipulating global affairs since antiquity, but that he and his sister are rare possessors of the immortal genes.

Problem is, Andrew might be too old to attempt the activation process. His sister, who is fourteen years his junior, barely made it through the transition, so the odds of him coming out of it alive, let alone immortal, are slim.

But fate may force his hand.

Helping a friend find his long-lost daughter, Andrew finds a woman who's worth taking the risk for. Nathalie might be a Dormant, but the only way to find out for sure requires fangs and venom.

8: Dark Warrior's Promise

Andrew and Nathalie's love flourishes, but the secrets they keep from each other taint their relationship with doubts and suspicions. In the meantime, Sebastian and his men are getting bolder, and the storm that's brewing will shift the balance of power in the millennia-old conflict between Annani's clan and its enemies.

9: Dark Warrior's Destiny

The new ghost in Nathalie's head remembers who he was in life, providing Andrew and her with indisputable proof that he is real and not a figment of her imagination.

Convinced that she is a Dormant, Andrew decides to go forward with his transition immediately after the rescue mission at the Doomers' HQ.

Fearing for his life, Nathalie pleads with him to reconsider. She'd rather spend the rest of her mortal days with Andrew than risk what they have for the fickle promise of immortality.

While the clan gets ready for battle, Carol gets help from an unlikely ally. Sebastian's second-in-command can no longer ignore the torment she suffers at the hands of his commander and offers to help her, but only if she agrees to his terms.

10: Dark Warrior's Legacy

Andrew's acclimation to his post-transition body isn't easy. His senses are sharper, he's bigger, stronger, and hungrier. Nathalie fears that the changes in the man she loves are more than physical. Measuring up to this new version of him is going to be a challenge.

Carol and Robert are disillusioned with each other. They are not destined mates, and love is not on the horizon. When Robert's three months are up, he might be left with nothing to show for his sacrifice.

Lana contacts Anandur with disturbing news; the yacht and its human cargo are in Mexico. Kian must find a way to apprehend Alex and rescue the women on board without causing an international incident.

11: Dark Guardian Found

What would you do if you stopped aging?

Eva runs. The ex-DEA agent doesn't know what caused her strange mutation, only that if discovered, she'll be dissected like a lab rat. What Eva doesn't know, though, is that she's a descendant of the gods, and that she is not alone. The man who rocked her world in one life-changing encounter over thirty years ago is an immortal as well.

To keep his people's existence secret, Bhathian was forced to turn his back on the only woman who ever captured his heart, but he's never forgotten and never stopped looking for her.

12: Dark Guardian Craved

Cautious after a lifetime of disappointments, Eva is mistrustful of Bhathian's professed feelings of love. She accepts him as a lover and a confidant but not as a life partner.

Jackson suspects that Tessa is his true love mate, but unless she overcomes her fears, he might never find out.

Carol gets an offer she can't refuse—a chance to prove that there is more to her than meets the eye. Robert believes she's about to commit a deadly mistake, but when he tries to dissuade her, she tells him to leave.

13: Dark Guardian's Mate

Prepare for the heart-warming culmination of Eva and Bhathian's story!

14: Dark Angel's Obsession

The cold and stoic warrior is an enigma even to those closest to him. His secrets are about to unravel...

15: Dark Angel's Seduction

Brundar is fighting a losing battle. Calypso is slowly chipping away his icy armor from the outside, while his need for her is melting it from the inside.

He can't allow it to happen. Calypso is a human with none of the Dormant indicators. There is no way he can keep her for more than a few weeks.

16: Dark Angel's Surrender

Get ready for the heart pounding conclusion to Brundar and Calypso's story.

Callie still couldn't wrap her head around it, nor could she summon even a smidgen of sorrow or regret. After all, she had some memories with him that weren't horrible. She should've felt something. But there was nothing, not even shock. Not even horror at what had transpired over the last couple of hours.

Maybe it was a typical response for survivors--feeling euphoric for the simple reason that they were alive. Especially when that survival was nothing short of miraculous.

Brundar's cold hand closed around hers, reminding her that they weren't out of the woods yet. Her injuries were superficial, and the most she had to worry about was some scarring. But, despite his and Anandur's reassurances, Brundar might never walk again.

If he ended up crippled because of her, she would never forgive herself for getting him involved in her crap.

"Are you okay, sweetling? Are you in pain?" Brundar asked.

Her injuries were nothing compared to his, and yet he was concerned about her. God, she loved this man. The thing was, if she told him that, he would run off, or crawl away as was the case.

Hey, maybe this was the perfect opportunity to spring it on him.

17: Dark Operative: A Shadow of Death

As a brilliant strategist and the only human entrusted with the secret of immortals' existence, Turner is both an asset and a liability to the clan. His request to attempt transition into immortality as an alternative to cancer treatments cannot be denied without risking the clan's exposure. On the other hand, approving it means risking his premature death. In both scenarios, the clan will lose a valuable ally.

When the decision is left to the clan's physician, Turner makes plans to manipulate her by taking advantage of her interest in him.

Will Bridget fall for the cold, calculated operative? Or will Turner fall into his own trap?

18: Dark Operative: A Glimmer of Hope

As Turner and Bridget's relationship deepens, living together seems like the right move, but to make it work both need to make concessions.

Bridget is realistic and keeps her expectations low. Turner could never be the truelove mate she yearns for, but he is as good as she's going to get. Other than his emotional limitations, he's perfect in every way.

Turner's hard shell is starting to show cracks. He wants immortality, he wants to be part of the clan, and he wants Bridget, but he doesn't want to cause her pain.

His options are either abandon his quest for immortality and give Bridget his few remaining decades, or abandon Bridget by going for the transition and most likely dying. His rational mind dictates that he chooses the former, but his gut pulls him toward the latter. Which one is he going to trust?

19: Dark Operative: The Dawn of Love

Get ready for the exciting finale of Bridget and Turner's story!

20: Dark Survivor Awakened

This was a strange new world she had awakened to.

Her memory loss must have been catastrophic because almost nothing was familiar. The language was foreign to her, with only a few words bearing some similarity to the language she thought in. Still, a full moon cycle had passed since her awakening, and little by little she was gaining basic understanding of it--only a few words and phrases, but she was learning more each day.

A week or so ago, a little girl on the street had tugged on her mother's sleeve and pointed at her. "Look, Mama, Wonder Woman!"

The mother smiled apologetically, saying something in the language these people spoke, then scurried away with the child looking behind her shoulder and grinning.

When it happened again with another child on the same day, it was settled.

Wonder Woman must have been the name of someone important in this strange world she had awoken to, and since both times it had been said with a smile it must have been a good one.

Wonder had a nice ring to it.

She just wished she knew what it meant.

21: Dark Survivor Echoes of Love

Wonder's journey continues in *Dark Survivor Echoes of Love.*

22: Dark Survivor Reunited

The exciting finale of Wonder and Anandur's story.

23: Dark Widow's Secret

Vivian and her daughter share a powerful telepathic connection, so when Ella can't be reached by conventional or psychic means, her mother fears the worst.

Help arrives from an unexpected source when Vivian gets a call from the young doctor she met at a psychic convention. Turns out Julian belongs to a private organization specializing in retrieving missing girls.

As Julian's clan mobilizes its considerable resources to rescue the daughter, Magnus is charged with keeping the gorgeous young mother safe.

Worry for Ella and the secrets Vivian and Magnus keep from each other should be enough to prevent the sparks of attraction from kindling a blaze of desire. Except, these pesky sparks have a mind of their own.

24: Dark Widow's Curse

A simple rescue operation turns into mission impossible when the Russian mafia gets involved. Bad things are supposed to come in threes, but in Vivian's case, it seems like there is no limit to bad luck. Her family and everyone who gets close to her is affected by her curse.

Will Magnus and his people prove her wrong?

25: Dark Widow's Blessing

The thrilling finale of the Dark Widow trilogy!

26: Dark Dream's Temptation

Julian has known Ella is the one for him from the moment he saw her picture, but when he finally frees her from captivity, she seems indifferent to him. Could he have been mistaken?

Ella's rescue should've ended that chapter in her life, but it seems like the road back to normalcy has just begun and it's full of obstacles. Between the pitying looks she gets and her mother's attempts to get her into therapy, Ella feels like she's typecast as a victim, when nothing could be further from the truth. She's a tough survivor, and she's going to prove it.

Strangely, the only one who seems to understand is Logan, who keeps popping up in her dreams. But then, he's a figment of her imagination —or is he?

27: Dark Dream's Unraveling

While trying to figure out a way around Logan's silencing compulsion, Ella concocts an ambitious plan. What if instead of trying to keep him out of her dreams, she could pretend to like him and lure him into a trap?

Catching Navuh's son would be a major boon for the clan, as well as for Ella. She will have her revenge, turning the tables on another scumbag out to get her.

28: Dark Dream's Trap

The trap is set, but who is the hunter and who is the prey? Find out in this heart-pounding conclusion to the *Dark Dream* trilogy.

29: Dark Prince's Enigma

As the son of the most dangerous male on the planet, Lokan lives by three rules:

Don't trust a soul.

Don't show emotions.

And don't get attached.

Will one extraordinary woman make him break all three?

30: Dark Prince's Dilemma

Will Kian decide that the benefits of trusting Lokan outweigh the risks?

Will Lokan betray his father and brothers for the greater good of his people?

Are Carol and Lokan true-love mates, or is one of them playing the other?

So many questions, the path ahead is anything but clear.

31: Dark Prince's Agenda

While Turner and Kian work out the details of Areana's rescue plan, Carol and Lokan's tumultuous relationship hits another snag. Is it a sign of things to come?

32 : Dark Queen's Quest

A former beauty queen, a retired undercover agent, and a successful model, Mey is not the typical damsel in distress. But when her sister drops off the radar and then someone starts following her around, she panics.

Following a vague clue that Kalugal might be in New York, Kian sends a team headed by Yamanu to search for him.

As Mey and Yamanu's paths cross, he offers her his help and protection, but will that be all?

33: Dark Queen's Knight

As the only member of his clan with a godlike power over human minds, Yamanu has been shielding his people for centuries, but that power comes at a steep price. When Mey enters his life, he's faced with the most difficult choice.

The safety of his clan or a future with his fated mate.

34: Dark Queen's Army

As Mey anxiously waits for her transition to begin and for Yamanu to test whether his godlike powers are gone, the clan sets out to solve two mysteries:

Where is Jin, and is she there voluntarily?

Where is Kalugal, and what is he up to?

35: Dark Spy Conscripted

Jin possesses a unique paranormal ability. Just by touching someone, she can insert a mental hook into their psyche and tie a string of her consciousness to it, creating a tether. That doesn't make her a spy, though, not unless her talent is discovered by those seeking to exploit it.

36: Dark Spy's Mission

Jin's first spying mission is supposed to be easy. Walk into the club, touch Kalugal to tether her consciousness to him, and walk out.

Except, they should have known better.

37: Dark Spy's Resolution

The best-laid plans often go awry...

38: Dark Overlord New Horizon

Jacki has two talents that set her apart from the rest of the human race.

She has unpredictable glimpses of other people's futures, and she is immune to mind manipulation.

Unfortunately, both talents are pretty useless for finding a job other than the one she had in the government's paranormal division.

It seemed like a sweet deal, until she found out that the director planned on producing super babies by compelling the recruits into pairing up. When an opportunity to escape the program presented itself, she took it, only to find out that humans are not at the top of the food chain.

Immortals are real, and at the very top of the hierarchy is Kalugal, the most powerful, arrogant, and sexiest male she has ever met.

With one look, he sets her blood on fire, but Jacki is not a fool. A man like him will never think of her as anything more than a tasty snack, while she will never settle for anything less than his heart.

39: Dark Overlord's Wife

Jacki is still clinging to her all-or-nothing policy, but Kalugal is chipping away at her resistance. Perhaps it's time to ease up on her convictions. A little less than all is still much better than nothing, and a couple of decades with a demigod is probably worth more than a lifetime with a mere mortal.

40: Dark Overlord's Clan

As Jacki and Kalugal prepare to celebrate their union, Kian takes every precaution to safeguard his people. Except, Kalugal and his men are not his only potential adversaries, and compulsion is not the only power he should fear.

41: Dark Choices The Quandary

When Rufsur and Edna meet, the attraction is as unexpected as it is undeniable. Except, she's the clan's judge and councilwoman, and he's Kalugal's second-in-command. Will loyalty and duty to their people keep them apart?

42: Dark Choices Paradigm Shift

Edna and Rufsur are miserable without each other, and their two-week separation seems like an eternity. Long-distance relationships are difficult, but for immortal couples they are impossible. Unless one of them is willing to leave everything behind for the other, things are just going to get worse. Except, the cost of compromise is far greater than giving up their comfortable lives and hard-earned positions. The future of their people is on the line.

43: Dark Choices The Accord

The winds of change blowing over the village demand hard choices. For better or worse, Kian's decisions will alter the trajectory of the clan's future, and he is not ready to take the plunge. But as Edna and Rufsur's plight gains widespread support, his resistance slowly begins to erode.

44: Dark Secrets Resurgence

On a sabbatical from his Stanford teaching position, Professor David Levinson finally has time to write the sci-fi novel he's been thinking about for years.

The phenomena of past life memories and near-death experiences are too controversial to include in his formal psychiatric research, while fiction is the perfect outlet for his esoteric ideas.

Hoping that a change of pace will provide the inspiration he needs, David accepts a friend's invitation to an old Scottish castle.

45: Dark Secrets Unveiled

When Professor David Levinson accepts a friend's invitation to an old Scottish castle, what he finds there is more fantastical than his most outlandish theories. The castle is home to a clan of immortals, their leader is a stunning demigoddess, and even more shockingly, it might be precisely where he belongs.

Except, the clan founder is hiding a secret that might cast a dark shadow on David's relationship with her daughter.

Nevertheless, when offered a chance at immortality, he agrees to undergo the dangerous induction process.

Will David survive his transition into immortality? And if he does, will his relationship with Sari survive the unveiling of her mother's secret?

46: Dark Secrets Absolved

Absolution.

David had given and received it.

The few short hours since he'd emerged from the coma had felt incredible. He'd finally been free of the guilt and pain, and for the first time since Jonah's death, he had felt truly happy and optimistic about the future.

He'd survived the transition into immortality, had been accepted into the clan, and was about to marry the best woman on the face of the planet, his true love mate, his salvation, his everything.

What could have possibly gone wrong?

Just about everything.

47: Dark haven Illusion

Welcome to Safe Haven, where not everything is what it seems.

On a quest to process personal pain, Anastasia joins the Safe Haven Spiritual Retreat.

Through meditation, self-reflection, and hard work, she hopes to make peace with the voices in her head.

This is where she belongs.

Except, membership comes with a hefty price, doubts are sacrilege, and leaving is not as easy as walking out the front gate.

Is living in utopia worth the sacrifice?

Anastasia believes so until the arrival of a new acolyte changes everything.

Apparently, the gods of old were not a myth, their immortal descendants share the planet with humans, and she might be a carrier of their genes.

48: Dark Haven Unmasked

As Anastasia leaves Safe Haven for a week-long romantic vacation with Leon, she hopes to explore her newly discovered passionate side, their budding relationship, and perhaps also solve the mystery of the voices in her head. What she discovers exceeds her wildest expectations.

In the meantime, Eleanor and Peter hope to solve another mystery. Who is Emmett Haderech, and what is he up to?

THE PERFECT MATCH SERIES

Perfect Match 1: Vampire's Consort

When Gabriel's company is ready to start beta testing, he invites his old crush to inspect its medical safety protocol.

Curious about the revolutionary technology of the *Perfect Match Virtual Fantasy-Fulfillment studios,* Brenna agrees.

Neither expects to end up partnering for its first fully immersive test run.

Perfect Match 2: King's Chosen

When Lisa's nutty friends get her a gift certificate to *Perfect Match Virtual Fantasy Studios,* she has no intentions of using it. But since the only way to get a refund is if no partner can be found for her, she makes sure to request a fantasy so girly and over the top that no sane guy will pick it up.

Except, someone does.

Warning: This fantasy contains a hot, domineering crown prince, sweet insta-love, steamy love scenes painted with light shades of gray, a wedding, and a HEA in both the virtual and real worlds.

Intended for mature audience.

Perfect Match 3: Captain's Conquest

Working as a Starbucks barista, Alicia fends off flirting all day long, but none of the guys are as charming and sexy as Gregg. His frequent visits are the highlight of her day, but since he's never asked her out, she assumes he's taken. Besides, between a day job and a budding music career, she has no time to start a new relationship.

That is until Gregg makes her an offer she can't refuse—a gift certificate to the virtual fantasy fulfillment service everyone is talking about. As a huge Star Trek fan, Alicia has a perfect match in mind—the captain of the Starship Enterprise.

FOR EXCLUSIVE PEEKS AT UPCOMING RELEASES & A FREE COMPANION BOOK

JOIN MY *VIP CLUB* AND GAIN ACCESS TO THE VIP PORTAL AT

ITLUCAS.COM

CLICK HERE TO JOIN

(OR GO TO: http://eepurl.com/blMTpD)

INCLUDED IN YOUR FREE MEMBERSHIP:

- FREE CHILDREN OF THE GODS COMPANION BOOK 1
- FREE NARRATION OF GODDESS'S CHOICE—BOOK 1 IN THE CHILDREN OF THE GODS ORIGINS SERIES.
- PREVIEW CHAPTERS OF UPCOMING RELEASES.
- AND OTHER EXCLUSIVE CONTENT OFFERED ONLY TO MY VIPS.

Also by I. T. Lucas

THE CHILDREN OF THE GODS ORIGINS

1: Goddess's Choice

2: Goddess's Hope

THE CHILDREN OF THE GODS

Dark Stranger

1: Dark Stranger The Dream

2: Dark Stranger Revealed

3: Dark Stranger Immortal

Dark Enemy

4: Dark Enemy Taken

5: Dark Enemy Captive

6: Dark Enemy Redeemed

Kri & Michael's Story

6.5: My Dark Amazon

Dark Warrior

7: Dark Warrior Mine

8: Dark Warrior's Promise

9: Dark Warrior's Destiny

10: Dark Warrior's Legacy

Dark Guardian

11: Dark Guardian Found

12: Dark Guardian Craved

13: Dark Guardian's Mate

Dark Angel

14: Dark Angel's Obsession

15: Dark Angel's Seduction

16: Dark Angel's Surrender

Dark Operative

17: Dark Operative: A Shadow of Death

18: Dark Operative: A Glimmer of Hope

19: Dark Operative: The Dawn of Love

Dark Survivor

20: Dark Survivor Awakened

21: Dark Survivor Echoes of Love

22: Dark Survivor Reunited

Dark Widow

23: Dark Widow's Secret

24: Dark Widow's Curse

25: Dark Widow's Blessing

Dark Dream

26: Dark Dream's Temptation

27: Dark Dream's Unraveling

28: Dark Dream's Trap

Dark Prince

29: Dark Prince's Enigma

30: Dark Prince's Dilemma

31: Dark Prince's Agenda

Dark Queen

32: Dark Queen's Quest

33: Dark Queen's Knight

34: Dark Queen's Army

Dark Spy

35: Dark Spy Conscripted

36: Dark Spy's Mission

37: Dark Spy's Resolution

Dark Overlord

38: Dark Overlord New Horizon

39: Dark Overlord's Wife

40: Dark Overlord's Clan

Dark Choices

41: Dark Choices The Quandary

42: Dark Choices Paradigm Shift

43: Dark Choices The Accord

Dark Secrets

44: Dark Secrets Resurgence

45: Dark Secrets Unveiled

46: Dark Secrets Absolved

Dark Haven

47: Dark haven Illusion

48: Dark Haven Unmasked

PERFECT MATCH

Perfect Match 1: Vampire's Consort

Perfect Match 2: King's Chosen

Perfect Match 3: Captain's Conquest

The Children of the Gods Series Sets

Books 1-3: Dark Stranger trilogy—Includes a bonus short story: **The Fates take a Vacation**

Books 4-6: Dark Enemy Trilogy —Includes a bonus short story—**The Fates' Post-Wedding Celebration**

Books 7-10: Dark Warrior Tetralogy

Books 11-13: Dark Guardian Trilogy

Books 14-16: Dark Angel Trilogy

Books 17-19: Dark Operative Trilogy

Books 20-22: Dark Survivor Trilogy

Books 23-25: Dark Widow Trilogy

Books 26-28: Dark Dream Trilogy
Books 29-31: Dark Prince Trilogy
Books 32-34: Dark Queen Trilogy
Books 35-37: Dark Spy Trilogy
Books 38-40: Dark Overlord Trilogy
Books 41-43: Dark Choices Trilogy
Books 44-46: Dark Secrets Trilogy

MEGA SETS

The Children of the Gods: Books 1-6—**includes character lists**

The Children of the Gods: Books 6.5-10—**includes character lists**

TRY THE CHILDREN OF THE GODS SERIES ON AUDIBLE

2 FREE audiobooks with your new Audible subscription!